The
Existence
of Pity

a novel by

JEANNIE ZOKAN

Unlocking New Worlds

Print ISBN-13: 978-1-940215-80-8
Print ISBN-10: 1-940215-80-3

Red Adept Publishing, LLC
104 Bugenfield Court
Garner, NC 27529
http://RedAdeptPublishing.com/

Cover and Formatting: Streetlight Graphics

For my family;
Mom and Dad—
for giving me room to grow,
Dan, Dave, and John—
each of you gallant and kind,
Chris—
for your unending love and support,
and Olivia and Natalie—
speak your beautiful truths, my darlings.

Chapter One

WHEN I FOUND OUT AARON had been shot, I fainted for the first time in my life. All the lights and colors of the emergency room darkened around me. I felt hot and cold at the same time, and a high-pitched ringing in my ears drowned out the nurse's words.

The worst part, though, was the dizziness. As the room pitched and swirled, I reached for Blanca. Standing was going to be impossible without help.

The smell of coffee pulled me out of the fog. My aching head was on a hard pillow in Blanca's lap, and when I remembered where I was, tears burned my closed eyes.

How could one summer go so wrong?

I should've known all was not right on the night before my last day of tenth grade, when summer was about to begin. Mom paced the hall between the living room and dining room while Aaron played never-ending scales on the piano. Dad still wasn't home from a revival. He had been late before, plenty of times, but he was at church in a dangerous *barrio* in the city of Cali, Colombia, half an hour from our house—and he was *really* late.

I tried not to think about the gruesome murders the newspapers splashed on their pages, but the harder I tried to push the images away, the more vivid they became.

"You kids should go on to bed," Mom said, looking at her watch.

Aaron stopped his piano banging and turned to her. "I could borrow the neighbor's car and track Dad down if you want."

"Then I'd be worrying about you, too," she answered, sounding annoyed at his suggestion.

My older brother shrugged. "Come on, Josie," he said, knocking my foot off the coffee table as he walked by.

I tossed aside the *National Geographic* and threw a couch pillow at Aaron but missed him completely. I went into the kitchen and flipped on the light instead of following him upstairs. The familiar smell of Ajax kept me company as I waited. Soon, our maid opened her bedroom door and saw me sitting on the counter.

"*¿Qué pasa?*" she asked. Blanca, a twenty-two-year-old Colombian native, knew if I was up after eleven on a school night, I would want to talk about it. She didn't speak English, but I'd grown up using both languages.

"My dad hasn't come home yet," I answered in Spanish then told her about the revival.

"Shall I stay?" she asked, leaning against the spotless stove, looking up at me with shiny black eyes.

"That's okay. I should go to bed."

"Do not worry, *chica*." She patted my arm. "He will be home any minute." She went back to her room and closed her door.

I walked up the stairs to my room and climbed in bed, hugging my pillow. "What time I am afraid I will trust in thee," made a loop in my brain and was about to put me to sleep when I heard the familiar sound of our Suburban stopping in front of our house. The driveway gate creaked, and Brandy, our big rottweiler-retriever mix, barked. A voice immediately shushed him. I sat up and looked out my bedroom window in time to see Dad's headlights bob through the entrance.

Giddy with relief, I jumped out of bed to see him, listening as he burst through the front door, full of news about the three converts. "And, Astrid, that church was packed," he was saying to my mother as I walked downstairs. "Ricardo is doing a great job as pastor."

"Keep it down," Mom hissed, her voice moving up the stairs toward me. "And don't scare me like that again. If you're going to be this late, call from a pay phone or something."

I turned and tiptoed back to my room. Hanging around with Mom while she was in that kind of mood was a bad idea.

"You knew I'd be okay, didn't you?" His voice followed hers.

She didn't answer.

I stood by my bedroom door, and Dad turned toward me, a wild look on his boyish face.

"G'night, Josie," he said, much too energetic for the middle of the night. When he hugged me, his white shirt and striped tie smelled more of coffee and antiseptic than church.

"See ya in the morning," I called to my parents, trying to make the strange interaction feel normal.

Their bedroom door clicked closed, muffling their conversation.

Hours later, I awoke screaming, as if I knew some cosmic wheels had been set in motion and wouldn't stop until everything in my life had changed completely. Of course, danger was an inherent part of growing up in such a wild and beautiful country, where stray dogs and beggar children made their homes in the street. Parts of the stunning Andes Mountains surrounding Cali were still so remote, they remained unexplored. But that night, I screamed because of a fresh fear, one I couldn't understand.

Mom and Dad ran to my room, and Aaron lurked at the doorway. When they saw I was unharmed, Mom gave me a glass of water, Dad prayed over me, and they all went back to bed. I didn't tell them that when I finally shook off the panic, the feeling of a presence lingered in my room and my thoughts refused to let me close my eyes again.

Thirty minutes later, I couldn't be alone anymore. I grabbed my robe and crept down the stairs and past the kitchen, to Blanca's room. Standing in the dark hallway, I tapped on her door and held my breath. Shame washed over me as I waited for her to let me in. At sixteen, I was way too old for such things, but I couldn't go back up those stairs. Sometimes, the house loomed over me.

When Blanca opened the door, she motioned for me to come in and sit in the easy chair by her door. She wrapped her blue robe around her and sat on the edge of the bed while I dropped onto the overstuffed burgundy seat. After a pause, she asked, "Your mother, is she okay?"

"Sure, I guess." I hugged my knees to my chest. "Why?"

"It is nothing, *chica*," she answered.

"Did you hear me scream?"

Blanca shook her head. "The world heard you scream."

"Tell me a story. You know, something about your brothers and sisters."

"Okay," she said, rubbing her eyes. "Have I told you about my brother's chicken?"

I leaned back, settling in. "No." Blanca's stories about her family and their farm, one mountain range and three bus transfers away, never failed to comfort me.

"We would search the countryside for eggs laid by my mother's chickens. One time, my cousins put an egg under my brother's pillow, but my brother must have found it before it broke." She smiled, adding, "It hatched and became my brother's pet chicken. He named it *Socorro*."

I chuckled, not knowing how much of the story to believe. Either way, "Help" was a funny name for a chicken. "Tell me more," I said, swinging my legs over the arm of the chair.

Blanca thought for a moment then said, "Here is something. One time, I was gathering wood for a fire, and a snake slithered out of the woodpile into the bushes. I dropped the branches and ran to my grandmother, screaming about the *culebra*. She told me seeing a snake means a big change is coming. Soon after I saw that snake, my father sent me to work here in the city."

"But that's a good thing, right?" I asked, knowing she'd moved in with us when she was seventeen.

She didn't answer.

"Dad found a snake," I remembered aloud. "The other day in the backyard. He tried to kill it."

"Maybe a change is coming here, too." Blanca eyed me.

I wasn't listening. My mind was on that vicious snake that had swayed out of the way of Dad's machete then slid into the grass and disappeared.

A few moments later, she asked, "Do you know why you screamed in the night?"

"Snakes?" I joked.

"I am serious."

I sighed. "No, I don't know why." I pulled my fingers through my hair, looking for split ends. The vise-like grip around my heart had softened in the warm light of her lamp, and I didn't want to talk about it anymore.

"Maybe many things are going on around you. You aren't seeing them."

"Like what?"

She studied my face before she spoke. "It is okay, *mija*. You cannot worry about everything."

"So how do you keep from worrying?" I didn't expect a real answer. No one's answers about how to stop worrying had ever helped.

"*Mi rosario.*" She reached down under her bed and pulled out a chain of beads. "*Tenga,*" she said, handing them to me. "Do the rosary. Trust me, you will feel better."

"I don't know, Blanca. Isn't that a Catholic thing?" I held the beads away from me, studying them. The rosary looked harmless enough, but my starry-eyed Baptist missionary parents probably wouldn't approve. They were dedicated to saving lost souls in a country where most people wore crucifixes and had cinders rubbed on their foreheads every Ash Wednesday.

"Just see if it helps you," Blanca answered.

Rain pounded on the window that late-May night when Blanca taught me how to say the prayers on the crucifix and the smooth beads. Every *"Dios te salve Maria, llena eres de gracia"*—"Hail Mary, full of grace"—soothed my fears until I was able to go back upstairs. I stole past my parents' room to my own, the rosary's crucifix jabbing my hand.

I still couldn't sleep, but it was from excitement. Tomorrow was the last day of school, and Alejandro would be there. Alejandro was my first crush, with those deep-brown eyes and that dark-blond hair. He was one of Aaron's nicer friends, and when one of my classmates told me Alejandro had asked about me, my heart had leapt into my throat. Weeks went by with nothing more than short conversations between us, smiles in the halls, and lots of wishful thinking on my part.

I had spent most of the evening picking out the next day's outfit. My final choices were a sailor top, blue jeans, and clogs. I fell asleep to the patter of raindrops, wondering if my blue peasant blouse might be best.

"Josie, get up, or you'll miss the bus!" Mom called from the stairs.

"I'm up," I yelled back, brushing my hair one last time as I checked my makeup in the mirror. Maybe today would be the day. Alejandro and I would have a real conversation, then we would see each other over the summer. By the time school started next year, we would be dating. I was smiling at the thought when I suddenly remembered screaming in the night. It came as a distant memory, and I pushed it away, but not before I checked under my pillow for Blanca's rosary.

I raced downstairs in time to hear Dad tell Aaron, "So this is it, your last day of eleventh grade."

"Yup," Aaron answered, not looking up from his breakfast.

Dad turned to me over his coffee and toast. "And it's your last day of the tenth."

"Then Aunt Rosie comes tomorrow," I said, leaning out of Blanca's way so she could set a plate of scrambled eggs and bacon in front of me. "*Gracias.*"

She nodded, patting my arm.

Aaron gulped a glass of chocolate milk. "I hope it's okay if I'm not here much to show her around. I want to hang out with my friends."

I rolled my eyes. Aaron always managed to let us know how popular he was.

Picking up the newspaper and shaking it open, Dad said, "I'm sure she'll understand."

"The bus is coming," Mom called from the front door.

Aaron and I grabbed our lunches and school bags and ran outside, reaching the gate just as the blue-and-white bus opened its doors.

The anticipation of three months of freedom made the ride noisy with banter about summer plans. At our perfectly landscaped private school, even the teachers finally loosened up, joking with us as everyone signed yearbooks and reminisced about the past year.

I was talking with some classmates in the hall before lunch when I turned and found myself face-to-face with Alejandro. I tried to act natural, even though my cheeks were burning. He was with his friend Maria Mercedes, as usual, but I ignored her.

"*¿Q'hubo?*" he asked.

"Not much," I answered in English, wondering how he could be so good looking and smell so nice, too. "You?"

He shrugged, smiling. "Maybe I'll see you this summer."

My heart banged, but I managed to keep the conversation going. "Yeah. We could play tennis at the club." As soon as the words were out, I flinched. Alejandro was the school's best tennis player, while I usually ended up as the ball girl in PE.

"I mean, I could teach you some te—I mean you could teach me." I looked down, mentally kicking myself for the mess I was making of things.

He just laughed. "*Chévere,*" he said, reaching out to touch my arm.

My skin prickled with electricity, and I looked up at him, breathing in the wonderful feeling, knowing my blue eyes were sparkling as much as his brown eyes were. The sun shone brighter, the trees seemed greener, and the voices around us sounded like a love song. Everything was perfect.

But then Aaron walked up and broke the spell.

"Alejandro, settle a bet for us." Aaron led him off, and there was nothing I could do but watch them leave and curse my brother.

Then I noticed Maria Mercedes staring at me. She giggled, no doubt because I must've looked pretty silly watching Alejandro walk away.

"You caught me," I said, shrugging.

She turned, tossing her ponytail, and ran to catch up with him. I stayed in the hall a little longer, not wanting to let go of that perfect moment, and when I joined my friends again, my mind was still on Alejandro, wondering how I could talk to him one last time.

When the final bell rang, I hurried between the rows of open-air classrooms toward the school library, in hopes of seeing Alejandro again. Sure enough, he was sitting on the low wall by his locker, about fifty feet from my destination, and he was watching me. When I saw him, I stopped short. I waved at him, but my smile faltered because something about his shoulders looked deflated and sad. I desperately wanted to walk to him, but those fifty feet might as well have been fifty miles.

I didn't have to wonder what had gone wrong—I knew the answer. I'd seen it before. As one of the privileged Colombians at our expensive prep school, his family expected a lot of him. They wanted him to stick with a Colombian girl, a Catholic girl. They didn't want him getting involved with a missionary's daughter, someone who attended this school on a scholarship.

Alejandro stood as if waiting for me to walk to him, but I couldn't do it. I turned away, my heart aching as I realized there was never going to be a day for us. We would never play tennis over the summer, and it was time to go home.

I said good-bye to my schoolmates still chattering on the bus and went straight to my room. I crawled under my happy-yellow bedspread, wishing it were black, and cried. My parents and brother weren't around, and after a few minutes, Blanca did something she'd never done before. She came upstairs to my room and asked to come in. I uncovered my head and stood to open the door.

"Alejandro?" she asked.

"He'll never go out with me, Blanca," I whispered in Spanish, leaning on her shoulder.

"I know you are sad"—she pulled away to look at me—"but don't drag out your misery. Try to think of something else. *¿Sí, Yo-si?*"

Blanca never called any of us by our given names; Mom and Dad were "*Señora y Señor Wales*," and Aaron and I had pet names like "*papi*" and "*mija*." When she called me "Josie" and made it sound like "yes, me," I had to smile.

"I mean what I say." She nodded, her black eyes glittering, her strong jaw set.

"I know." I sat on the edge of my bed. "But what do I do now?"

"The rosary will comfort you, but you must keep your chin up. As my father always said, there will be another boy. A better one." She sat beside me. "A black cat ran in front of you two days ago. It made me afraid that something bad was going to happen. I should have known it would be a broken heart." She patted my arm.

"Just a broken heart." I sighed, wondering if I would ever feel that wonderfully perfect feeling again.

"Come have a snack." Blanca put her hand out to me to pull me up. "And tell me about your *Tía* Rosa."

I brightened at the thought of Aunt Rosie's visit. "And do we have more of that pineapple upside-down cake?"

"*Claro que sí,*" she answered.

Of course we did. Cake and Aunt Rosie couldn't unbreak my heart, but I appreciated the distraction. "I'm glad summer's here," I said, walking down the stairs.

"*Sí,* and there will be another boy," she said, following me. "A better one."

Chapter Two

THE SOUND OF A PAN flute sliding up and down the scale woke me the next morning. It was the knife sharpener's way of letting the maids know he was in the neighborhood. As the music drifted down the street, I thought about the three months ahead, assuming this summer would be like the lazy ones in my past. The days wouldn't be any longer; the sun always rose at six every morning and set at six every night in the equatorial city. They would feel long, though, since I would be free to do what I wanted: sleep late, read the books stacked by my bed, and not much else.

Watching the mango tree swaying outside my window, I thought of Aunt Rosie's visit. She'd been my favorite aunt when I was younger, but she hadn't seen me in over two years, and I'd changed a lot, what with braces working a small miracle on my smile and contact lenses saving me from dreadfully thick glasses.

My thoughts turned to the camera I had asked Aunt Rosie to buy me in the States. She would also bring peanut butter and American candy bars we couldn't get in Cali. Oh, and Dr Pepper. Aaron would get some shoes, since Mom had given up on finding size-twelve sneakers. Mom had asked for Whitman's chocolate, American panty hose, and Shalimar perfume.

Her voice interrupted my mental list. "I don't know where you put it, Henry," Mom said as she passed my room, heading downstairs.

I grabbed the rosary from the floor by my bed and shoved it under my pillow.

"Is it on the piano?" The sound of shuffling papers told me Dad was in his study.

"No." The piano bench creaked open. "It's not down here," Mom called. "You better find it before tomorrow. I need that music for the service."

"I will, Astrid," Dad said. "Maybe it's in my office at the seminary. I'll head across the street later."

Dad stopped at my door. "Hey, kiddo," he said, his tone happy again. "Has your brain turned to mush yet?"

"Very funny," I answered. "Did you ask Aunt Rosie to bring you anything?"

"I told her to surprise me. And today's the big day."

I jumped out of bed. "Can't wait!"

"Henry?" Mom called from downstairs.

"Coming." Resentment tightened his voice.

I followed him downstairs for breakfast.

Mom had a long list of things she wanted to get done before her sister's visit, and she asked me to help clean the house. Within five minutes, Blanca told me I was slowing her down and sent me outside to sweep. Brandy raced over to me with a stick in his mouth, so I tossed it for him to fetch. After a few throws, he sat down and started chewing on it. He growled when I tried to take it from him, so I gave up on the game.

I turned to my chore of clearing the leaves off our driveway. It was long enough to park five cars under the trees alongside our two-story brick house. The house wasn't especially beautiful, but whenever I was outside, I knew to expect the stares from dark-eyed strangers as they walked by. My life, so different from theirs, seemed to fascinate them. So did my blue eyes and long blond hair.

I breathed in the sweet smell of burning sugar cane and listened to a street vendor selling avocados. Those were parts of everyday life in Cali, and I loved it. As I worked in the sunshine on my first free day, the easy traffic on the street and the chirping birds in the trees calmed me like the prayers of the rosary. I thought of how I had screamed in the night, but the memory was packaged up and stored away, so I left it alone.

Alejandro came to mind again, and I winced, wishing I hadn't fooled myself into thinking we would get together over the summer. I was considering what I might say to him on the first day of school in September, when a woman with a baby in her arms came to the gate, snapping me from my reverie. Brandy was sitting by our front door, still gnawing at the stick. He lifted his head toward the woman. His ears perked, but he remained silent, which seemed strange. Usually, our guard dog went crazy when someone stopped at the gate. That was why we had him.

The woman, probably the wife of one of the Colombian seminary students, shifted the blanketed baby in her arms and asked to see my father.

"He's gone to his office at the college," I told her, touching the child's soft hair. "Your baby is beautiful."

"I need to speak to Señor Wales," she answered, drawing the baby away from my hand. "I will look for him there."

"Can I help you with anything?"

"*No, gracias,*" she called over her shoulder.

I watched her cross the street and enter the huge wrought-iron gates of the seminary, then I continued my work. After the driveway was cleared, I left the broom in the corner of the garage and went to the kitchen.

Blanca nodded at me and said, "Are you more relaxed now, *mija*?"

"Yeah, but all that work made me hungry."

"You see why it's nice to sweep the driveway," she said, handing me a banana.

I hopped onto the counter. "Two geese flew over the house while I was out there. They were flying really low."

"Someone is traveling," she told me, turning back to the dishes in the sink. "Of course it may be your *Tía* Rosa, but it may be something else. Are your parents planning to take you on a trip?"

"Not anytime soon. My mom just came back from having that operation in the States, and we don't go back home for another two years."

"*Ya veremos.*" She shrugged.

It took an hour to reach the airport, but watching the bustling city with its million people made the time fly. Cali was especially nice in the breezy afternoon. The sun, surrounded by impossibly fluffy white clouds, shined on the green mountains that nestled Cali into a lush valley. Three concrete crosses, the Tres Cruces, towered on a nearby mountain, and the eight-story statue of Cristo Rey, Christ the King, stood with open arms on a distant peak.

By the time Aunt Rosie's airplane landed at twilight, I had adjusted my wrap-around skirt and white blouse and tightened the barrette in my hair about two hundred times. But as soon as she stepped from the jet and waved, I knew we would still be close. As stylish as ever, she was wearing a long sweater and plaid pants, her brown shoulder-length hair curled around her rosy cheeks. Dad and Aaron were allowed into the customs room to help her collect her luggage and communicate with the officers. Mom and I had to wait on the other side of the glass doors, watching her charm the military police and other passengers with her friendly smile.

After her many bags were checked, the workers stamped her passport and visitor's papers. Then she ran to my mom and me and threw her arms around us. "It's so good to see you!"

"You, too, Aunt Rosie," I said, breathing in her soft perfume.

"And how are you, Astrid?" She turned to look up at Mom.

Mom hugged her again, tighter. "So glad you're here," she

whispered. Tears glistened in her eyes, and she didn't let Aunt Rosie go.

Finally, Dad touched Mom's shoulder. "Okay, we better get this show on the road."

"I can't tell you how excited I've been about this trip," Aunt Rosie said, following Dad away from the customs entrance. "Aaron, what are you doing, lifting weights?" She squeezed his biceps then reached up to tousle his curly brown hair. She linked arms with me, adding, "And, Henry, you must be beating the boys off with a stick. This girl is such a beauty!"

I tried, and failed, to hide a big grin as we walked behind Mom and Dad through the airport.

"How was your trip?" Mom asked. She seemed to have regained her composure.

"It was fine. Uneventful. I didn't see anything like this along the way." She looked around the spacious terminal. "This place is as big as Grand Central Station."

"I like how this whole side is open to the outdoors," I told her as we passed thick columns that supported the roof four stories away. "It's neat to see the airplanes flying in and out."

"What, no weather to worry about?" she asked.

"Rain blows in sometimes, but not too often," Dad told her.

"Oh, that's right. It's always sunny and seventy-five degrees here."

We laughed as we walked to the parking lot to find our Suburban in the cool night. I liked having fun with my family again. It had been awhile.

"Why did everyone on the plane cross themselves and clap when we landed?" Aunt Rosie asked, setting her bag down by the car.

Mom's hand hovered over the handle for a moment before she opened the door. I knew what she was thinking: South Americans never took flying over the Andes lightly. A few years earlier, a jet had collided into the mountains, stranding the few survivors on the treacherous peaks for over two months before they were rescued. Bringing that up didn't seem like a good idea, though. This was Aunt Rosie's first overseas flight since Uncle Lloyd's death in a plane crash four years earlier. No one knew why his Cessna 150 went down over New Mexico one clear November day, killing him and one of his fellow pilot friends. Those things happened, they said.

An image of Aunt Rosie at his grave flashed through my mind. She had looked like a movie star, with big glasses and the perfect dress, but as Uncle Lloyd's casket lowered into the ground, she had crumpled into my mother. Her sobs were so loud and sad; I would never forget them.

"They always clap like that," Aaron told her with a casual smile, bringing me back to the present. "They're just glad to be on land again."

"Well, I'm glad to be on land, too," Aunt Rosie said.

I hated to admit it, but my brother knew how to smooth things over.

"I'm ready to go somewhere fun tonight," Aunt Rosie added. "What do you say?"

"How about pizza?" Mom turned to Dad and added, "We could go to Salerno's."

"Pizza? In Colombia?" Aunt Rosie asked.

"We're breaking you in slowly," Mom answered. "Trust me, you'll love it."

And so Aunt Rosie's whirlwind visit began. She spent half the trip to the pizza place telling us about President Jimmy Carter and the two-hundredth birthday of the States. The other half, she filled with asking questions about the city as we drove through. The huge paper mill fascinated her, even its reeking steam billowing white against the dark sky. The crazy traffic, still busy late at night, kept her pointing out close calls, ancient cars, and tightly packed buses.

A huge brick oven dominated the center of Salerno's, and the only thing better than watching flames leap out of it was tasting the pizza, which overflowed with sauce and cheese.

Aunt Rosie snapped her fingers to the lively music pulsing through the restaurant, and Aaron told her, "That's salsa. Cali is famous for it. The dancing and the music."

"They play that stuff all night sometimes," my dad added. "On holidays, no one sleeps for the noise."

"Do you ever want to get out there and dance with them?" Aunt Rosie laughed when I turned to her, my eyes wide. "I'm kidding," she added, patting my knee. "I know Baptists can't dance."

"Some of us can," Aaron said with a wink that made Aunt Rosie laugh even more.

After our meal, Aaron persuaded Mom and Dad to let him drive us up to the statue of Cristo Rey to get a view of Cali. Aunt Rosie had promised she wasn't too tired from her long day of travel, and Mom and I sat in the backseat, with her between us, discussing plans for the next ten days.

We were talking about shopping when I noticed Dad grip the dashboard with both hands. The Suburban's headlights weren't much help against the darkness on the road to the top of the mountain, and just as I was about to ask my brother to slow down, Dad yelled, "Aaron, look out!"

Aaron swayed off the edge of the winding road then swerved directly into the path of an oncoming van. With my heart in my throat, I reached for Aunt Rosie's hand as Dad grabbed the steering wheel and jerked our car back into our lane. Headlights blinded me as the van whipped by. Aaron stopped the car by the road, and we sat motionless until my brother looked around at us and started to laugh.

Dad wiped his brow with his hand. "Son, what on earth is so funny? You could've gotten us killed!"

I gasped for air. I hadn't realized I was holding my breath.

"You should see your faces," he said. "You all look like you've just been mugged!"

I was staring at my crazy brother when Aunt Rosie put her hand on the window. "I can barely make them out, but aren't those little white crosses on the side of the road? And aren't they for people who've died right here?"

"Oh, it wasn't that bad." Aaron started the engine.

"Yeah, it was," I said, trying to slow my pounding heart.

"Henry, don't let him drive," Mom ordered.

Dad jumped out of the car, ran around to the driver's seat, and pushed Aaron to the passenger side.

"Well, if I wasn't awake before, I am now," Aunt Rosie said, patting Aaron's shoulder.

We were quiet as Dad maneuvered the Suburban onto the road and drove slowly up the hill. Safely at the top of the mountain, Aunt Rosie and I hopped out of the car and stood under the concrete Christ.

"This looks like the one in Rio de Janeiro," she said.

"Ours is a little smaller, but they are a lot alike," Dad said as he and Mom joined us.

"I love his face," I said.

Aunt Rosie followed my gaze to his kind, but serious, eyes. "I think it's neat that you live in a city Jesus is watching over."

"Yeah," Aaron added from the car. "Someone has to keep an eye on the road up here."

My parents and Aunt Rosie laughed, but I shook my head. Aaron could get away with anything.

I looked down on the sprawling city, vibrant with life even at night. Its golden lights warmed the darkness. As Dad pointed out Cali's landmarks, I wondered if he loved the place even more than I did. There was so much opportunity, so much beauty hidden among the painful realities of life in Colombia. And although I couldn't explain what was so special about it, I was going to enjoy sharing my adopted country with Aunt Rosie.

Chapter Three

IT WAS ALMOST MIDNIGHT WHEN we arrived home, but Aaron and I couldn't wait another minute to see what Aunt Rosie brought us from the States. We dragged her four suitcases into the living room and helped her unpack. Shoes, T-shirts, perfumes, chocolate chips, and American candy—it felt like Christmas morning. Blanca was watching from the hall, and I held up the extra-large jar of peanut butter and my new Kodak Instamatic camera for her to see.

Mom admired her new stationery and smiled at the box of chocolates Aunt Rosie insisted were only for her. Aaron tried on his sneakers and ran the loop through our living room, dining room, breakfast nook, and kitchen. Dad held up white dress shirts and one of his new ties, a wide one with a purple paisley design.

"Promise me you won't wear that to church," Mom said, wrinkling her nose at it.

"They'll love it, Astrid!" Dad beamed at Aunt Rosie.

She nudged my mom. "Come on, sis, you know it's so cool."

Mom shook her head.

"I guess it's time to divvy up the candy." Dad reached for the bags of Snickers and M&Ms.

"Hold it right there," Aaron said, snatching them away. "Last time, you ended up with more than the rest of us. I think Aunt Rosie should do it."

"I appreciate you trusting me with such an important job," she teased. "Give me four bowls to sort them into. Then I've got to hit the hay. All that traveling's catching up with me."

I awoke the next morning to Aunt Rosie standing over me, shaking my shoulder. "It's a gorgeous day in paradise, Josie. Let's go to the seminary for a run."

"What time is it?" I flopped onto my stomach.

"Six thirty."

"Can't we run later?" I asked into my pillow.

"It's perfect now. Come on, Miss Longlegs." She nudged me as she sat beside me on my bed. "You know you want to."

I rolled over and sat up. "Okay, but only because after you go back to the States, I can sleep all day."

"Jeez, Josie, that's a depressing reason." She zipped up her jogging suit then jumped up. "Oh well, whatever works! Come on, kiddo."

On that first early-morning run on the seminary grounds, we rounded a curve in the road and saw the Nevado del Huila. The eighteen-thousand-foot mountain was about one hundred miles away and almost always hidden in a bank of clouds, but that day, the white snowcap glowed pink from the sunrise. Aunt Rosie slowed her pace then stopped running as she stared at the clear and commanding mountain.

"It's always right there," I told her between breaths, "but most of the time, we can't see it. Wish I had the camera you brought me."

"Yeah," she answered, not taking her eyes off the peak. As we watched, clouds drifted around the mountain, concealing it.

Aunt Rosie turned to me. "Mountain break is over." She dashed down the road. "Bet you can't catch me!"

I raced past her. "What did you say?"

"Hey!" she called.

I slowed down, and we ran together until we arrived at our front gate. I closed it behind us and sprinted to the front door, just ahead of Aunt Rosie, as Brandy chased us into the house. Once we stopped panting, we joined Mom and Aaron for breakfast. Dad was in his office upstairs, getting his sermon ready.

"Okay." Aunt Rosie held up an *arepa*. "I get that papayas grow as big as watermelons here, but what is this? A pancake, only thicker?"

"Arepa," we said in unison.

"And it's made out of corn," Mom added.

Aaron reached for the plate. "Pass me one."

"Astrid, you didn't tell me how stunning Colombia is," Aunt Rosie said, handing the bread to Aaron. "And all this luxury," she added, looking around her.

We were eating at the long dining room table, which overlooked a sunny patch of bright-red flowers in one window and purple bougainvilleas in another.

"That says a lot, coming from you," I said. "You've been everywhere."

Aunt Rosie had worked as a flight attendant for American Airlines before Uncle Lloyd died.

"It is beautiful," Mom answered. "But a lot of people are hurting and need our help." She sipped her coffee.

"Well, for today, we're going to help them by being happy ourselves. What's on the agenda, my dear?"

Mom looked at her watch. "Church, of course, and we don't have much time."

"I haven't been here twenty-four hours, and you're already taking me to church." Aunt Rosie shook her head.

"Hey, it's what they do," Aaron said.

"Will I get to hear you play the piano?" Aunt Rosie asked him. He shrugged. "Sure."

"Then what're we waiting for?" Aunt Rosie jumped up, and I followed her out. Maybe I would enjoy going this time, too.

Despite the language barrier, everyone at the Baptist church loved Aunt Rosie for her genuine interest and infectious giggle. During Dad's sermon, I even caught some of Mom's choir members looking back and forth at the two sisters and whispering to each other. I could tell they were wondering how such different people could be related. I wondered the same thing. Aunt Rosie seemed soft and kind while Mom was stiff and aloof.

After lunch, Aunt Rosie sat with me on the couch, and I translated the Sunday newspaper's comics section for her and told her some of the headlines. Riots had broken out at the local university, a new art gallery had opened in town, a Cali soccer team had won an important game... I skipped over the week's list of murders.

At church again that evening, Aaron played a classical piece during the offertory. My parents and Aunt Rosie seemed mesmerized, watching him play the piano. He really was amazing, but I couldn't separate the beautiful music from the fact that my brother could be about as sensitive as a stump. So I went back to seeing how many words I could create from the letters in "*Digno es el Cordero*," the Spanish version of the hymn "Worthy is the Lamb."

We stopped for ice cream at Mimo's on our way home and sat on the benches by the small shop.

"He really has a gift, you know," Aunt Rosie told my parents.

Dad nodded, licking his chocolate-dipped ice cream cone. "It sure is nice to have him around to play for our services."

"No," Aunt Rosie said. "I mean he's really good. Maybe he should be in the States, studying piano."

My parents looked at each other. "I guess we never thought about it," Dad said.

Aaron was already finishing off his cone and eyeing Mom's. "You gonna eat that?"

Aunt Rosie had me up and running again on Monday morning, and after breakfast, Dad drove all of us to Silvia, a town where native Colombians sold handmade goods. As we traveled along curving roads through lush green mountains, I watched Mom. She'd been so serious lately, but Aunt Rosie had her laughing about the many pets they'd owned while growing up in Albuquerque. I wondered why I couldn't bring out this carefree side of my mom like her sister could.

Over the two-hour trip, Dad pointed out the sights along the road, and Aunt Rosie took pictures of everything: the coffee beans drying in the sun, the farmers with their burlap sacks, and the large red cacao beans hanging from tree trunks. When a brightly painted *chiva* bus careened by, overflowing with passengers, I leaned out my window and snapped a few photos, too.

As we climbed in altitude, the air became cooler and crisper and the landscape took on an even more vivid green. We rounded a bend, and in the distance, Silvia looked like an Alpine village in the summertime. Aunt Rosie caught her breath. "That's really beautiful."

Dad parked the car by a grassy area down the street from the market, and we pulled out the picnic lunch Blanca had packed.

"I think I see the town square," Aunt Rosie said. "Josie, let's walk over there."

"Sounds good to me."

After lunch, we walked the cobblestoned streets past cafés, *tiendas*, and offices to the market, leaving the others on a blanket in the sunshine. I admired the Catholic church that dominated the center of Silvia, but Aunt Rosie's eyes were on the Guambiano Indians selling their wares in the outdoor market. The men and women, their faces ruddy from the high altitude, were dressed in skirts and *ruanas*, woolen wraps similar to ponchos. The women wore black braids down their backs and several strands of white beads around their necks. Everyone had on dark bowlers. The native

South Americans, unlike many in the larger cities, weren't in awe of Americans. If anything, they hardly looked up when we walked by. They were proud of their way of life and intended to maintain it.

"I want a picture of that little girl and her baby brother," Aunt Rosie said, pointing her camera toward them.

I shook my head. "They don't like to have their picture taken. They believe a part of their soul leaves if an image is made of them."

Aunt Rosie nodded but looked disappointed. A small shoulder bag caught my eye, and I picked it up to examine it. I turned to show it to Aunt Rosie in time to see her trying to sneak a photo of the children. Their mother noticed, too, and yelled, motioning for my aunt to leave them alone. I ran over and apologized in Spanish, steering my aunt away as the Guambiano kept haranguing us.

"I told you not to do it," I whispered to her.

"I'm sorry, Josie, but they're fascinating. No one'll believe me when I try to describe these people. Those men are wearing long blue skirts! The women are wearing hats like your grandpa used to wear!"

"I know, but can't you just let them be?"

She gave me a surprised look, making my cheeks burn. "I'm sorry, Aunt Rosie."

She raised a hand. "No, Josie, you're right. If they don't want their picture taken, I won't take it." She put her camera away, adding, "So what if nobody believes me?"

"I'll back you up," I told her, guiding her to another stall.

By the time we headed back to the car, Aunt Rosie had something from almost every one of the vendors, and I was buried under a pile of woolen wraps, wall hangings, purses, knit caps, and belts. I tossed my armload in the back of the Suburban, and Aunt Rosie held up a royal-blue *ruana* for Mom to see. "I can't believe these prices. This only cost five dollars!"

"That's a nice one," Mom said as we hopped in the backseat.

"I'm driving," Aaron announced, walking to the driver's side.

"Are you kidding?" I asked.

Dad tossed him the keys. "He needs the practice, Josie."

"You better be careful." Mom shook a finger at him.

Aunt Rosie tousled Aaron's hair when he sat at the wheel. "We're behind you all the way, kid. Literally."

Dad sat next to my brother, warning him to slow down every few miles as he drove us down into the valley. Brightly colored blankets surrounded Mom, Aunt Rosie, and me, and I rested my head on one of them. Keeping up with my aunt wore me out.

"There wasn't a purse exactly like yours, Astrid, but this one's pretty close," Aunt Rosie said about her new shoulder bag.

"And it matches your turquoise bracelet," I pointed out. "So what do you think of Colombia so far?"

"I love it. I wish I could live here."

"Really?" Excitement at having her there bubbled inside me. "Why don't you?"

"Well, there's a reason," she said, looking at me.

"What is it?"

"I've met someone. We're going to get married." She glanced at my mom, but Mom kept staring ahead.

"Oh." My bubble popped. "But wait, that's good, isn't it?" I looked at Mom.

Aunt Rosie shrugged. "Yeah, it's great. Your mom's just upset because he's Catholic. But he's a really nice guy. He has two sons, so I'll be an instant mom. Do you want to see a picture?"

"Sure."

While Aunt Rosie dug through her purse for her billfold, I wondered why Mom wasn't happy for her sister.

"Here we are on a bike ride around Will's neighborhood," Aunt Rosie said, showing me the photo. "The little redhead is Thomas. He's five. Warren is eight. And that's Will."

"They look really nice," I said.

A balding man with kind eyes had his arm around Aunt Rosie

and his other hand on a boy's shoulder. With a toothless grin, Thomas stood in front of the others.

Mom took the picture and studied it. "That redhead looks like a handful," she said, giving it back to Aunt Rosie.

"Yes, he is," Aunt Rosie agreed. She tucked the photo away and looked out the window, her lips a thin line.

It seemed sad my mom would withhold her blessing just because Will was Catholic. Catholics weren't so different from Baptists, and Aunt Rosie had been through enough. I put my hand on her arm. "I'm glad you're here, Aunt Rosie."

Her face softened. "I'm glad I'm here, too, sweetheart."

When we arrived back home, Blanca had dinner ready for us, and afterward, I helped her take the dishes to the kitchen. She laughed when I told her about the trip and how we had to drag Aunt Rosie away so she wouldn't buy every *ruana* in the market.

Aunt Rosie walked in and gave me a questioning look. "What's up, kiddo?"

I switched to English. "I'm just telling Blanca about our day."

Blanca looked over at Aunt Rosie. "Good to shop," she said in broken English.

Aunt Rosie's eyes lit up. "Very good to shop."

I followed Aunt Rosie to the living room to listen to Aaron play the piano. We sang along while he played "Leaving on a Jet Plane" and "Memories," but when Aaron switched to a classical piece, Aunt Rosie took a seat on the rug. I joined my parents on the couch, where they were reading the newspaper, and watched Aunt Rosie sit with one knee up, turning at her waist to look behind her.

"What are you doing?" I asked.

"Yoga. Have you heard of it?"

"Just in magazines."

"Come try a spinal twist." She patted the floor beside her. "It feels so good, especially after sitting in a car all day."

I was following her lead when Dad set aside the newspaper,

stood, and checked his thick brown hair in the living room mirror. "I need to run a quick errand, Astrid. Ricardo wants to show me a book he's been talking about."

"Okay," she answered, reaching for his newspaper section. "Don't be gone too long. You two can get to talking."

"I'll be back soon," he called, grabbing his keys from the hall table.

"Who's Ricardo?" Aunt Rosie asked.

"One of the pastors in town." Aaron stopped playing and watched from the window as Dad drove away. "He's not heading the right way."

"What do you mean?" Mom asked without looking up from the paper.

Aaron turned. "It's probably nothing." He sat on the floor with Aunt Rosie and me. "Come on, Mom. If I can do this yoga, you can."

"No thanks," Mom answered. "You three be careful. I know someone who hurt her neck doing that stuff. Besides, it's from some Eastern religion."

"Yes, and it's been around a long time. But don't worry, Astrid," Aunt Rosie said. "We don't plan on chanting *Om mani padme hum* just yet."

Mom checked her watch, ignoring her sister. "I'm going upstairs. Don't forget we have a luncheon with the American Women's Club tomorrow, Rose. I'm looking forward to introducing you to my friends."

"Okay," Aunt Rosie answered, twisting in the other direction. "But we have to stop at the juice stand Aaron told me about."

"I'm worried you're being too adventurous for your stomach. And for your belief system," Mom answered, standing. "See you in the morning."

When Aaron figured out he wasn't flexible enough to touch his toes, he followed Mom upstairs. A few minutes later, his new Elton John album was playing on the stereo.

After a couple more stretches, I asked Aunt Rosie, "So, do you do that chanting stuff?"

"Sure. That and meditation help me handle life's problems." She glanced at the stairs and lowered her voice. "I find peace and comfort in a lot of things I've learned from Buddhism."

"Would you say that chant again?" I whispered.

She found a pen and a piece of paper on the telephone stand, wrote out the words *Om mani padme hum*, and handed me the paper. "It's a request for blessings of compassion. But let me tell you something else. Chanting the name of Jesus is powerful, too. The answers are all around you. You're a seeker, but you don't have to look far."

I wanted to cry, hearing her say I was a seeker, because I knew she was right. "Is it okay to be like that? I'm so different from Mom and Dad, and even Aaron. They know what's true for them, but I'm just not sure." I thought of how hard it was to sit through church three times every week, where everyone assumed I was one of them, and how easy it was to give the rosary a try when I was afraid. I wanted to know about my Jewish friend's synagogue, and I had a million questions for my classmates in their beautiful white dresses at their First Communion. But those friends and classmates had thought my questions were strange and that the answers were none of my business since I had my own religion.

"It's perfectly fine for you to be more like your Aunt Rosie than your parents." She hugged me then put her hands on my shoulders. "But you should be talking to me about boys! You're young and beautiful. Where are the dates?"

I sighed. "Maybe if I lived in the States, I would have a boyfriend. But the Colombian boys are so different from me. We don't have anything in common. And the American ones are more like brothers."

"That's too bad," she said.

"There is one boy." I looked down at the paper in my hands, folding it into a square.

"Really?"

"Yeah, but I think I'm just too American for him. It doesn't matter."

"Sure it matters. You're sixteen! Don't wait for something to happen. Get out there and create your own life."

"I don't know where to begin," I said, trying hard to keep the tears from my voice. "What should I do?"

"Get a boyfriend this summer," Aunt Rosie said with a nod. "You don't want to play it too safe, pretty girl." She hugged me again, and I rested my head on her shoulder, wanting to stay in her warm embrace forever. We finally said good night, then I went to bed smiling, feeling better than I had in a long time.

Chapter Four

I SHUDDERED AWAKE A FEW HOURS after going to bed, catching myself just before screaming. A strange nightmare about stolen souls in mountain villages and blinding headlights on hillside roads wouldn't let me go. No amount of praying the rosary could shake my fear, so I crept down the stairs and tapped on Blanca's door.

She motioned me to come in and sit. We were silent for a few moments before she asked, "What woke you tonight?"

I thought about telling her of the dream but changed my mind. "I don't know," I answered, trying to forget.

"Maybe you are too much in your own world. Many things are going on around you, but you are not seeing them."

"You said that before. What are you talking about?"

She studied my face then smiled. "It is nothing, *mija*."

"Good." I knew I should want to know what was going on around me, but somehow, I didn't think it would make life better.

"Your *tía*, she's nice."

"Yes," I said, grateful for the subject change. We giggled about all the things she'd bought at Silvia and how she had said the only way she could get it all back to the States was to wear everything on the plane.

"But you will miss her when she's gone," Blanca said.

I sighed. "Yes, I will. I want to buy my own rosary. Maybe that will comfort me. There's a picture in the newspaper of a rosary with black beads and an emerald in the crucifix. Can you take me somewhere that sells something like that? I have birthday money."

"I don't know about rosaries with emeralds, but some churches have *tiendas* where they sell books and religious articles."

"Good," I said. "Can we go tomorrow?"

"What will you tell your mother and father? And your *tía*?"

I shrugged. "Dad has to work, and Mom and Aunt Rosie are going to meet some of Mom's friends. Besides, we can come up with another reason to go shopping, can't we?"

"Your mother did say she would teach me to sew," Blanca answered. "I only need material to get started, and then I can make clothes for my brothers and sisters. But not tomorrow. My *novio* is taking me to visit his family."

I frowned. Blanca's boyfriend was a police officer who worked in our neighborhood. Juan Fernando was nice enough, but I couldn't help feeling jealous of their time together. Besides, when she was gone, there was no escaping the emptiness of this oversized house.

"We will go to a fabric store and a rosary shop another day. Now try to get some rest."

Even though Blanca hadn't made me feel much better, I fell asleep and was up and ready to run with Aunt Rosie the next morning. Breakfast was rushed, and soon, Mom and Aunt Rosie were out the door to the American Women's Club meeting, taking Aaron with them to his piano lesson. Dad had left for work already. The house, which had been so lively, was suddenly quiet.

I was reading in my room when Blanca called up the stairs. "It turns out Juan Fernando has to work today. If you like, we can go shopping."

"Really?" I ran to the railing and leaned over it. "That's great. I mean, I'm sorry you can't see Juan Fernando."

"It's okay, *chica*. Come on, we must go soon."

I rummaged through my sock drawer for the money I kept

hidden next to my supply of American candy. Before rushing downstairs, I put some money and a comb in my purse and dressed in jeans, a collared T-shirt, and tennis shoes. Blanca, in her usual cotton dress that tied in the back, seemed as excited about our adventure as I was.

We walked down our street to catch the bus into the city. I sat by the window, enjoying a much more elevated view than I was used to in our Suburban. Our driver kept so close to the curb that I could smell the cologne on the men walking along the sidewalk. Two women in the seat across the aisle from us began chatting with Blanca. They smiled when they learned I wanted rosary beads.

"She doesn't have her own already?" one asked, pointing to me.

"No one in the family has one," Blanca answered. "Until today."

They both nodded in satisfaction.

"Get one for your mother, too," the second one told me.

Although Colombians watched my every move, they didn't usually include me in their conversations, so I welcomed the rare connection. I didn't want to bring it to an end by saying there was no way I would be buying my mom a rosary.

Downtown, we hopped off the bus, and Blanca led the way to a fabric store. She bought sturdy cotton material for her little brothers and pretty prints for her sisters while I found buttons to match. We left the store, walked through a park along the Rio Cali, then crossed the river on a wide bridge. A few paces ahead, Blanca stopped and put her hand on my arm. "We are here."

I looked up at the church ahead of us. "Really? The most beautiful church in Cali?"

Blanca smiled. "I wanted to show you this one."

All my life, I had seen La Ermita in passing, and I studied the gray-and-white spires that were so ornate, they looked as though they belonged in Europe. I smiled at La Ermita's elaborate steeple, which reached toward heaven, not one bit sorry for its extravagance.

"*Venga, mona*, we don't have all day," Blanca said, pulling me inside the sanctuary. "I still have work to do when we get home."

She opened one of the heavy doors, and the beauty of the church stole my breath. I took two steps in, admiring the stained-glass windows, the large statues, and the altars. Our Baptist church was nowhere near as beautiful. In our church, simple rows of wooden pews faced a pulpit and a pool to baptize those who wanted to be born again. In La Ermita, I could feel the presence of something greater than myself, something that had been there long before me and would remain long after I was gone. Our church had love, but in the Catholic church was... majesty.

"Bless yourself with holy water," Blanca whispered, dipping her fingers into a bowl by the entrance.

"No, Blanca, I shouldn't." Anyone watching me would know I wasn't a Catholic, that my actions were those of an impostor. "Let's go." I put my hand on her arm.

Blanca led me to a small store off the sanctuary that sold crucifixes, rosaries, and statues of saints, and I blended in with the other shoppers. Although there were no emeralds, I found the perfect rosary for me: dark-blue beads with gold medallions and a not-too-lifelike crucifix. I liked praying the rosary, but seeing the tiny body of Jesus hanging on a cross was disconcerting. In that regard I was a Baptist, preferring to concentrate on a Christ who was resurrected, not in horrible pain on the cross. I also bought a four-inch statue of Saint Michael, the patron saint of protection. I liked his oversized wings.

The nun behind the counter wore a black-and-white habit that revealed only her hands and face. She handed me a brown paper bag with my purchases, and when I told the nun her church was beautiful, her face became so radiant, I caught my breath.

Outside, Blanca and I walked for a while before I broke the silence. "I have some money left. Let's go to the bookstore. The Librería Nacional."

"Where is it?" Blanca asked.

"Just down the street," I answered. "We can get some Neapolitan ice cream. It comes in tall sundae glasses with sugar wafers."

"*Sí*, but we cannot take too much time."

"Well, come on then," I said, pulling her along. The bookstore's smell of fresh ink and new paper was intoxicating. Books of all sizes were piled everywhere, each one a colorful invitation to a different world, each one in Spanish. I flipped through a few books, but Blanca didn't leave my side, so I led her to the café.

"Thanks for taking me to La Ermita," I said as we sat on barstools, eating ice cream.

"Did you like it?"

"A lot." I clinked my long spoon in my glass. Thinking of the woman in La Ermita's store, I asked, "What's it like to be a nun? Aren't they brides of Christ?"

"One of my aunts is a nun." She looked at her watch, a gift from my parents at Christmas. "We should go. I need to get home to make dinner. Besides, I am tired of the stares."

I turned and caught the eyes of a couple who must have thought it didn't make sense for a *gringa* to be eating with a Colombian native at the upscale bookstore. I stared back, but when Blanca stood and whispered, "*Vamonos,*" I was right behind her.

Cali's midday heat had passed, and the city bustled with people in the cool afternoon sunshine. I breathed in the satisfaction of being part of the crowd with somewhere to go, but when we arrived at the bus stop, Blanca grabbed my hand. "That's our *buseta*!"

We chased after it, calling for the driver to stop, but the bus lurched away. There was nothing to do but wait for another one.

An older man saw what happened and said, "That was the last Cañaveralejo bus. You will have to find a different way home."

A woman holding a compact umbrella made room for us on the bench. "What will you do?"

Blanca shrugged and patted my arm. "There will be another

bus," she whispered as I hugged my purse and bag containing the statue and rosary.

"There are no more buses tonight," the woman insisted.

"And it is difficult to find a taxi at this time of day," the man added. "You should call someone right away."

I had enjoyed the camaraderie of Colombians before, but now I wished they would leave us alone. Blanca set her jaw and said, "She will be fine."

We checked every few seconds for a bus to come as we waited in silence. After a while, I asked about her aunt who was a nun.

"She lives in a convent in Bogotá," she told me.

"What's her name?"

"Maria de las Lagrimas."

"Mary of the Tears?" I repeated.

"Yes. Her name had been Sara, but she was given a new name at the convent. My mother says they called her 'Mary of the Tears' because she cried every night for six months."

"Why did she cry?"

"She had to leave a boy in her hometown."

"Oh." I thought of Alejandro. Although there was really no hope of us getting together, at least I would be able to see him again, and it occurred to me I wasn't ready to give him up. We could be Romeo and Juliet, defying our parents' wishes.

Imagining our own balcony scene, with him knocking a tennis ball to my window, I didn't notice the shadows lengthening around me until I shivered. I looked around to see the two who had spoken to us earlier were gone. I wrapped my arms around my waist, wishing I'd brought a sweater.

Four men walked toward us on the street, joking loudly with one another. My heart beat hard as I turned away, praying for our bus—any bus—to come. This rowdy gang looked like trouble.

One of them called, "*Oye, mona, ¿qué tienes ahi?*"

Blanca stiffened.

The men stopped in front of us, waiting for a reply.

"We were at La Ermita," I answered. Looking up at the one who'd spoken, I pulled my new rosary and statue of Saint Michael from my bag and offered them to him.

For a long, frightening moment, he didn't speak. His friends watched him, waiting for a cue. I didn't lower my eyes, even though my hands were shaking. Finally, he laughed. His friends joined him, cackling like fighting roosters.

Blanca jumped up to hail a cab that was driving by, but two of the men intercepted her. "Where are you going?" one of them asked with a wolfish grin.

Blanca sat back down. "*La policía,*" she said, pointing. When the group turned to look at the police car approaching us, Blanca ran in front of the cruiser. It screeched to a halt, almost hitting her.

I used the distraction to slip past the gang and join Blanca. "Are you okay?"

"*Sí,*" she answered, grabbing my arm and dragging me to the officer's car window. I looked back in time to watch the men saunter away, still joking about the *gringa*.

Blanca explained to the officer she was Juan Fernando's girlfriend and needed to get in touch with him. The policeman's eyes met mine as he spoke into his radio, and within minutes, a taxi pulled up to the bus stop.

"Don't worry about her," the officer told Blanca, nodding in my direction as I rushed to open the cab's back door. "Juan Fernando will be in touch with her family."

Safely in the cab, Blanca said, "I hope we do not get into trouble for this."

I nodded, limp with relief, and stared at the neon signs as they flickered against the purple sunset.

She shook her head. "I should have listened to those people and called Juan Fernando."

I reached over and held her hand, wondering what Aunt Rosie would think and how upset my parents were going to be.

I didn't have to wonder for long. Dad was standing outside our wrought-iron gate with Juan Fernando. Dad raised his hand to our taxi as we pulled up, his wallet already out. "How much do I owe you?" he asked the driver as Blanca and I scrambled from the backseat.

"What happened?" Juan Fernando joked with Blanca. "Don't you know you can't take the *gringa* with you when you hit the town?"

Without answering, she slipped away from him and into the house.

After the driver took his fare and drove away, I hugged my father, tears stinging my eyes. "Thanks, Pop," I said into his shirt. "Our bus didn't come pick us up." Once I was safely home, the potential danger of our situation gathered in my chest. Over my shoulder, Dad shook Juan Fernando's hand. "Thanks again for your help. I'll try to keep Josie closer to home next time."

"*No se preocupe*, Señor Henry. I will make sure she is safe." Juan Fernando smiled at me, then he slid into his cruiser and drove off, waving out the window.

"I'm sorry, Dad," I said, reaching out to pat Brandy as we walked toward the house.

"Just try not to let it happen again. Now let's see about supper. I think your aunt is cooking up something special."

Dad had an unwavering belief that my life was in God's hands, that I would be okay, and most of the time, I wished he would show a little more concern for my well-being. That night, though, I appreciated his easygoing attitude. I ran my bag from La Ermita upstairs then returned to see what was happening in the kitchen.

Aunt Rosie was chattering with our parrot, Roberto, as she made sloppy joes. Blanca, who had started setting the table, looked up at me with wide eyes when I walked in.

"*Está bien,*" I said, taking the silverware to help. It was okay, but she didn't look convinced.

"Come and get it," Aunt Rosie called. "I bet you're hungry," she said to me.

"Yeah," I lied. Food was the farthest thing from my mind.

When Mom, Dad, and Aaron filed into the dining room and took their usual seats, Aaron asked me, "Why were you so late?"

"We went to a fabric store in town," I explained, sitting at the table. "Then our bus was pulling away just as we got to the stop. We chased after it, but it kept going. We waited forever for another one, until Blanca spoke to a police officer, who got us a taxi. I'm sorry, Mom," I added, looking at her. "I'll be more careful next time."

"I don't like it, Josie," she said after an angry silence. "We all had to wait for dinner, and now I'm going to be late for choir practice. And we were worried about you."

"Didn't you mean to say you were worried about her first?" Aunt Rosie asked. "And then that we had to wait for dinner?"

I glanced up in time to see Mom silence my aunt with a look and continue her tirade. "Maybe you should spend less time with Blanca and more time at the seminary. I know they could use your help shelving books in the library. You could even make a little money."

I focused on my sloppy joe, trying to hide my dismay. The Baptist Seminary across the street was a huge college with classrooms, apartment complexes, a library, cafeteria, and soccer field. Although I loved everything about the place—from the rows of sixty-foot-tall palms at the entrance to the maze of sidewalks around the apartments—I couldn't work there with my parents. I took a bite of my sandwich and stared at my plate, wishing the whole thing would blow over.

Aunt Rosie asked Aaron about his piano lesson, and everyone's attention shifted to him. I caught my aunt's eye and gave her a grateful smile. With a wink, she nodded and passed Aaron the potato chips.

Mom stood to leave for choir practice and called Blanca to the table. Holding a packet of music against her thin frame, Mom straightened her cardigan sweater over her shoulders and told Blanca what needed to be done the next day. Blanca nodded at the list of chores she had been doing every day since she started working for us.

I wanted to save Blanca from the lecture, but there was nothing I could do. I mouthed an apology and crept up to my room, where I flopped on my bed to read.

Aunt Rosie popped her head into my room. "You okay, kiddo?"

"Yeah." I didn't look up.

"That must've been scary, missing the bus and all." She sat on the edge of my bed.

I put down *Pride and Prejudice* and looked at her. "It was. But I wish Mom didn't have to be so mean to Blanca."

"I know. But your mother's been going through a lot lately, Josie. Maybe give her some slack." Aunt Rosie picked up Richard Bach's *Jonathan Livingston Seagull*. "Say, what's in this pile of books?"

"Have you read that one?" I asked.

"Yes, and I loved it," she said. "When you finish it, we can talk about it."

I smiled. "That would be great."

Just then, Aaron leaned against my doorframe. "So tell us the real reason."

"What are you talking about?" I asked.

"Why were you so late?"

"I already told you," I said then added, "well, we also went to the Librería Nacional for ice cream."

"Really?" Aaron asked. "I still don't think you're telling us the whole reason. Did you meet your boyfriend somewhere?"

"Blanca's boyfriend? You saw him outside."

"No, stupid, *your* boyfriend. Alejandro."

"Josie, who's this?" Aunt Rosie asked, smiling.

I glared at Aaron, but I knew my face was pink. "Alejandro *isn't* my boyfriend, and we *didn't* meet up." Wondering how Aaron knew, I turned to Aunt Rosie. "He's just a boy from school."

"Don't have a fit," Aaron said. "I'm just not sure a trip to the fabric store and the Librería Nacional would take all day. My only guess is Blanca's helping you see some guy."

"Well, you're dead wrong, Aaron. How could there possibly be guys in my life when everyone is so intent on keeping them away from me?"

Aaron laughed, clearly glad to have succeeded in riling me up.

"Leave her alone, Aaron," Aunt Rosie told him. "I can see how the time could get away from a person when she's having fun in the big city. Isn't that right, Josie?"

"Yeah, that's right." I turned away, and my eyes caught sight of the top edge of the brown paper bag sticking out of my desk drawer. I opened my book again, hoping the long afternoon at the bus stop wouldn't haunt my dreams.

Chapter Five

ON FRIDAY, MY PARENTS WENT to work at the seminary, and Aaron left to play tennis at the club. Aunt Rosie and I had a morning to ourselves, so we decided to take a trip downtown.

I mentioned our plans to Blanca as she carried the breakfast dishes to the sink. She raised her eyebrows. "La Ermita?"

"Don't worry," I answered, turning to go upstairs. "If we end up there, we'll take a taxi home. I don't want to miss another bus."

Her only reply was an especially loud clattering of pots and pans.

After dressing in jeans and a pink blouse, I met Aunt Rosie at the bottom of the stairs, smiling at her outfit. She was wearing a blue jumpsuit along with one of her belts from Silvia. She modeled her look with a twirl. "How's this?"

"It's great. You'll fit right in with the Colombians on the bus," I answered, opening the door for her.

"I don't want to fit in. I want to stand out."

"I was kidding, Aunt Rosie. You'll stand out, trust me. Jumpsuits haven't made it down here yet." We walked down the block, and when the Cañaveralejo bus stopped for us, I dropped coins into the metal box to pay our fare. Fellow passengers gave us sidelong glances as we found seats close to the front, but no one spoke.

We were on a busy four-lane street heading into town when Aunt Rosie asked, "Do you get American movies here?"

"Yeah, about six months late. They're in English, but they have Spanish subtitles. Why?"

"There's a movie Will and I saw a little while ago called *The Outlaw Josey Wales*."

"Really?" I asked. "Like my name?"

"Pretty close. Isn't that funny?"

"A movie about me, and I'm an outlaw."

"Trust me, it's not about you. Josey Wales is played by Clint Eastwood, and he'd just as soon shoot you as give you the time of day. He has this one line where he says, 'Are you gonna pull those pistols or whistle Dixie?'" Aunt Rosie mimicked Eastwood's raspy voice through gritted teeth.

I laughed. "Will must like westerns."

"Yeah," she answered, looking out the window. "You know, he was married before, but his wife died. He's a widower, like I'm a widow."

"Wow." I shook my head. "How'd she die?"

"He said she caught pneumonia. One day she was fine, and the next, he was planning her funeral." After a few moments, Aunt Rosie sighed. "I'm glad we found each other."

"Me, too," I said, thinking back to how devastated Aunt Rosie was when Uncle Lloyd died. "How long have you known Will?"

"About a year. A mutual friend of ours kept telling him he had to meet me and kept telling me I had to meet him. I didn't think it was going to work out at first, but he kept hanging around until it got to the point where I couldn't imagine him not being there." She chuckled.

"When's the wedding?"

"End of August. It'll be a small wedding." She paused and smiled at me. "You'd love the dress I'm going to wear. It's hot pink. If it can't be white, at least it'll be memorable!"

"Only you, Aunt Rosie," I said, smiling. "I wish we could be there."

"Who knows? Maybe you can make the trip up to Albuquerque. But don't worry; I'll take pictures."

Going to her wedding sounded fun, but I knew my parents wouldn't consider it. Pictures would have to do. "Our stop is coming up," I said, pointing over her head. "Will you pull the chain?"

We hopped off the bus a few blocks from La Ermita. There had never been any doubt in my mind that I would take her there. I had to share it with her.

"Let's go this way," I said, steering Aunt Rosie across Rio Cali. I pointed out the graceful trees that lined the rocky river as we walked across the bridge toward the church.

When La Ermita came into view, she stopped and stared. "What a beautiful building!"

"It's a Catholic church. Pretty impressive, huh?"

"I'll say. It reminds me of a smaller version of the Notre Dame Cathedral in Paris. Can we go inside?"

"I was hoping you'd ask." As we walked toward the ornate building, I told Aunt Rosie how Blanca had taught me to pray the rosary. "We were here the other day. We came so I could get a rosary of my own."

"So that's what took you so long," Aunt Rosie said. "And you didn't think your folks would understand."

"Not one bit. Do you still want to go inside?"

"Sure. Maybe I'll learn a little about Catholicism, for Will's sake."

We were quiet as we entered the building. I motioned toward the ceiling, and Aunt Rosie looked up with wide eyes at the distant dome and its stained-glass windows. When we moved on to the small store, the nun Blanca and I had met a few days before recognized me, waving me toward her.

"This is my aunt," I told her in Spanish. "She's visiting from the States."

The nun smiled and cradled Aunt Rosie's hand in hers, saying, "*Bienvenida.*"

"Thank you. I mean, *gracias*," Aunt Rosie answered, bowing slightly.

The nun's face lit up as it had before, and she gestured to the contents of the glass case.

"I love these statues. What is that one?" Aunt Rosie pointed at a man with a tiny dove on his shoulder.

The nun explained it was Saint Francis, and I translated.

"It would be perfect for Will's son Warren," Aunt Rosie told me. "He loves nature."

After Aunt Rosie learned about the saints, she chose two others: Saint Anthony of Padua, the Patron Saint of Lost Articles, for Thomas, who was always misplacing things, and Saint Joseph, the Patron Saint of Families, for Will.

The nun wrapped each statue in brown paper and placed them in a bag. "Will you be staying for the service?"

"Do you want to stay?" I asked Aunt Rosie.

She nodded. "Let's go for the whole experience."

We walked to the entry and joined the small crowd assembled in the hushed church. I blessed myself with the holy water and walked halfway up the aisle to a pew. I noticed others had knelt before sitting down, so I did the same, and Aunt Rosie followed my lead. As we absorbed our surroundings, my gaze kept returning to the Virgin Mary's serene face behind the altar.

A man holding a cross in front of him walked past us, followed by the priest in a long robe, and the sweet smell of incense filled the air. We began a process of standing, kneeling, making the sign of the cross, and reciting from the missal. Reading from the red prayer book, I noticed almost every passage mirrored Baptist beliefs. There were differences, of course. Blanca had been baptized as a baby, and she confessed her sins to the priest in a little closet. I'd been baptized in the second grade, when I chose to be. I admitted my sins to God, and the thought of listing them to a priest made me shudder. On the other hand, one of the new members of our church was terrified at the idea of walking into the deep baptismal pool to be plunged completely under water.

Aunt Rosie and I watched the congregants take communion, then we stood with the others and crossed ourselves one final time. As we walked out into the midday sunshine, Aunt Rosie said, "That was beautiful, and so peaceful. Thanks for taking me there."

"Do you think you would ever confess your sins to a priest?" I asked.

"Not unless I had to. What's next on the agenda?"

I stopped and looked around. "Let's go to the Plaza de Caycedo."

Cali's downtown streets swarmed with people as we headed toward the park to sit on thick concrete benches under towering palm trees. Some Colombians were dressed for work, moving quickly past us, while others relaxed with their friends in jeans and T-shirts.

"That looks fun," I said, pointing to a group kicking a soccer ball around.

"Yeah." Aunt Rosie leaned back and closed her eyes. "Do you realize, Josie, we could be anywhere in the whole world?"

"What do you mean?"

"I don't know; it just seems like people are the same wherever you go. Every city has a park for people to hang out in, and it usually has a statue of an important person in the middle." She opened her eyes and pointed to the bronze image of a man clutching a flag. "Who is that, anyway?"

"I'll go find out." I jumped up to read the plaque. Returning, I told her the statue was of a man who helped Cali gain its freedom from Spain. The park had been a public market in the 1600s.

As cathedral bells rang out, I looked around the old park with new eyes, wondering how much—or how little—had changed in three centuries. When the bells finally stopped chiming, I pulled out my camera to take pictures.

"I'm glad you like your new camera," Aunt Rosie said.

"Maybe I'll become a photographer for *National Geographic* one day." I took a picture of the statue with palm trees behind it then one of the soccer ball flying in the air. "I'll travel the world, visiting all those parks."

She nodded to a group of men standing at the corner. "What are they doing?"

"They're selling lottery tickets."

She stood up, opening her purse. "I want to buy one. I want a piece of the Colombian dream."

"What if you win?" I had never known anyone who gambled.

"Don't worry," she said as we approached the men. "They won't track me down to give me the money."

One man told us the price, and she gave him the pesos. As we walked away, Aunt Rosie was clutching the colorful strips of paper, and I overheard the group joking about the *gringas* buying lottery tickets. When I told Aunt Rosie, she turned back and laughed along.

We wandered by the cafés and trendy boutiques on Sixth Avenue, and I was opening the door to a perfume store when Aunt Rosie stopped me. "Your mom is probably home from the seminary by now. Let's head back and see what she's up to."

My aunt's words were almost a physical blow to me, and I winced. It hurt to hear that she wanted to end our day together. I took a deep breath and slowly closed the door to the shop, realizing it was because her visit, which had only just begun, would end too soon. I would miss her terribly when she was gone: our morning runs, our conversations, and the yoga. We would all miss the lively family meals and card games, but I needed her more than they did. She was the one family member who really knew me and accepted me as I was: a seeker. When she left, it would be even worse than before, because I knew what it felt like to be understood. A thought came to me, something I hadn't been able to express before: I wished she were my mother. But she wasn't, and she was ready to go.

"We'll catch a cab," I said, walking away from her toward the street. Everything that had seemed so perfect moments ago—La Ermita, the impossibly old park, the clanging cathedral bells, and the laughter of strangers—felt sad.

The sound of my own screaming shook me awake and left me panting, my heart pounding. I sat rocking myself in the night, not sure what would happen next. But nothing happened, making me wonder if I'd really screamed or if it had been a bad dream. But I couldn't remember a dream, and all I could think of was Aunt Rosie and me genuflecting toward the statue of Mary at La Ermita.

The clock read midnight, and I wondered if Aunt Rosie and Aaron were home. They had gone to see *Taxi Driver*, which Aaron knew Mom and Dad wouldn't let me see. I had spent the evening flipping through the three stations on our small television then read myself to sleep.

Wide awake, I opened Aaron's door and saw his bed was empty. Back in my room, I prayed the rosary to keep from worrying about them. The movie had to have ended hours ago. I was about to start the prayer again when a car rolled to a stop in front of our house.

I slipped out of bed and peeked through the window in time to see Aunt Rosie climb out of the taxi while Aaron thanked the driver in Spanish. I heard them sneak into the house and go into the kitchen, where a light flipped on. The sounds of the refrigerator and cupboards opening meant they were looking for a late-night snack. I grabbed my robe and crept downstairs to join them.

"Why are you guys home so late?" I whispered.

Aunt Rosie jumped. "Josie! You scared me." She patted my arm and asked in a hushed voice, "You hungry? We're starving."

I smelled cigarette smoke in her hair, but that wasn't surprising. People smoked everywhere in Cali. "I'm not hungry. Where were you guys?"

"None of your business," Aaron said, putting bread and cheese on the counter.

"We can tell her." Aunt Rosie opened a bag of potato chips. "We went dancing at a discotheque after the movie. I love how friendly everyone is here."

"It was her idea." Aaron pointed a thumb at our aunt, his head in the refrigerator. "Where are the pickles?"

I pushed him aside, pulled the pickle jar from the refrigerator door, and handed it to him. I knew Mom and Dad wouldn't approve of their trip to a nightclub, but I wasn't about to tell. I had a secret of my own, and I hoped Aunt Rosie was keeping it to herself.

Aunt Rosie giggled as she tried to salsa across the kitchen floor.

"I'm going back to bed," I told her. "See you in the morning?"

"Bright and early," she said. "Well, maybe not too early."

I went upstairs, trying to understand why I felt let down by Aunt Rosie. It occurred to me, as I lay holding my rosary, that Aaron saw a different side of my aunt, a side she didn't share with me. I wondered what else I didn't know about her.

The next morning, she was my Aunt Rosie again, but we barely ran at all, and she downed two cups of black coffee at breakfast instead of one.

"So tell me about last night," I said between bites of buttered toast.

"I mostly learned Spanish from some nice Colombian men. They gave up teaching me to salsa early on." She put more papaya on her plate. "Aaron had a good time. I think he met a girl he likes."

"Really? He never settles on just one girl."

"Well, he spent most of the night dancing with a cutie in a party dress and high heels. I was glad to see him enjoying the evening. I want you two to get out there and have fun!"

"Just do me a favor," I said, looking around to make sure we were still alone. "Don't tell anyone about La Ermita."

She gazed at me with big blue eyes. "I wouldn't dare, angel. That's about your search for meaning, and I don't want anyone to stop you."

I blinked back unwelcome tears.

She reached for my hand and squeezed it. "Tell me, Josie. What adventures do you have planned for the summer?"

I looked away. All I could think of was the adventure I wouldn't be having—dating Alejandro.

"You're thinking of that Colombian boy Aaron was talking about, aren't you?" she asked.

I shrugged.

She held her coffee cup with both hands and took a long drink. "You're young. It's summer. Surely you'll be doing something fun."

"There's always the stack of books by my bed."

She ignored me. "You can take lots of pictures with your new camera."

"Yeah," I agreed halfheartedly. "We'll be going swimming and playing tennis at the tennis club, too. Oh, and Mission Meeting is coming up."

"What's Mission Meeting?" Aunt Rosie asked as Aaron joined us in the breakfast room.

"It's when all the missionary families in Colombia get together," I answered. "We all stay at the seminary for about two weeks. The parents go to a bunch of meetings to talk about their work while the missionary kids hang out together."

"What's that like?" Aunt Rosie asked, watching Aaron rest his head on the table.

"It's good to see other MKs—you know, missionary kids," I said. "Some years are better than others."

"Well, I predict this will be the best Mission Meeting yet with your MK friends."

"Can you two keep it down?" Aaron mumbled. "My head is killing me."

"You look like you could use a cup of joe." Aunt Rosie poured coffee for him.

"He doesn't drink that stuff," I said.

"There's always a first time." She gave Aaron a devious smile as he took the cup and drank it down. "So what shall we do today? Maybe play tennis again?"

"Count me out," Aaron said.

Aunt Rosie's final days with us were a blur of morning runs, tourist activities, and conversations on the living room rug. On Aunt Rosie's last evening in Cali, we all wore our Sunday best and ate dinner at the nicest restaurant in town, the Suizo Chalet.

Walking to the car after our excessively large fondue meal, Aaron asked, "Should we go up to Cristo Rey again?"

"No way!" Aunt Rosie and I answered in unison.

Aaron laughed. "Then how 'bout a drive around the city?"

Mom and Dad agreed, and Aaron drove us through Miraflores, the neighborhood where my family used to live. The hillside streets were steeper than I remembered, and the houses were closer to each other, but the stairs to our big front door and the patch of grass I used to play on were the same.

Aaron slowed down next to our old house, and I pointed to the second story. "That was my balcony."

"Cool," Aunt Rosie said. "Did you like living there?"

"Yeah. Sometimes trios of *boleros* would serenade our neighbors in the night. That was fun."

"It was nice being surrounded by Colombians," Dad said. "Where we live now is more convenient for work, though."

Aaron put the Suburban in gear and headed up the hill. "Can I drive us over to Arboleda?"

"That's a really nice neighborhood," I explained.

"Okay by me," Dad said, looking over his shoulder at Mom.

"We have to go home eventually," Mom answered with a sigh.

It was late when we arrived at our house. Dad and Aaron went upstairs, but Mom lit candles in the living room and sat down on the couch, patting the seat for Aunt Rosie to join her. I sat in a rocking chair across the room while they talked about their childhood and old friends. I closed my eyes and listened to their murmured conversation, comfortable in my chair.

"I feel fine. I'm just not sure what I did was the right decision," Mom's words floated by.

"You did what was best for you, Astrid," Aunt Rosie answered.

"I wish that made me feel better about it."

"You'll have to find a way to put it behind you," Aunt Rosie said as I dozed off.

Mom shook my shoulder, pulling me out of sleep. "Come on, Josie, time for bed."

The candles were gone, and Aunt Rosie was already in her room. I trudged upstairs, dressed for bed, and reached for my rosary. I desperately needed Mother Mary to keep the sadness away, because I knew what tomorrow would bring.

The next day was all business. We ate breakfast, and Aunt Rosie took a few more pictures while Dad loaded her suitcases, each crammed with souvenirs, into the Suburban. During the drive through Cali, Aaron made jokes, and Aunt Rosie laughed along, but I couldn't bring myself to join in.

Before I knew it, we were at the airport, and I was choking on tears as I hugged my aunt and promised to write. Then she boarded the plane, it lifted off, and Aunt Rosie was gone.

Chapter Six

THE BAPTIST COLLEGE CAMPUS WAS the only place where I felt truly safe in Colombia. Even in my house, with Brandy barking at anyone who passed by, I felt a vague sense of unease, that I wasn't completely protected. But the seminary was surrounded by a high brick-and-metal fence, and a gun-wielding guard was on duty at all times. I could roam the wide-open spaces in peace, missing Aunt Rosie and thinking about Alejandro.

I wandered around the campus the day Aunt Rosie left, ending up in the library on the second floor of the main building. Only a few students were sitting at the tables between the bookshelves, and I walked out to the balcony, where bougainvillea was taking over. I liked to study the scale model of old Jerusalem on display in a glass case, with its tiny people and elaborate temple. After a glance at the model, I looked around to make sure no one was watching me. I stole inside the library again and searched among the concordances, books on ancient languages, and inspirational stories, until I found a book about the saints. Flipping through its pages, I came across the perfect saint for my problems. I wrote his name on a piece of paper and headed back home.

Blanca was dusting the living room furniture when I found her.

"When do you think we can go to La Ermita again?" I asked.

"Why?"

"I want a statue of Saint Jude, the Patron Saint of Lost Causes," I told her.

"*Ay, muñeca*, life will go on. You will see. Things will get better for you." She looked at my pitiful face and stopped. "Come with me." Blanca put down the dust rag and led me to her room. "I have the statue of Saint Jude. You can borrow it."

"Really?" I asked.

"I am far from my family," she said, smiling as she dug in her chest of drawers and handed me a statue. "And I had boy troubles of my own, too."

I had expected the statue of Saint Jude to be prince-like, wearing a cape over his strong shoulders, a sword in his hand. The Helper of the Helpless and Patron Saint of Lost Causes was an old man leaning heavily on a cane, with a yellow flame on his bald head. I had put so much hope in Saint Jude that when I saw the uninspiring statue, I laughed. Blanca raised her eyebrows, but I ignored her. I grabbed the saint and hurried to my room.

The tired old saint seemed to smile at me as I studied it, and I hugged it to my cheek. It had already given me what I needed: perspective. Maybe, just maybe, I could live through this. I would see my aunt again, and there would be other boys. Life would go on. Besides, summer was here, and I would make sure Aunt Rosie's prediction came true: this Mission Meeting would be the best one yet.

Over the next few days, Mom and I helped Blanca pack for her annual trip to her home. We filled a suitcase with canned food, several Spanish New Testament Bibles, and candy for Blanca to take to her family. She had bought a bus ticket to Huila, the town near her family's farm, and when a taxi came to take Blanca to the bus station, I stood beside the gate with my hand on Brandy's collar and waved her off. Then it was my turn to load my suitcase with what I would need for Mission Meeting.

My family always stayed at an apartment in the seminary for the ten-day retreat, and it felt like a vacation, though we were just across the street from home. Mission Meeting would be like a family reunion; we MKs even called each other's parents aunts and uncles, making us cousins of a sort. The missionaries weren't family like my Aunt Rosie, but it would be good to see everyone again, especially my best friend Anna.

After crossing the street with my bags and claiming my room in our apartment, I headed to the dining hall. As long as I stayed within the seminary gates, I could go where I pleased. As I walked past the gardenia bushes toward the cafeteria, it occurred to me that I felt more self-assured since Aunt Rosie's visit. Her acceptance had given me confidence.

I was in the cafeteria lunch line when someone came up behind me and covered my eyes. I turned, and squealed when I saw it was Anna. We grabbed hands and jumped up and down, laughing. Although she hadn't reached my height, Anna had grown taller over the past year, and she had a new look. Her dark hair was brushed and clipped to the side, her jeans were stylish, and she was wearing lip gloss.

"So how was your year?" I asked. "How many horses are on your ranch now?"

"Just five," she answered. "My dad got a mare, and we think she's pregnant. The foal will be mine if she is."

"Wow, how cool! What will you name it?"

"If it's a female, definitely Josie."

"Hmm," I said with a laugh. "I'm not sure I like the idea of you riding around on Josie all day. Or putting a feed bag on Josie or smacking Josie with a riding whip."

"I could call her Aunt Agnes," she whispered.

We looked around for our least-favorite missionary. An older woman who wore conservative dresses and kept her hair in a tight bun, Aunt Agnes had been on the mission field longer than anyone else. Anna saw Emily and called her over. Emily's parents were the only missionaries in the small town of **Tumaco,** and she was one of the few MKs who went to a public Colombian school. Two years older than Anna and me, Emily loved to bring up our age difference while tossing her waist-length brown hair.

"Josie, you've changed a lot in the last year," Emily said, looking me over with her big brown eyes. "No braces? No glasses? And you've got curves!"

I blushed, thrilled she'd noticed but not sure how to respond.

"Are you dating anyone?" she asked, giving her signature toss.

"No, are you?"

"Yeah. His name is Dario, and he goes to our church. I don't know what we're going to do when I leave for college in August." Emily sighed.

"Really?" I asked. "And your parents let you date him?" Maybe it was just in Cali, but not dating the church members was an unwritten rule.

"Sure." She shrugged as we inched forward in the line. "Why not?"

"I don't know. There aren't any guys to date at our church. There was a boy at school, but..." I turned to Anna, not wanting to finish my sentence. "How about you? Are you dating anyone?"

"No," Anna said. "I'm interested in someone, but he doesn't know I'm alive."

Emily grabbed Anna's elbow and looked me in the eye. "Josie, please tell me you know that Anna is in love with your brother."

"Oh no!" I turned to Anna. "That's not true, is it? You don't know my brother like I do!"

"Emily, you promised you wouldn't say anything." Anna pulled her arm away and glared at her. "Remind me not to tell you any more secrets."

"Don't worry, Anna," I told her. "I'd just as soon forget I heard it." I glared at Emily, too, but she didn't seem to notice either of us.

"Hey, it's the Westin twins," she said, waving at the two MKs who were walking in. Jack and Tom Westin lived in the capital city of Bogotá and were eighteen. They were tall and athletic but not as smart as my brother, who liked to tease them when they didn't keep up with his jokes. Most people couldn't tell the two blond, blue-eyed boys apart, but those of us who'd grown up with the twins knew their subtle differences. Jack was shorter but not by much. Tom always kept a comb in his back pocket.

When Emily went to greet them, she left Anna and me in an uncomfortable silence. Anna's infatuation with Aaron would strain our friendship if we weren't careful. "Listen," I said. "I'm okay with forgetting how you feel about Aaron."

"Just tell me: does he ever mention me? Is there a chance he could be interested in me?"

"What do you think, Anna?" I motioned in Aaron's direction. "Do you see him over there?"

Anna looked where I was pointing. He stood outside, surrounded by a group of girls. They were laughing at something he had said.

"He doesn't talk about any of them, either," I added.

"I suppose you're right."

She sounded so dejected, I tried a different angle. "Listen, you're too good for him. You win awards at rodeos. You're on your way to becoming an important scientist—"

"Preferably a veterinarian, but go on."

"You are so much… better than he is." It was a lame finish, but we had arrived at the front of the food line. We pushed gray trays toward the servers, who dished rice, fried chicken, and green beans onto our dinner plates.

"*Muchas gracias,*" I said, smiling at the Colombian cooks in their matching aprons.

We sat with other MKs, joining the conversation about the

youth group traveling from Florida. Every Mission Meeting, a group of Baptist teenagers and adults came from somewhere in the States to lead the MKs in discussion groups and Bible studies while our parents attended meetings about their work in the churches around Colombia. Each day was one long Sunday school class. Then we were on our own for dinner, and we kids met on the darkened seminary grounds for Capture the Flag. The adults talked over coffee or played card games in the cafeteria.

Suddenly, Anna looked behind me and beamed. Aaron had arrived. "Hey, guys," he said. "Someone tied a rope onto the big tree by the soccer field. You can swing really high on it."

A few of the kids took their trays to the servers and followed Aaron out the door. After our lunch, Anna and I walked over to the rope swing, too. The tree was enormous, about seventy feet tall, with a huge canopy of leaves. I had a healthy respect for the old tree because bats lived in its decaying trunk. The erratic creatures flapped around it at sunset, and no amount of telling me they ate mosquitoes made them less creepy, especially when there was the chance they could get caught in my hair.

When we arrived, my brother was swaying from a rope hung from one of the tree's highest branches. Aaron was fearless. He was standing on a large knot in the thick rope, swinging in an arc that took him from one edge of the tree to the other. Some MKs were catching the rope and running with it to pull him higher.

After a few scary pendulum swings, Aaron called, "Slow me down." When the rope stopped swinging, he jumped off and brushed his hands on his jeans. "Who's next?"

"I am," Anna said, stepping forward.

"Are you sure?" I asked her under my breath. It seemed senseless, hanging onto a string and sailing twenty feet in the air. But even as I thought of its stupidity, I wished I had the nerve to try it.

Anna stared at Aaron, walked up to the rope, and climbed on. "I'll do it. Swing me."

Aaron grabbed the bottom of the rope and ran with it, pulling her into the air. Her first swing wasn't high, but each time Aaron pulled the rope, she went closer to the edge of the tree's canopy.

"This is so cool!" Anna said, sounding more afraid than excited. I wondered if she would lose her lunch when she came down.

"I gotta tell you, Anna, I'm impressed," Aaron called. "What do you think of the view up there?"

At the top of the arc, Anna said, "I can see the tennis club behind the wall. I can see the pool!" But as she turned toward the seminary, her smile froze. When she swung closer to us, her eyes were wide. "Stop me. Aunt Agnes is heading our way."

Sure enough, our missionary aunt stomped toward us in her sensible shoes, scowling. Aaron grabbed the rope and slowed it down. By the time Anna was stepping off the knot and rubbing her hands, Aunt Agnes was calling to us. "What are you kids doing in that tree?"

Anna's younger brother, Isaac, sat on the knot and calmly moved back and forth, dragging his feet on the ground.

Aaron said, "Just swinging on this rope, Aunt Agnes. Would you like to give it a try?"

Anna and I could barely keep from laughing, and Isaac had to pretend he was coughing.

"Now listen, young man"—she wagged her bony finger at Aaron—"what you're doing is very dangerous. That rope doesn't look strong enough to hold your weight, and neither does that limb." She looked up then around at us. "Do you want me to tell your parents what you children are doing out here?"

Most of the MKs didn't meet her eyes, but Aaron wouldn't back down. "Actually, Aunt Agnes, I don't think my parents would mind us having some fun. Life is dangerous. Didn't you realize that when you became a missionary?"

"Well!" She puffed up. "Such insolence! I came here to tell lost souls about Jesus. If I die leading someone to Christ, that's very different from your falling off a rope and dying of stupidity."

I could see Aaron wanted to keep the conversation going, but I didn't think talking about it any more was such a good idea. I put my hand on his arm. "We're sorry, Aunt Agnes."

"That's more like it." She gave a firm nod, turned on her heel, and marched back to join the other missionaries.

"Why do you aggravate her?" I asked my brother once Aunt Agnes was out of earshot.

He shrugged and tousled Isaac's scruffy hair. "Guess the fun's over for now."

"Come on, Anna," I said. "Let's get back to the cafeteria. It looks like more families have arrived."

Aaron joined us as we walked.

"Look at my hands," Anna said, showing us her pink palms.

"Look at mine," Aaron answered, lifting his hands. They were covered in blisters.

"Aaron, you always go too far," I said.

"Yes, I do." He puffed up, just like Aunt Agnes had done. I shook my head.

Later that afternoon, my parents drove Anna, Emily, Aaron, the Westin twins, and me to the airport to welcome the American youth group. Uncle Bruce, a missionary doctor who worked at one of Cali's hospitals, followed in the seminary van. We would need it to carry the visitors back to Mission Meeting. As we rode through town, Emily asked who we thought the captains of the Capture the Flag teams should be.

"Tom and I want to do it," Jack said. "We'll be heading for college in the States soon. This will be our last Mission Meeting."

"Aw, I didn't know you were so sappy," Emily said, elbowing Jack.

"I'm not; it's my twin here." He nodded in Tom's direction.

Aaron and Anna started teasing Tom for being sentimental, and I turned to him, about to join in. But an image of him as a child came to me. He'd cried a lot, but then again, I'd been the one hiding behind thick glasses, my nose in a book. Aaron wet his pants until he was seven, and Jack was accident prone, showing up to each Mission Meeting with a cast on an arm or leg. Emily sucked her thumb, and who could forget that Anna didn't like to wear clothes? Up to her sixth birthday, she was snatching off her shirt and shorts as soon as her mom looked away. This was the problem with growing up in a missionary family: we knew too much about each other.

I touched his knee and smiled up at him. We were at a stoplight, and I noticed a man by the road with a squirrel monkey in his arms. I pointed the pair out to the others, and when the monkey caught sight of us, it jumped onto the man's shoulder, screeching as it bobbed its head. We laughed at its antics, and as my dad drove on, the conversation moved away from Tom.

Tom was flipping a small stone in his palm, and a few blocks down the road, he took my hand and put the stone in it. I liked how his big hands were strong but smooth.

"I want you to have my pet rock," he said.

"What's its name?" I played along, studying the flat gray stone.

"Rocky."

I laughed. "Thank you, Tom."

"No, thank you, Josie."

"No problem," I said, unable, for some reason, to stop smiling as I clutched the stone.

We pulled into the airport parking lot and jumped out of the Suburban, racing each other to the airline desk. The plane was running behind schedule, so our group meandered toward the center of the terminal. We didn't know how long we would be waiting, so Tom and Jack wandered off to play hacky sack with

Aaron. Emily, Anna, and I sat on the floor in front of Uncle Bruce and my parents to play Gin Rummy. I always carried my orange deck of Braniff Airways cards in my purse for times like this.

Anna was shuffling the cards for a third game when Uncle Bruce and my dad walked back to the check-in desk. A few minutes later, Dad hurried toward us. "They're already here," he called, motioning for us to follow him. "They came in from the far end of the terminal. Bruce is with them, and they're almost through customs."

Anna handed me the cards, and we ran to the glass-enclosed customs room. When we saw the teenagers surrounding Uncle Bruce, Anna and I gaped at each other. Every single one of them was tan, had perfect hair, and was wearing clothes straight out of a magazine.

Aaron and the twins came up behind me, and Aaron let out a low whistle. "Look at the girl with the blue jean jacket," he said to Jack.

"Try to stop being a jerk, Aaron," I said, but my eyes were on the gorgeous boy talking to Uncle Bruce. He looked like a Greek god with dimples, and I wanted to drink in everything about him, from his perfectly messy blond hair to his perfectly scuffed topsiders. Uncle Bruce led them out of customs, and we walked together downstairs to the van and car. Aaron managed to walk next to the girl in the jean jacket. Emily was chatting with the Greek god. The rest of the American visitors stayed together, laughing at inside jokes as we studied them with sidelong glances. In the end, all ten visitors rode in Uncle Bruce's van, but that was okay. I wasn't ready to spend an hour in a van with a bunch of strangers.

After arriving at the seminary, the visitors put their suitcases in their rooms and came to the cafeteria for a snack. Their leader, Larry, was full of energy as he led us in games to get to know each other. He smiled nonstop, making the hard work of getting our two groups to cooperate look effortless. We MKs had played most of the games in past Mission Meetings, but the Grouping Game was new.

In this game, Larry asked us questions like what month we were born in, what state our parents were from, and if we had a dog or cat. The people with the same answers found each other and talked until he called out another question. Larry worked with a college student named Martin, and almost every answer I gave was the same as his. We were both born in April, had a dog, and came from Texas.

"So what else do you and I have in common?" Martin asked me, his dark eyes sparkling. Though six inches shorter than Aaron and the twins, he was muscular and had a kind face.

"What's your favorite color?" I asked.

"Blue," he answered.

"Me too! And what's your favorite food?"

"Italian."

"Not Colombian?" I joked.

He laughed. "Not yet."

I looked around for the Greek god, Erik. We hadn't been in the same group even once. I noticed, though, that he kept checking his hair and watching Aaron make a fool of himself with Molly, who was still wearing the jean jacket. I turned back and smiled at Martin.

At nine o'clock, Larry dismissed us for the evening. Aaron and I ran to our apartment for dark jackets, and when we arrived at the soccer field, sixteen kids had gathered for Capture the Flag. Though Aaron had invited the visiting kids to play, none joined us. Isaac and some of the younger MKs might have scared them off, talking about the wild animals that might be lurking in the playing field.

The Westins picked their players. I was on Jack's blue team with Emily and Isaac, while Tom picked Aaron and Anna for his red team.

I waved to Anna as we walked in separate directions. "Maybe next year we'll be on the same team."

"Next year, we'll be the captains," she called back, disappearing into the darkness.

"Come on already," Aaron called as Tom and Jack stood in the center of the field, deciding on the boundaries and where the jails and flags would be. Anticipation and excitement were getting to all of us. Finally, the twins shook hands, and we were off.

My plan was to lie low and watch the other team, looking for holes in their defense. One first-timer was captured almost immediately when he foolishly crossed the line, and Tom dragged him to their prison. Aaron acted like a drill sergeant, pushing him to the ground and yelling, "Drop and give me twenty!"

Soon, I heard Anna tell Aaron in Spanish, "You better cool it. He might pass out. He's scared enough."

Our team captured another of the younger set, and Jack and Emily tied his hands behind him. They were teasing him with a harmless shell of a huge scarab beetle when the boy fought the rope from his hands and ran off the field.

"Toby, come back," Jack yelled after him. "Look, I'm sorry. Your initiation's over. You're in."

The boy turned around, and Jack patted him on the back. Out of the corner of my eye, I saw Anna use the distraction to pop out of the darkness and steal the blue bandana that was our flag. My heart pounded as I chased her down. I grabbed her around the waist, but she kept running, dragging me along. Jack stopped her and yanked the flag from her hand.

"Nice try, Anna," Jack told her. "Now get in jail."

Anna and I fell on the ground, panting and laughing, and when we could breathe again, I escorted her to our prison while her teammates cheered her valiant effort. As the game continued, Aaron almost caught me in his territory, but I made it back to my side. I couldn't help but taunt him as I stood out of his reach.

"Don't you worry, sis," he said. "I'll get you before the night's over."

I had no reason to be afraid, but I still shivered with anxiety. There was a fine line between reality and fantasy in the game, and that was why I loved to play. I slipped back to the safety of our territory to watch for a while. Sometimes, I needed to regain my courage.

When I'd grown bored with watching the others, I sneaked into enemy territory, using mango trees for cover. Ten feet from their home base, I ran to their red flag, grabbed it, and turned to head back to our side. Foolishly, I waved it over my head and whooped as I ran. Tom reached me within seconds. He pulled me to the ground, and I wrestled to get away. But he was on top of me, and he wasn't letting me go.

"I give, Tom. Here's your flag back," I gasped, trying to stand.

He took the flag and held my hands against the ground with his hands, not saying a word. Stuck under his weight, I breathed his musky scent mixed with the freshly mown grass. Spellbound, I realized, all at once, how good looking he was. His eyes sparkled as they stared without apology into mine. His strong chin hovered over me. It didn't seem to matter that I could barely breathe. I didn't want him to go. Could he feel my heart pounding? Was that his heart beating against my chest?

Too soon, Tom moved off me and stood, offering his hand. I took it and jumped up, leaning into Tom. He steadied me then let me go, walking toward his home base, flag in hand. He stopped, turned around, and pointed at me. "You're in my territory. That makes you my prisoner."

His words sent a delicious shiver down my spine.

Aaron walked toward the center of the field. "Let's call it a night."

"Yeah," Jack said, coming out of the shadows. "Come out, everyone. We're done for tonight."

"Josie's our prisoner tomorrow," Tom said as MKs materialized out of the dark field.

"What, we don't start fresh every night?" I asked.

"No way," Tom said.

Aaron laughed. "Sorry, Jos. Looks like you're too dangerous out there."

"Fine," I grumbled, but my heart was doing somersaults. I walked off the field with Anna, and as she shared stories of the game, I put my hand in my back pocket, reaching for the stone Tom had given me. As it moved through my fingers, I smiled. Blanca had been right. Life would go on, and things would get better for me. And maybe Tom would be the reason.

Chapter Seven

AFTER LUNCH THE NEXT DAY, Anna and I met in front of the seminary to take a tour of the city. It was Larry's idea, but only Martin and two girls from the youth group joined us. Anna was showing me a bruise from the previous night's Capture the Flag game when Tom walked over. "Heard you were going downtown," he said.

"Join us." Larry beckoned to him. I looked away so Tom wouldn't see my big grin.

We were waiting for a bus when Larry pointed to a huge structure down the road. "What's that?" he asked. "It looks like a giant bowl."

"It's the Plaza de Toros," I told him. "It's where they have bullfights. We can hear them yelling '¡olé!' from our house. It's pretty awful, really."

"Do that many people want to see a bullfight?" Martin asked.

"Sure," Anna answered. "Bullfighting's popular here."

"Aaron and I went once," I said. "I don't know what was worse: seeing the bull stumble after being stabbed or watching the crowd in a frenzy at the sight of his blood."

"One bullfight was enough for me, too," Tom added, kicking his hacky sack.

"I don't know," Anna said, her arms crossed. "If a bull is really aggressive, they let him live to fight again. And bullfighting's been around forever. It's part of Colombian culture. I think we should accept it."

The four Americans looked at me. I didn't want to disagree with Anna, but some traditions needed to be changed. "Look, here comes the bus," I said, grateful for the distraction. "Does everyone have their money?"

After clinking the coins in the bus's metal box, Daphne and Donna, the two girls from the youth group, sat together and bent their heads over Daphne's *Seventeen* magazine. Larry stayed near them, and Tom sat next to me, leaving Martin with Anna across the aisle. I saw Martin give Tom a disappointed look. Could it be that the college boy from Florida wanted to sit by me? I remembered how much we'd had in common during the Grouping Game, and I had to admit, having two guys interested in me was a nice problem.

"Tell Martin about Siloé," Anna said over the seat. We were passing a large hill crowded with tin-roofed shacks. Laundry drying on clotheslines fluttered outside each home along busy dirt roads that zigzagged up and down the steep hill. People were everywhere.

"It's a *barrio* of poor people, and it's really dangerous," I told Martin, who had turned to face me. "What's weird is at night, the whole mountain lights up with television sets. You can see right into the houses, and almost every one of them has a blue light shining out of it."

"That's sad," Martin said.

"Yeah, television's a waste of time," Anna said. "And kids are always asking how big our house in the States is. They think we all live like those people in the American soap operas."

"Wait," Martin said. "I wasn't talking about their TVs. I mean it's sad they have such terrible living conditions."

"These aren't terrible conditions," Tom said. "It's a dangerous place, and I don't recommend going there, but these people have food and water. And homes."

As we looked at the hill and its mass of humanity, Tom asked, "Would you like to see some really poor people?"

"Where are they?" Martin asked.

"Out in the country," Anna answered, just as Tom said, "On the streets."

I nodded. "Maybe both of you are right."

We were quiet until the bus jostled past the Parque de las Banderas.

"Cali hosted the Pan American Games a few years ago," I told the others, showing them the flags of thirty countries behind a wide fountain.

"Is the US flag there?" Martin asked.

"Yeah, somewhere," I answered.

"It's weird to see the Colombian flag on all the buildings, not the stars and stripes."

"You're not in Kansas anymore," Anna joked.

When we were closer to the heart of the city, I reached up and pushed the button. "The next stop is ours."

"What's there to see?" Anna asked.

"A really cool church," I said.

"First Baptist?"

"No." I smiled at her. "Come on, I'll show you."

The *buseta* stopped on the other side of Rio Cali. As we walked through the park and over the river toward La Ermita, I didn't point out the cathedral. I wanted them to discover it as Aunt Rosie had, and I thought of Blanca. She'd done the same for me. She'd let the beauty of the church pull me in.

"This park is really nice," Martin said, looking around at the green landscape and the shade trees with benches under them. "And look at that church!" Martin's eyes opened wide as he pointed to La Ermita ahead of us.

"That's what I wanted to show you."

"Can we go inside?" he asked, pulling out his camera to take pictures.

"Why would you want to do that?" Anna asked.

Martin shrugged. "Why shouldn't we? You know, I was raised Catholic. I've only been a Baptist since my senior year in high school."

We watched as Martin took pictures. He must have been oblivious to how strange his words sounded to the rest of us, all born-and-bred Baptists.

"I've always admired the stained-glass windows and the altars in Catholic churches," he added.

"I like them, too," I said, taking my own pictures of La Ermita. "Something else we have in common."

Anna and Tom didn't go into the church, and Larry, Donna, and Daphne stood right inside the doors. Martin and I walked to the entrance and stepped in for a quick look. I smiled when Martin kneeled.

He looked guilty as he said, "Force of habit, I guess."

"That's okay," I told him as the smell of burning candles drifted our way. "Rituals are good for us, I think."

Without answering, he put his camera away and gazed at the stained glass circling the dome above us, each window a different saint with a golden halo. "Ready to go?" he whispered.

As we walked toward the others, he said, "It's beautiful, but it doesn't hold the key for me."

"What do you mean?" I asked.

"It's just me, I guess, but Catholicism was only ceremony. No substance."

"But I like how the ceremony connects me to others," I said as we walked outside. "I like how the service is so—I don't know… active. It's like the rituals give me peace. Didn't that happen to you, too?"

Martin gave me a puzzled look and was about to say something when Larry joined us. "I know this is wrong," Larry said, "but I wasn't expecting these high-rise buildings, the nice church, this beautiful park..." He gestured around us. "I guess I expected it all to be dirt roads and shacks."

"Huh," Martin said, turning to see what Larry was talking about. "I see what you mean. There's all this development, then look over there. Those women are doing their laundry in the river. It's all mixed together."

"Welcome to Colombia," Anna said.

For a while, we watched the women wash clothes and lay them on rocks to dry as three children played in the water. One boy caught something and hopped along the rocks to show it to the others.

"Wonder what he caught," Larry said.

"No telling," I answered. "Let's head toward Sixth Avenue."

I kept thinking about my conversation with Martin as we visited a few shops on the busy city street and bought trinkets from street vendors. I had put my hand on his arm to bring it up again, when Tom said, "Anyone want a Coke?" He was standing in front of a sidewalk café.

"Are they safe to drink?" Donna asked.

"Yeah, just don't get the ice," Anna answered, already walking into the restaurant. After we bought bottles of Cokes and a bag of *pandebono* to share, we sat on rickety metal chairs around a small table. Martin sat beside me.

"This is excellent bread," Larry said, looking at the puffy, warm *pandebono*. "What's in it?"

"Cheese," Anna answered. "Colombian cheese. I don't think you can get it in the States."

"It is tasty," Martin said, "but I don't know. I think the bread Josie made this morning was better."

I smiled. The MKs and youth group had made bread, and it was no surprise that mine was a disaster. "Yes, my brick is doing a good job holding down the cafeteria."

"*Pandebono* is one of the best things about living in Colombia," Anna said, ignoring Martin and me.

"What do you like about living here?" Larry asked, turning my way.

"The mountains," I said right away. "And being able to speak Spanish."

"I love living on a ranch outside Medellín," Anna said. "I don't think we could afford to have horses if we lived in Texas."

"Something else I like about Cali is how green it is," I added. "Everything is always growing, and there are so many amazing flowers—"

"Like bird of paradise," Anna put in.

"And fruits—"

"Mango, chontaduro," Anna added.

"Trees—"

"The saman." Anna nodded.

"And bugs," I finished.

Anna laughed in agreement; there were lots of bugs.

"What about you, Tom?" Larry asked.

Tom sat back. "I like living in Bogotá. I like how big it is. It's way bigger than Cali. And my parents are always coming up with new ways to work with Colombians." He shrugged. "I like helping them."

"Yeah?" I asked. "What else?" After seeing him in a new light, I wanted to hear all about him. Besides, the longer he talked, the more I could study his rugged features and tousled blond hair.

"I like taking prisoners in Capture the Flag." He stared across the table at me.

My heart beat faster at the memory of last night's game, and I leaned back in my seat, trying not to blush.

The conversation moved to the popularity of soccer in

Colombia, and as I sat with my friends on that sunny afternoon, I began to sense that something wasn't quite right. It was too quiet. There were no birds singing, no dogs barking, and no cicadas chirping. People were talking, and car horns were honking, but the underlying sounds of nature, usually relentless, were gone. We were still in our wobbly chairs when Tom sat up, his eyes alert. I felt it, too, and reached for Anna's hand.

With fear in her eyes, she said, "Earthquake!"

Tom stood, his hands gripping the table. "Everyone stay calm. It'll be over soon."

Daphne and Donna ignored him, leaping onto Larry, crying and screaming. Larry put his arms around the girls while Martin clung to my chair, his face white. Bottles along the café wall fell against each other and shattered on the ground. Our drinks fell off the table and fizzed on the floor. I held Anna's hand and watched, helpless, as the world shook around me. It seemed the earth itself intended to swallow us whole, and there was nothing we could do about it.

The waitress rushed outside and immediately knelt, making the sign of the cross, then prayed loudly as the earthquake rumbled on. Cars swerved and stopped in order to avoid the people who ran into the street. A transformer exploded nearby, creating more panic. The red-and-white-striped canopy above us shuddered, the neon Coca-Cola sign sputtered off, and the world just shook, and shook, and shook.

When the earthquake finally slowed to a stop and the terrible rumbling became quiet, Anna and I looked at each other with relief. As I waited to be sure the shaking had ended, I thought of Blanca again and hoped the earthquake hadn't reached her town. What would she have to say about it? Such an upheaval couldn't be a good sign.

"Glad that's over," Anna said, letting go of my hand.

Donna and Daphne clung to Larry, as pale as ghosts. Donna looked like she might throw up.

"I've never been so scared in all my life," Daphne said.

"That was a long twenty seconds," Tom said, running his hand through his hair.

"Twenty seconds? That was only twenty seconds?" Larry slumped into his chair. "Sit down, girls." He motioned to Donna and Daphne, but they didn't move.

"Wait," Martin said, putting his hands out. "Did you feel that?"

"Aftershock. Or maybe nothing at all," I told him.

"Once you've been in one, you think you feel tremors all the time," Anna added. "You'll be walking along, and suddenly, you'll stop just to make sure the ground isn't moving underneath you."

"The earth isn't the dependable place you thought it was, Martin," Tom said.

"I guess not." Martin shook his head.

The waitress started picking up bottles, so Anna and I helped her put the café in order. Out on the street, a police officer was trying to get traffic moving, and the horn honking began again. Tom walked to the sidewalk then came back inside. "It looks like a window blew out of a building down the street. Let's go see what happened. Maybe we can help."

Although the earthquake had been minor, it had shattered the picture window of a bakery. People were looting from the exposed pastry cases, even though pieces of glass stuck to the baked goods. The owner of the store yelled at the shoplifters, his hand wrapped in a bloody rag.

"Can we help you?" Tom asked him.

"*¡Sí!*" The baker looked like he might cry with relief. "Help me move the bread off the street."

Tom, Martin, and Larry dragged the display cases toward the back of the store while the others gathered the ruined bread and pastries. I was sweeping glass into a pile when someone said my name. I looked up and into the smiling eyes of Alejandro, who leaned against the doorframe.

"What, for the love of God, are you doing in this bakery?" he asked in Spanish.

My knees nearly buckled with the shock of seeing him again, and I had to look away to keep my cool. "We're helping the owner get his store back together." My eyes darted back to his handsome face, and I leaned on the broom handle for strength. I'd forgotten his soft brown eyes.

Alejandro came over to me and kissed my cheek—I could never get used to that Colombian custom. It seemed so intimate. I didn't mind breathing in his expensive cologne, though, and I noticed Tom and Martin were watching.

"Want to help us?" I asked Alejandro.

He laughed, his hand on my arm. "*Claro que sí.*"

Of course he would, and my knees almost betrayed me again.

I introduced everyone, and we went back to cleaning. The initial elation of seeing Alejandro evaporated, making way for discomfort as these separate worlds collided. I couldn't think of a thing to say to anyone as we worked in this bakery.

It seemed strange that less than a month ago I had been crying over him. Sure, he was good looking, but he was so different from me. What else did I see in him? Had he changed since the last day of school? I stole a glance his way and realized he hadn't changed—I had. A girl couldn't work so hard to move on from someone and be the same person when she saw him again.

Alejandro didn't stay long. He helped move a few racks of bread then said he had to go. When he kissed my cheek again, I had to crush the impulse to reach out and stop him from leaving. I felt like a part of my life was ending forever, and I wasn't sure I was ready. I shook off the feeling. Alejandro leaving this bakery didn't have to signal the end of an era. I turned to see Tom watching me, but he got back to work when Alejandro walked out the door.

While the guys moved boards to cover the front window, Anna, Donna, Daphne, and I filled trays with fresh bread.

"Was he the one you were talking about the other day?" Anna whispered.

"Yes." I sighed. "Pretty cute, huh?"

She nodded. "Very."

"Alejandro goes to my school," I told Daphne and Donna.

"He has great hair," Donna said.

I laughed.

When Daphne and Donna moved out of earshot to set up a tray of *buñuelos* in a display case, I told Anna, "I'm not sure Alejandro is the one for me."

"Why not?" she asked, helping me with a basket of pastries.

I wanted to tell Anna all about how I had been so in love with Alejandro, but after glancing at Tom and Martin, I just shrugged. She and I could talk later. Maybe I would tell her I'd moved on to other interests.

When our work was complete, the baker thanked us and asked us to visit soon, offering us all the bread we wanted. Anna joked that we could eat a lot of his bread, but he was serious.

"It's the least I can do," he said.

Tom checked his watch. "We'd better get back to the seminary. I hope everyone's okay there."

I looked at Tom, my eyes wide. I hadn't thought about my parents. "We can probably catch a bus home from that stop." I pointed up the street.

While we waited to go home, the chaos around us seemed to drain the enthusiasm from our group. "Why don't we get two taxis?" I suggested. "It won't cost much more, and we'll get home quicker."

"Yeah, we've had enough adventure for one day," Larry said. "And I need to check on the others in the youth group."

It took a few minutes, but Tom stopped two taxis, and we split up. Martin ended up in one cab with Anna and Larry, and Tom sat next to me, with Donna and Daphne squeezed in beside him.

I leaned forward to tell the driver to take us to the seminary, and when I sat back, Tom's arm was around me. I rested against his strong chest and could hardly concentrate as his leg pressed against mine. My brain went fuzzy, and I looked past Tom out the window. The mountains, the sky, the buildings, the people... everything looked wonderful, even after the earthquake. I wished the taxi ride could last forever.

"There's something else I love about Colombia," I told him.

"What's that?" he asked, looking down at me. His lips looked so soft, I wanted to reach up and touch them.

"I love how beautiful the sky is," I said, remembering my train of thought. Fluffy cumulus clouds floated across a deep-blue backdrop. Tom nodded, smiling, with his hand on my shoulder. His touch turned my mind to mush, but it didn't matter. I just leaned into him and enjoyed the moment.

When our cab driver turned down the road to the seminary, he must've read my mind, because he drove slowly under the long and graceful archway of trees. Too soon, he stopped at the college entrance, and I reluctantly pulled away from Tom. We gathered our pesos, paid the driver, and headed into the seminary.

Anna walked beside me, leading me away from the others. "What's up with you and Tom?" she whispered.

"I don't know," I said, suddenly embarrassed. I looked around for him, but he had disappeared.

"Well, I think it's obvious he likes you. But do you like him?"

"I don't know," I said again. "I never noticed how nice he was until now, but—"

"Good gravy, Josie, you do like him," she said, nudging my arm.

I felt my face flush. "Please don't turn this into anything," I begged. "I don't want you to scare him off. Please. Just let it be."

"Fine, Josie, but where's the fun in that?"

"Thanks, Anna."

"I've gotta see how my parents are doing," Anna called as she dashed off. She left me to walk to our apartment on my own, wondering about Tom, Martin, Alejandro, and the earthquake that seemed to have shaken everything into a very interesting mess.

Chapter Eight

DAD WAS IN HIS ROOM when I returned to our apartment. "That was some earthquake, huh, Dad?" I called as I changed out of my dirty clothes into jeans and a sweater.

"Sure was," he answered. "Glad you're okay."

"You, too." I walked into his room and brushed my hair in front of the mirror. "Still feel a little shaky, though. How 'bout you? Did you check the house?"

"Yeah," he said, shoving his wallet in his pocket. "I found a few things on the floor, but everything's all right."

"How was my room?" I asked, picking up a fat envelope from his dresser.

He grabbed the envelope from my hands. "Sorry, Josie, I didn't check. I'm sure it's fine, though."

"What's that?" I asked, pointing at the packet he was stuffing into a drawer. Dad wasn't usually so secretive.

"It's nothing. Come on, let's get to the cafeteria. We don't want to miss supper."

"If it's nothing, why don't you tell me what it is?" I asked, following him out the door.

He stopped so suddenly that I ran into him. And the look he gave me made my eyes widen. It was *not* nothing. And I would have to find out what Dad was hiding later.

"Brandy was a nervous wreck," Dad said, changing the subject as we walked down the stairs. "I gave him some meat and a bowl of rice from the fridge, and he calmed down."

"Have you been feeding him?" I put the awful look behind me.

"Uh-oh. I forgot the maid isn't around to take care of him."

I shook my head. "Poor dog. You may want to remind Mom she has a pet."

"I'll feed him again tomorrow."

"Feed the parrot, too."

In the cafeteria, we looked for Mom among the missionaries and found her eating with Anna's parents. I put my arm around her shoulder, and she patted my wrist but didn't look up. I wanted to tell her what had happened to us in the city, but she kept talking to Aunt Lucy.

Dad stayed with her, and I joined Isaac in the food line. He told me the worst thing about the earthquake was calming the American kids. Erik had been the biggest baby.

"You should have seen him cry," Isaac said, mimicking a snuffle.

When I set my tray beside Emily and Anna, Emily looked up and said, "Sounds like you all had an exciting trip this afternoon."

I studied her expression and decided she wasn't implying anything about Tom and me. Maybe Anna could keep a secret, which was a good thing, because Tom and Aaron were eating at the table next to ours.

"Do you think we'll play Capture the Flag tonight, since the earthquake and all?" Anna asked.

"I don't want to sit around and talk about it, do you?" I answered.

"Not really."

Jack and Isaac walked over to Tom and my brother. "We're ready to show you how to play tonight," I heard Jack say. "Or would you girls rather hand over the flag now, before anybody gets hurt?"

Tom looked up from his plate but not in time to stop Jack from slipping an ice cube down his shirt. Tom jumped up and untucked his polo, sending the ice clattering to the floor.

"Save it for the game, Jackie boy," Tom told his twin, re-tucking his shirt before he sat down again.

I might have laughed too hard at the exchange—Aaron turned to stare at me. I blushed and looked at my meatloaf. Luckily, Larry and Martin walked over, and everyone turned their attention to the leaders.

"Martin and I need to go over some things, so we don't have anything planned for tonight," Larry said. "But if you want, we could meet for a little while and talk about the earthquake."

"What earthquake?" Jack said. "That little shake may have been inconvenient, but it sure wasn't a disaster."

"I can see how you'd take it that way," Larry said. "All right then, we'll meet again in the morning."

After dinner, the two Capture the Flag teams ran toward the field. Our blue team had come up with a plan to capture the red flag, and we were ready to play. Jack quickly freed me from their jail, and before long, Isaac was running across their territory and into our field, red bandana in hand, with Jack pushing members of the red team away from him like a linebacker. After a great deal of celebration on our side, we started playing again.

While patrolling our boundaries, I spied a figure crouching behind a tree. It had to be Tom; his size and confidence gave him away. I tiptoed behind him to grab him by his big shoulders. Unfortunately, my foot sank into a hole, and I fell on him. Before I could react, he turned and rolled me on my back, pinning me down—again.

"Tom, it's me! I know it's a rough game, but try not to kill me, okay?" I said, keeping my voice low.

"Sorry," he answered, but he didn't get up. He kept looking down at me, those soft lips inches from mine. I stared back at him, not sure what to expect, until he kissed me, a gentle, sweet kiss. My first. I kissed him back, coming off the ground to meet him. After a lingering moment, he pulled away from me, and I watched him run to his side of the field. He should have been my prisoner, but I let him go. All I could think of was his warm, wet lips on mine.

Then I realized I couldn't move. My leg must have twisted when I stepped in the hole, and it hadn't helped when Tom threw me down. My entire left side felt like lead. I rose to a sitting position, my knee and ankle throbbing, but fell back when the pain turned into sharp stabs. I must have cried out, because Jack whispered, "Who's there?"

"Jack, come here."

"Josie, is that you?" he asked, moving toward me.

"Yeah, I need help."

"Are you okay?"

"I don't know. My leg hurts like crazy."

"What happened?" Jack asked, kneeling beside me.

"I must have twisted my foot."

"Josie, Josie, Josie," he said, shaking his head. "Let me help you get up."

I tried to stand, but the pain in my leg was so severe, I gasped.

"Here." Jack picked me up easily and carried me to our prison. How strange that someone else—with exactly the same strong arms, broad chest, and easy kindness—had kissed me only three minutes before. Looking up at Jack's firm jaw, a duplicate of Tom's, I wondered how they might be different. Then I went back to worrying about my knee.

Jack set me down on the prison bench and sat beside me. He put his arm around me to steady me while our team gathered around us. No one seemed to know what to do. When word of "man down" made it to the other team, Tom and Aaron jogged over.

"What's going on?" Aaron asked when he saw me surrounded by my teammates.

"Josie's hurt," Jack answered.

"What?" Tom knelt beside me. "What happened?"

I didn't answer. He lifted me and carried me toward a streetlight near the seminary road. I temporarily forgot my pain as I laid my head on his chest, listening to his heartbeat.

"Did I do this to you?" he asked as he walked, careful to keep his voice low so the others wouldn't hear.

"I just told them I twisted my foot," I whispered back.

Tom was quiet, a grim look darkening his face.

"I'm going to survive," I added. "I'm pretty tough, you know." I felt his heart beat harder.

"We should probably get help." Tom turned around and called to Jack, "Try to find Uncle Bruce. And, Aaron, do you want to get your folks?"

Jack and Aaron trotted off to the cafeteria, where missionaries sat around tables, talking and laughing as they played cards. We were on a bench under the streetlight when Tom took off his jacket and draped it around my shoulders. I hadn't noticed I was shivering.

Anna and Emily came over and sat beside me. "Can I see what happened to your leg?" Anna asked.

"I thought you wanted to be a veterinarian," I joked.

"We're all animals. Now let me see your injured limb."

Pain rolled through my leg when Anna touched it, and I jerked away. "That's really swollen, Jos," Anna said, her eyes wide. "It looks broken. If you were a horse, they'd probably have to shoot you."

"Thanks, Anna. Great bedside manner."

"Sorry. Don't listen to me. We'll see what Uncle Bruce has to say."

Emily pulled her away from me, and not a moment too soon. Anna's knee-patting was killing me.

"Maybe we should get her to the cafeteria," Tom said.

"No, please. I don't want to have all the parents hovering over me. They'll want to know what we were doing out there." My teeth were chattering, and I tightened his jacket around me.

"Well, the truth is we were running around like fools on the soccer field. They don't have to know it's Capture the Flag and Torture the Prisoners," Emily said.

"She's right." Anna nodded.

Uncle Bruce and my parents hurried around the corner of the cafeteria and rushed to my side. Uncle Bruce felt my leg just as Anna had, and my dad put his hand on my shoulder. Relief at having them there mixed with the pain, and I bit my bottom lip to keep from crying.

Mom studied my leg and asked, "What were you doing?"

Emily was our spokesperson. "We were running in the field, and she tripped and fell."

"Well, it looks like a nasty sprain, maybe both your ankle and your knee," the missionary doctor said, and I heard Tom sigh. "Let's take you to your apartment and get you comfortable."

Dad leaned over to lift me, but Tom was quicker, reaching down and picking me up in an easy move.

"You got her?" Dad asked, following Tom.

"Yes, sir," he answered. As we headed toward our building, Tom leaned his head toward mine. "I'm sorry, Josie."

"No, I'm sorry," I said.

"Why are you sorry?"

"Because our apartment is on the third floor."

Tom smiled down at me. "It'll be good exercise."

Dad opened our apartment door, and Tom set me down on my bed. Everyone crowded around me while Uncle Bruce arranged my leg on a pillow. He surrounded my ankle and knee with bags of ice from our kitchenette and gave me pills for the pain.

"Let me know tomorrow morning how she's doing," Uncle Bruce told my parents. "If the swelling doesn't go down, we'll need to take x-rays."

"Are you going to be okay?" Dad asked. "Are you comfortable?"

The ache in my leg had subsided, making me aware of my parched throat. "I could use another glass of water, but I'll be okay."

My mom refilled my glass and brought it to me. "Aaron, watch out for her and let us know if she needs anything," she said, resting her hand on my shoulder. "And if it's okay with you, we're going back to the cafeteria."

"I was just about to beat Emily's dad in Hearts," Dad said. "I hope they held the game for me." He kissed me on the forehead and added, "We'll be back soon, okay?"

I nodded up at him. After the adults left, Anna sat on the edge of the bed. I looked at Tom then the others. "You know what really happened? I was just about to catch Tom in blue territory when I stepped in a hole and fell on him. He threw me on the ground and twisted my leg. So it's his fault, and he's my slave until I'm healed."

"Let's all put our hands on her and heal her right now," Tom said.

I knew he was joking, but I answered, "Hey, do it. I've always wanted to see if that really works."

"You've gotta believe, or it won't work, silly," Anna told me.

"Okay. I believe I can be healed. I really do. Put your hands on my leg and pray. Please?"

They stared at me, not moving.

"Why won't you do it?" I asked, knowing full well healings weren't a common practice in our church.

"God doesn't like to be tested." Aaron crossed his arms as he repeated Mom's words.

"Our parents are missionaries! If we can't pray for healing, who can?" I insisted.

No one answered.

"Do it just this once," I begged. "I really want to be healed." I didn't tell them I planned on having the best Mission Meeting ever, and being crutch-free was an important part—or that I needed to know if our Baptist belief could bear up to being tested. "I think it's God's will you heal me."

"Okay," Tom said with a sigh. He put one hand on my leg, raised the other in the air, and closed his eyes. One by one, the others joined him and put their hands on my leg. I trembled at the level of energy that surged through me.

"Jesus, we believe you are the great healer," Tom prayed. "If it's your will, heal Josie's knee and ankle. Release her pain and let her sleep easy tonight so she won't be a mean slaveholder. Amen."

Anna and I smiled at the ending of Tom's prayer, then a deep calm settled on the room as I looked at my friends, under the spell of God's presence.

"Well, do you feel any different?" Emily asked, breaking the silence.

"Should I try to stand up? The pain is definitely not as bad as it was, but..." I grimaced as I shifted on the bed.

"I'd wait until tomorrow morning to try anything," Tom said. "It would still be considered a healing if you can walk in the morning."

"Fine. So now what do we do?" I asked.

"I'm going to watch Dad's Hearts game," Aaron said, ignoring Mom's request to take care of me. It didn't matter; I preferred Tom's care.

"There's no way your dad can beat mine," Emily countered as they walked out of the apartment. "Sleep tight, Josie," she said over her shoulder.

"My dad's got that Hearts game in the bag," I called back.

Anna gave a wistful look after them, and I motioned her away. "Shoo. Leave me with my slave."

She jumped up. "Hope you feel better. See you tomorrow!" Anna followed Aaron and Emily out, giving me a quick smile as she shut the door behind her.

Jeannie Zokan

Tom sat next to me on the bed, picking up my hand. "I'm sorry I hurt you."

A dizzying warmth crept over me, and I rested my head on the pillow. "I guess there was just no other way to get you all to myself. I mean, get me all to yourself," I said. The pain pills had made me bold, but Tom didn't seem to mind; he kept playing with my hand and smiling.

We were quiet, and I might have drifted off for a few minutes. Standing, Tom flipped the overhead light switch off then turned on a lamp by my bed. He sat next to me again and put his arm around me. I snuggled up to him, my hand on his firm stomach.

"Aaron lifts weights every morning," I said. "You must work out, too."

"Jack and I use a gym near our house. We go every day before school. On the days we don't have soccer practice, I take a run through the *barrio.*"

"I like to run, too. Around the seminary. But I guess I won't be doing that for a while."

"Poor baby," he whispered into my ear. He turned my face to his and kissed me—a long, slow kiss. I pulled away for air, but he kissed me again then shifted onto his side to face me. He looked at me with a smile, touching my cheek with the backs of his fingers.

I didn't know what was about to happen. One part of my brain pulled away and talked to me, telling me I really didn't want to go all the way with him right then. The other part of my brain just followed what my hands wanted to do: pull him closer. My body yearned for him to touch me. We looked into each other's eyes until he turned and rested his head on the top of mine. I had forgotten that getting any closer would have been impossible since my leg was encased in ice, and I giggled.

"What?" he asked.

"Nothing." After a few moments, I added, "If someone had told me last week that I'd be in your arms tonight, I'd have thought they were crazy."

"Hmm," was all he said. We were side by side, and everywhere his body touched mine, I trembled. Breathing in his musky scent reminded me of a fireside on a cool night in the mountains. We listened to the nighttime sounds of the seminary together: the whoosh of cars in the distance, the soft murmur of people talking and laughing, and the intermittent calls of night birds. A far-off salsa song floated in the air, and Tom sang the smooth Spanish in my ear. "Your kisses reach my soul. I want to conquer your heart, my beautiful girl."

I wished the moment would last forever, but an overwhelming sleepiness engulfed me. I woke up to find him disentangling himself from my arms.

"See you tomorrow, Josie," he whispered, kissing my cheek and turning off the lamp before slipping out of my room.

"G'night, Tom," I mumbled as sweet dreams slowly mixed with reality and lulled me to sleep.

Chapter Nine

BIRDS CHIRPING OUTSIDE MY WINDOW woke me the next morning, and I remembered Tom's warm embrace, hugging the pillow where his head had rested the night before. I pulled back the covers to inspect my ankle and knee and found the swelling had gone down. When I tried to sit up, though, sharp pain jolted my leg. Refusing to believe the healing hadn't worked, I steeled myself to try again, stretching as the pain loosened to a dull throb.

When I managed to stand and limp from my room, Mom asked, "How are you feeling today?" She was sitting at a table by the window, and her Bible lay open in front of her.

"I can move, at least. Will you help me get dressed?"

"Sure, Josie. But you should probably take another pill with breakfast."

"Okay." The pain was bearable if I kept my thoughts on Tom. The pill could be my backup plan.

The whole time Mom helped me pull on blue-jean shorts, a pink T-shirt, and one sandal, I couldn't stop smiling. Soon, I would see him again. Mom and I layered a pair of my dad's white socks over my swollen ankle, and when I was ready for the day, she called Aaron. I put a few pain pills in my purse and lengthened the strap to sling it over my shoulder. With my arm around Aaron's neck, we headed out the door.

"I wish Tom would show up," Aaron said, breathing hard as we lumbered down the stairs. "Are you guys, like, dating?"

"I don't know," I said, hiding a smile. Inside, I was singing, "Yes, yes, yes, we are."

Aaron set me down on a ledge in front of our building and held my arm while I hopped onto the sidewalk that led to the cafeteria.

"It's a miraculous recovery," Uncle Bruce said, walking toward us. "I was just coming to check on you. I'm amazed you're moving so well already. How are you feeling?"

"I feel great, but Aaron could use an oxygen tank, and all he did was carry me down the stairs."

Uncle Bruce laughed and gave Aaron a playful punch in the arm. "It's good for you to work those muscles, son." He turned back to me. "Josie, I asked around, and Agnes has a crutch you can borrow. She said she'd bring it to breakfast this morning. You can get it from her then."

"Oh, um, thanks," I said, wishing it could have been anyone but her. At least I hadn't gotten hurt falling off the rope swing. She would never have let me hear the end of it.

"Lucky, lucky you, Josie," Aaron said after the doctor left. "You will definitely be in Tom's care when you get that crutch from Aunt Ug-nes."

"She'd have a cow if she knew I was running around the seminary like a banshee last night." I put my arm on Aaron's. "All right, let's get this show on the road. Is it me, or is this the most beautiful day ever?"

"No, it's just you. Come on."

I breathed in the scent of gardenias, basking in the fresh morning air. Every morning in Cali was springtime. But when I saw Tom leaning against the wall by the cafeteria door, clouds rolled in. He was wearing a very ugly knit cap pulled down over his ears.

"Hey, Tom," I said with a weak smile. "What's with the hat?"

"I got it when we visited Machu Picchu," he answered.

Aaron laughed. "Tom, you're such a goofball. Well, my sister's all yours."

Aaron walked away, and for a moment, I wanted my normal-looking brother back. Quashing that feeling, I turned to Tom. "Uncle Bruce found someone who has a crutch I can borrow. Guess who it is."

"Who?"

"Aunt Agnes."

"Huh," he said, not reacting as I'd expected. "Well, let's get you inside." He put his arm around my waist but couldn't open the heavy glass door to the cafeteria and steady me at the same time, so we stood awkwardly until Isaac came along and held the door for us.

"So how are you doing?" Tom asked once we were in the dining hall.

"Pretty good, actually. When Uncle Bruce saw me, he said it looked like I had a miraculous recovery. Maybe your healing hands worked."

Tom smiled, but it was wrong—all wrong. How did anyone ever fall in love? There were so many things that could mess it up, like dumb hats and awkward moments.

We found Aunt Agnes eating breakfast at a table near the food line, the crutch leaning on a chair next to her.

"Oh, there you are, child," she said, standing. She helped me adjust the crutch to my height and showed me how to use it.

"Thanks, Aunt Agnes," I said after a trial run. "I hope I won't need it for long."

We were leaving her table when Aunt Agnes said, "You kids be careful now."

I turned around to tell her we would be, and the spinster winked at me with a smile that said she knew something was going on between Tom and me. I couldn't control a shiver as I hobbled away.

94

We were in the food line when Martin appeared behind us. "What happened to you?" he asked, looking at my leg.

"I was running, and I tripped. But don't worry, I was healed last night. This crutch is only for show."

Tom looked at me like I was crazy, but Martin said, "Your faith only has to be the size of a mustard seed to work."

"And I believe it. But I'm super hungry right now, so I'm going to limp over to the servers and get myself some bacon, eggs, and papaya. Then maybe I'll try walking without this crutch."

Martin laughed. "What is it you missionary kids sneak off to do every night?"

I looked at Tom, hoping he would answer the question, but he wasn't listening.

"Just hang out." We were at the head of the line, so I turned my attention to the food, complimenting the servers on the delicious-looking bacon and warm biscuits.

Tom took my tray for me and found seats for us at a table with other MKs. We ate in silence, and I thought about my situation. Tom was a good guy, and I really liked him, but did I like him enough to overlook things like his stupid hat? And he was so quiet. Would I always have to lead every conversation? I remembered how it had felt to have his arms around me last night and was flooded with a confusing warmth.

At the table next to us, Aunt Beth and Uncle Craig were eating breakfast with their daughters. The young missionaries were laughing about something their four-year-old daughter, Sarah, had said. Aunt Beth was fun and pretty in her nice skirt and blouse, her brown hair pulled into a ponytail. Uncle Craig was tall and reserved, like Tom. It was easy to see he was devoted to his wife and daughters.

"How are you, Josie?" Aunt Beth asked from her table.

"I'm okay," I answered.

"What happened to your leg?"

"I tripped running last night." Even though Aunt Beth would probably be okay with our Capture the Flag game, I wasn't going to change my story. "Your girls sure are getting big." I gestured at Sarah and her baby sister, Allison.

Just then, Allison flung a spoonful of oatmeal at Uncle Craig, and it landed on his cheek. He looked at Aunt Beth, who handed him a napkin, trying to keep from smiling. Allison, her eyes wide, said, "Uh-oh," and we laughed as Uncle Craig wiped the food off his face.

Aunt Beth pretended to be stern with Allison. "Say you're sorry to Daddy."

Then the moment was forgotten, except that I couldn't forget the look Aunt Beth had given Uncle Craig. Nothing could make him look stupid in her eyes, not even a glob of oatmeal stuck to his cheek. I wanted that; I just wasn't sure I could have it with Tom.

I took a pain pill from my purse and swallowed it, and not only because of the pain in my leg.

Halfway through the morning Bible study, my leg started feeling stiff. I picked up my crutch and limped away from the others and into the hall, where I attempted some standing yoga stretches I'd learned from Aunt Rosie. Just as I was trying to walk without the crutch, Martin came out of one of the classrooms and caught me in the act.

"Hey, your leg really is cured," he said.

"It's getting there," I answered. "It still hurts, but moving seems to help."

"Want to take a walk? That might loosen it up."

"Sure," I answered.

Martin held the door for me, and I hobbled into the sunshine. As we walked along the road in front of the seminary, I pointed across the street. "That's where we live. We're only staying at the seminary for Mission Meeting."

"Nice place," he said, studying our house.

"Yeah. While we're here in Colombia, we have it good. But when we go to the States for furlough, the government offers us food stamps. Last time we went back home, my dad didn't sign up for them. I guess he was embarrassed."

"I grew up on food stamps," Martin said. "My dad was always drunk, and Mom finally kicked him out when I was nine. I tried to do odd jobs to make money for us, but it was hard. Then she married this guy who had a decent job. I don't think Mom loved him, but he took care of my sisters and me, so she was happy."

"How is she now?"

Martin shrugged. "She's getting used to the idea of me being a Baptist youth minister."

"You said you were Catholic. How did you become a Christi—I mean a Baptist?"

Martin laughed at my slip. "So Catholics aren't Christians?"

"Sorry." I shook my head. "You were saying you became a Baptist…"

"I was a stock boy at a grocery store in high school, and the boss was the kind of guy who'd jump in and help anyone out. One day, he and I were shelving canned vegetables, and he invited me to his church. They were having a potluck dinner, he said, and I didn't feel like I could say no. He was my boss and all."

I nodded, and he went on. "I almost didn't go, but I'm glad I showed up. The food was great, and the people were friendly. The preacher talked about making a difference in the world and having a personal relationship with Jesus Christ. I went forward when he asked if anyone wanted to accept Jesus as their savior. Since that day, being born again has made me a better person. I have hope, a reason to live."

"Good testimony," I said.

"What about you?"

"I was in the second grade, and I saw the preacher giving everyone who got saved a cool three-ring binder. I wanted it for my drawings, so I got saved, too."

"Not very inspiring," Martin said, chuckling.

"What do you expect from someone who's spent most of her life in church? And I was eight." We had turned around and were heading back to the classrooms. "Let me tell you something that happened to me," I said, deciding to confide in him. "About a month ago, I couldn't sleep. I, uh, had a lot on my mind." I took a deep breath. "I talked to our maid, and she gave me some beads and taught me to pray the rosary. I've prayed the rosary ever since, and it's really helped me feel better about stuff."

Martin smiled. "It's okay, you know. If that's what you need, good for you for finding it."

"Really? I'm surprised to hear you say that. My parents wouldn't feel the same way."

"Have you told your boyfriend?"

"Who? Tom?"

"Isn't he your boyfriend?" My cheeks must've flamed red, because Martin laughed. "Never mind. I'm prying."

We sat on the swings near the cluster of apartment buildings and kept talking until Martin looked at his watch and jumped. "We gotta get back, Josie. I'm not being much of a leader out here."

It didn't take long to get back to the classrooms. I seemed to have acquired the knack of using the crutch. Martin walked ahead and opened the door for me, and I noticed his clean-cut good looks again. But our connection went deeper than that. I could talk to him, and he seemed interested in me. I didn't know there were guys out there I could have such an honest conversation with, and I couldn't help but wonder if his lips were as soft as Tom's.

The Americans had brought the score for the musical *Godspell* so the youth could perform it at the final meeting, and I heard

Aaron playing one of the tunes on the piano. We followed the sound to the chapel, where the MKs and youth group were rehearsing. When Martin and I walked in, everyone stopped singing to stare at us. Something was wrong. I slid into the pew next to Anna, and she grabbed my arm and whispered, "Where were you?"

"I needed to stretch my legs," I explained. "Martin took a walk with me. Why?"

"No one knew where you guys were." Her tone was curt, and her eyes looked hurt, as if she wished I had let her in on a secret. Then I realized the group thought it was strange that Martin and I had been alone together. At first, the insight made me smile, but the thrill disappeared when I thought of Tom. How had he felt when I'd walked in with Martin?

Larry glanced at his watch. "We have a few minutes before lunchtime. Aaron, do you want to go through some more songs?"

"Sure," Aaron said. "Let's sing 'Day by Day.'"

After practice, Tom and I walked together to lunch. He wasn't wearing his silly hat, but I didn't mention it in case he decided to put it back on. "So, where were you?" He sounded nonchalant, but I could tell by the way he was staring at the ground that my explanation needed to be good.

"My leg was feeling stiff, so I took a walk with Martin. What did I miss?"

"Not much. Daphne and Donna talked about what happened on our trip to the city yesterday. They want to go help more people today." After a few seconds, he added, "How's your leg?"

"It's healed, I tell you." I smiled up at him, trying to apologize for leaving with Martin, but for the life of me I didn't know why. If I had to choose between them right now, Martin would win. I liked being with Tom, who was attentive and kind, but talking to Martin was so easy. I gave up trying to figure out my conflicting emotions.

"Well, since you're feeling better, you can play Capture the Flag tonight," he said.

"I doubt it. But maybe we can play something else." When Tom raised his eyebrows, I added, "You know, like cards."

Tom most likely knew I wanted to find a way into his arms again, but I didn't care. No matter how confused my mind was, my body knew where it wanted to be. When he finally smiled down at me, my head felt light and warm.

If mornings in Cali felt like springtime, then noon was summer, and the only place to be was inside. I sat at a table in the cool cafeteria with my fellow MKs and laughed at Aaron's imitation of Erik running his hand through his hair and puffing his chest out. Anna told stories about the chickens on her ranch and how they tormented her dog, while Tom and Jack played a rowdy game of table football with a small paper triangle.

I basked in the simple pleasure of time with good friends until Uncle Craig ended our fun. "A group is going visiting in the *barrio* behind the seminary this afternoon," he said, his hand on Tom's shoulder. "Any of you want to come?"

Tom looked at me for permission.

"I'm not up for it, but you should go if you want to," I told him, glad my hurt leg gave me an excuse not to go. I didn't enjoy going into peoples' houses to share our beliefs. It was better, I thought, to offer sewing classes or singing lessons. Then, when they showed up at church, we could tell them about being born again.

"You sure you'll be okay?" he asked.

"I'll be fine. Anna will keep me company, won't you?" I looked over at her.

"You bet," she said. "What shall we do? Teach the Americans how to play soccer? Run a few miles?"

"Sounds great." I laughed. "Then we'll hike the mountain behind the seminary."

Tom looked baffled, and Anna rolled her eyes. "I'm kidding! I'll take care of her."

"Let's go to my house," I told her. Our big house with its high ceilings and thick walls would be cooler than the seminary apartments, which were bright and sunny.

"Okay," Anna said. "I've been wanting to see Brandy."

"He's probably starving." I grabbed my crutch and stood, wondering if my dad had forgotten to feed the dog again.

Martin and the twins piled into Uncle Craig's car while Anna and I headed toward my house.

"So, what's going on with you and Tom?" Anna asked as we passed the swing set.

"He kissed me," I told her, trying to act casual.

"Really? Are you going out?"

"Oh, Anna, that's the problem. I was crazy about him last night, but this morning…"

"What happened?"

"I don't know. What do you think of his hat?"

"The one he had on at breakfast? It's cool. I want to get one like it. Why?"

I concentrated on the cracks in the sidewalk as I swung my crutch forward with each step.

She stopped short. "You think it's ugly!" She started walking again and added, "You know, every girl at the American school in Bogotá wants to go out with Tom. He was dating the most-popular girl there, but he broke up with her."

"How do you know that?"

"Some of the MKs were talking about it."

"Did they know why he broke it off?" I asked.

"No."

"Oh, Anna. That doesn't make me feel any better. Now I'm wondering what's wrong with me that I'm not crazy about someone as wonderful as Tom."

"Maybe you should give him another try."

"Maybe. Meanwhile, Martin is really nice."

Anna stopped again and put her hand on my arm. "Josie, stay away from him. He's four years older than you, and he's going back to the States in"—for some reason, she looked at her watch—"in seven days. Just leave him alone, okay?"

"Fine! For Pete's sake, Anna. They aren't all bad, you know." I regretted the words as soon as they came out of my mouth. It seemed like every year, someone from the American youth group broke an MK's heart, and last year, it had been Anna's. She and one of the boys had a fling, and when he left, he'd promised to write but never did. For six months, Anna's letters to me were about how she missed him and what she should have done to keep him. She lost fifteen pounds pining over him. Anna may have been a strong country girl, but she had a fragile heart.

We walked in silence to the gate of our house until I changed the subject. "So how are things with you and Aaron?"

She sighed. "Nothing to report. He's nice to me, but then he's nice to every girl. How do I stand out from the crowd?"

"Good question," I said.

I opened the front door while Anna played with Brandy. The dog tore around the yard, thrilled with Anna's attention.

"Your dog is crazy, Josie," she said as Brandy tackled her, his tail wagging. "Makes me miss mine."

I stepped inside, and Anna followed. Uncomfortable silence met us. The house was never quiet when Blanca was home.

We put food in Brandy's bowl then checked the first floor for earthquake damage Dad might have missed. A few cereal boxes had tumbled off the pantry shelf in the kitchen, and some knickknacks had fallen from the dining room cupboard.

"Not too bad," Anna said after we put everything where it belonged.

"Yeah, that's a relief," I answered. "Let's go upstairs to my room."

Blanca's statue of Saint Jude, which had been on my nightstand, was in pieces on the floor. A chill ran down my spine when I saw it hopelessly shattered; it couldn't help me anymore. I hopped over to the mess before Anna noticed it. If she realized it was a saint, she would ask questions, and I didn't have any answers. Unlike Martin, Anna wouldn't understand my interest in Catholicism.

"What was that?" She was too quick for me.

"Just a figurine." I gathered the fragments into a pile and shoved them under my bed. I'd have to get a new Saint Jude for Blanca at La Ermita.

Anna sat on my bed and paged through the books on the nightstand. I had just opened the back of my camera to load film into it when I heard my dad's voice downstairs. I tossed the camera on my bed, reached for my crutch, and hopped to my bedroom door.

"No, I can't come over right now," he was saying in Spanish. "I shouldn't even be calling. I should be at the seminary, but I wanted see if you were hurt in the earthquake yesterday. How are you and the baby? Do you need anything?"

I walked toward the stairs. Dad wasn't making any sense.

"Good. Well, the apartment is the safest place to be." He paused. "*Sí, sí,* I know you need the money! I'll take care of everything. I'll come by when I can get away. *Hasta luego.*"

My dad hung up the phone and looked up. When he saw me at the top of the stairs, his face froze, his mouth open. I felt heat rush from my heart to the top of my head. A knot formed in my stomach. Something was terribly wrong. He climbed the steps toward me, and I wanted him to stop.

"Dad, what's going on?" I asked, my voice unnaturally high. "Who was that?"

"No one you know." He reached out to hug me, but my crutch was in the way, and I wasn't about to move it. He dropped his arms.

"Then who was it?"

"Don't you worry about anything, okay?"

He started to move away, but I grabbed his shirtsleeve, pulling him toward me. "What's going on?"

"Nothing, Josie," he said. "Don't worry about it."

He tried to free himself, but I wouldn't loosen my grip on his shirt.

"You're going to have to explain everything, or I'll think the worst. It sounds like you're giving money to someone. Is it Ricardo from church?"

"No. Let go of me!"

I didn't let go. "It sounds like the person has a baby and lives in an apartment. Why are you paying that person?"

He jerked away from me, no longer trying to console me.

I'd forgotten about Anna until she raced past us down the stairs. "I'm going to go now," she called behind her.

Dad's face was ashen as he watched her leave.

I didn't take my eyes off him. "Why, Dad?"

Anna slammed the front door. The sound carried a distant finality. Dad immediately walked downstairs, and I thought he was going to follow Anna out, but he dropped onto the bottom step and put his head in his hands.

I hobbled down the stairs as I waited for him to speak, the silence reverberating through the house. When he finally did, his voice was unusually calm. "It's my baby. I'm helping the mother buy the things she needs. I had an affair, Josie."

His words were undeniable, earth-shattering evidence that gathered around me like physical things. I had to sit down. I leaned against the wall and slid onto the stair next to him.

"Look, I never meant to hurt anyone. I only saw Samara a few times."

"A few times?"

"But then she was pregnant, and I had to take care of her. It's over now, but I check on her and the baby, and give them money when I can. Your mom—"

"What were you thinking?" I interrupted. "How could you, a missionary, do such a thing? Why would you do this to us? To Mom?"

Dad took my rant, head bowed, without answering my questions. I grew quiet as we sat together at the entrance of the house. Finally, I asked another question. "Who is she?"

Dad sighed. "Samara's a woman I met one day when I was out visiting. It ruined things for her, too, having a baby. She—"

"You went to convert her, and instead, you got her pregnant?" Anger boiled up again.

"I wish you hadn't found out, Jos." He put his head back in his hands.

"I wish it hadn't happened."

"Oh, Josie. That's the understatement of the year."

Suddenly, I couldn't be in the house another second. I stood, grabbed my crutch, and hopped to the door. But I turned back to him, my curiosity outweighing my anger—I had to know one thing. "What is the baby? Do I have a brother or a sister?"

His face softened, as if he couldn't help himself. "Her name is *Piedad Maria*."

"Piedad? Her name is Pity?" I stared at him, still trying to take it all in, then pulled open the door. I needed air.

I was already outside when Dad called after me. "Josie, wait."

Turning, I stopped to glare at him.

"I know this sounds crazy," he said, "but I'm glad you found out. Now I'm not the only one who knows about this mess."

A wave of disgust washed over me, followed closely by sadness, hurt, and fear. "I need to get out of here."

"Just… don't tell your mother. Don't tell anyone."

Without answering, I closed the door behind me, and when Brandy bounded over and licked my hand, I pushed him away.

Chapter Ten

MY PLAN WAS TO LIMP along the road around the seminary grounds to clear my head, but when I passed the chapel, I heard piano music. It was Aaron again, helping some kids practice for the musical. I slipped in and sat on the back pew to listen. The midday heat and my heavy heart made walking the seminary road more than I could bear.

As my brother played the piano, I thought about the disaster my father had created. What was Mom going to say about the affair? Of course she would find out, wouldn't she? I hoped I wouldn't have to be the one to tell her.

Scenarios of Mom finding out about the baby whirled in my mind as Aaron played "Turn Back, O Man" for Emily. It seemed strange to hear Aaron talking and laughing as he helped her with the song. He didn't have a care in the world, and for the first time in my life, I felt sorry for him. His life was about to be turned upside down, like mine had been.

When Anna came in with Daphne and Donna, I plastered a smile on my face. To my relief, Anna smiled back as if nothing had happened. She'd probably guessed my father's awful secret the same way I had, but I trusted her to keep quiet. It didn't really matter; no one would believe her if she told. My dad, the great teacher of theology and pastoral leadership, was the last person anyone would expect to commit adultery.

Anna slid in next to me while Daphne and Donna sat in the pew in front of us. Daphne pulled a *Seventeen* magazine out of her oversized purse and showed us pictures of the latest stars. My eyes kept shifting to the articles "What to Do When He Cheats" and "Time to Pick Mr. Right."

I listened as they discussed the Bee Gees, and when Donna put down the magazine, I reached over the pew and grabbed it, reading through the two articles. But all I learned was if a man cheated once, he would probably cheat again, and when it comes to picking between two or more dates, a girl should follow her heart. Frustrated, I tossed the magazine down.

Aaron stood and stretched. "That's enough practice for now. Let's go to my house for a Ping-Pong tournament."

Anna shot a worried look my way, but I just shrugged. There was nothing more to see at our house. Dad was surely long gone. "Sounds good to me," I said, turning to Donna and Daphne. "Do you want to come over?"

"It'll be cool to see your house," Donna said. She was looking at Aaron, and I realized she had a crush on my brother, too. I shook my head.

As we were walking across the street, Uncle Craig's car pulled up to the seminary entrance. Tom, Jack, and Martin got out.

"Hey guys," Aaron called. "Come on over. We're going to play Ping-Pong."

"Uncle Ted needs our help," Jack said. "The earthquake knocked some bookshelves down at his house, and we're gonna lend him a hand."

"Change of plan, then," Aaron said, leading us to Uncle Ted's, four houses down the block.

Martin and Tom came my way, and I turned to Martin. His presence would feel more comforting than Tom's right now.

"Tom was terrific at translating my testimony," Martin said

as we walked down the street. "There were so many people who wanted to talk to us, we ran out of tracts."

I couldn't help thinking how my dad had visited Samara to tell her about Jesus. He had given her a tract, invited her to church... and then what had happened? I didn't want to know.

Uncle Ted met our group at the door, and we followed him into his house. He showed us the library, where most of the damage had occurred. It was a small room, more like a closet, so only Tom and a few others were able to fit inside to put the bookshelves and their contents back in order.

"Come see Uncle Ted and Aunt Lily's backyard," I told Martin as we stood in the hall. "She's an amazing gardener." I led the way, hoping to talk to him alone. Martin turned one of the many pots hung around the patio so he could see the orchid bloom inside. "These are really beautiful."

"Yeah, they are," I answered.

I was considering telling him about my dad's affair when Martin went on. "My girlfriend is really into flowers."

"Oh?" I had to force myself to think of something to say because my brain was screaming, *What? You have a girlfriend?* Finally, I said, "I guess they're easy to grow if you know what you're doing. I don't, uh, I don't have a green thumb," I ended stupidly, searching for a way to get out of there.

"Look at this one with all the tiny dots on it," he said, showing me a purple orchid.

"Yeah, and this one. It's so bright." I pointed at a hot-pink one.

"My mom grows orchids like these," Anna said as she and Jack joined us on the patio. I reached out and grabbed her arm, keeping her by my side. I didn't want to talk to Martin anymore. I should have known he had a girlfriend... I had only imagined he was interested in me, and I'd been a complete fool.

Martin turned to follow Jack to the backyard, and I stood with my hand on Anna's arm.

"Are you all right?" she whispered.

I watched Martin and Jack walk away. "No, I guess I'm not."

"How about I get you home?" Anna asked.

"I don't want to go there," I answered, my eyes brimming with tears.

"We'll go to my apartment at the seminary," she said, taking charge.

I told Tom I was leaving with Anna, and he didn't miss a beat. "Okay, see you at dinner."

"What just happened?" Anna asked as we walked down the street.

"Oh, nothing. I just found out Martin has a girlfriend."

"Would it be okay if I said I told you so?" Anna asked.

"No." I shook my head.

"I bet Larry told Martin to stop hanging out with you so much," Anna said.

"What do you mean?"

"He's one of the leaders, Josie. He shouldn't be hanging out with you even if he wanted to. Especially not alone like this morning."

We passed a few houses in silence before Anna asked, "Do you want to talk about your dad?"

I thought for a moment as I swung my crutch in front of me. I shouldn't tell her about my dad's horrible mess, but I had to talk to someone. It occurred to me that if Blanca were there, I would be crying on her shoulder right now. Finally, I answered, "Well, there's not much to say, really. Basically, I have a half sister named Piedad. Piedad Maria."

"Her name is Pity?"

"I know, right? But he says the affair is over, and he's just helping the mother with money. Do you think I should tell my mom?"

"Yeah," Anna said with a sigh. "It's better than not knowing. It'll break her heart, I suppose. I mean, how would you feel?"

"I feel pretty broken-hearted just being the daughter of the jerk. Such a jerk!" It felt good to get mad. I looked over at Anna. "I guess you know you're sworn to secrecy."

"Yeah. Wow. And you never knew anything was going on, did you? What will people think, him being a missionary and all? Do you think your parents will be fired? I remember they fired the missionaries in Santa Marta because they found out Uncle Perry was stealing money from the church."

Anna looked so concerned, I didn't have the heart to tell her she was being about as sensitive as an ox. She kept babbling about how bad the situation was, not noticing the tears that ran unchecked down my cheeks.

The rest of Mission Meeting, I just wanted to lock myself in my room at home. I couldn't disappear, though, since everyone would want to know what was wrong. Instead, I hid in plain sight, everything blurring around me.

My leg felt fine within twenty-four hours of the mishap, so I considered it a miracle and returned the crutch to Aunt Agnes. Tom was always nearby, it seemed, and his calm and quiet presence comforted me, since I had so much on my mind.

I avoided Martin. I had been foolish to think he, a youth group leader, could fall for me. It wasn't his fault his kindness had given me the wrong impression, but I didn't need to hang around him and be reminded of it. Several times, he tried to start a conversation, but I politely included other people.

My dad left me alone, which was just as well. I might have made a scene if he'd tried to talk to me. I had nothing to say except to yell at him for doing such a horrible thing. It was bad enough I had to live through the daily Bible studies, where my mind kept seizing on my dad's hypocrisy.

Capture the Flag was my only diversion. Our blue team was ahead by two when suddenly, Tom's team came alive. Anna and

Aaron worked together to capture our flag three times over the next few days, and they gloated insufferably. Emily and I managed one more capture, but Tom took our flag twice on the last night we played, running with impossibly long strides. If he wanted to impress me, it worked.

To celebrate the red team's victory, the twins insisted the MKs and the youth group go into town and see the movie *Rocky*. The exciting fight scenes, Tom's warm hand in mine, the salty popcorn, and the sweet Coke all gave me a reprieve from the torture of my thoughts.

"We're getting ice cream, and blue team's paying," Aaron announced as we left the theater.

"Who?" Donna asked.

"They've been playing some game every night," Erik explained. "Sounds like the blue team lost."

"Yeah," Anna told her. "And I want three scoops!"

"I've got you covered," Jack told her as we took over the shop. "So long as I like the flavors, too."

Anna put her hand up to him. "No way am I sharing. I earned this."

I offered to pay for Tom's ice cream, but he refused, buying my rum raisin as well as his mint chocolate chip. We ate the cones outside, sitting side by side on a low brick wall, and when it was time to head toward Sixth Avenue to catch cabs back to the seminary, Tom and Jack kept us laughing. They quick-stepped down the road, mimicking Rocky's boxing moves, then staggered, calling, "Adrian! Adrian!" Even passersby smiled at them.

The day before Mission Meeting would end, I awoke as the sun brightened the sky. Every time I turned around, there was another good-bye. It was a good thing our last day was packed with activities; there wouldn't be time to think about everything I was losing. I threw on running shoes, shorts, and a T-shirt then took a few minutes to pull my hair into a ponytail and brush my teeth before heading over to Tom's apartment building.

I tossed pebbles up at his window on the second floor, and he came out to the balcony. He smiled down at me, his hair tousled and his bare, muscular chest inviting. I had brought my camera along, and I snapped his picture.

"What are you doing up so early?" he asked, leaning over the railing, ignoring my camera.

"Come on, sleepyhead; let's go for a run. I bet I can beat you at a sprint."

"You're on." He disappeared into his family's apartment.

Before long, we were walking on the road that encircled the seminary. "I was just kidding about beating you," I told him. "There's no way that could happen."

"Forget it; bet's on. And I get to choose what the loser has to do."

"Great." I was pretending to be sarcastic, but inside, I quivered at how he'd taken control.

The dew sparkled on the grass around us, and the cool air was sweet with the smell of orange blossoms and gardenias. As we ran, our feet crunched the gravel in unison. I tried to remember everything about our time together so I would have the memory of Tom beside me during every morning run after he was gone. My feelings for him had grown during our time together, and it didn't seem like it was only because he distracted me from Pity.

As we neared the big tree with the swing, we sprinted toward it, and Tom pulled ahead to win.

"So what do I have to do?" I panted, walking in circles with my hands on my hips.

"You're going to swing on the rope."

"You're kidding, right? I'm no Aaron, you know."

"It'll be fun. You'll see," Tom said.

With the last of my energy, I tried to run away, but he caught me easily. Standing behind the tree, he held me in his arms and kissed me again. His lips were so soft, and I melted. I held him close, my head on his chest, hearing the drumbeat of his heart.

Too soon, he said, "All right, come on. No more putting this off." He dragged me to the swing.

As I was studying the faraway tree limb and the rope that looked a little too frayed, Blanca's words came to me. On one of the many nights I'd gone to her room, she had told me to treat fear like a young child. "Tell that little girl you will look after her, *mija*," she said. "Then go ahead and embrace life. You will be protected."

I stepped onto the knot and held on tight as Tom pulled the rope back and back and back. He released the rope, and I lurched through the air toward the other end of the tree's mammoth canopy. It took some time for my stomach to catch up with me, but after a few good swings, I opened my eyes, thrilled at the feel of the wind rushing by and the dappled sun shining on me through the leaves.

"Geronimo!" I called as I sailed through the air.

Tom laughed and took a few photos of me as I spun around and around.

"Do you want to take a turn?" I asked, jumping off and steadying myself.

"No, we'd better get ready for breakfast."

I pulled him to me. "Thank you, Tom," I said into his chest.

He smiled, but as we walked back, hand in hand, he seemed sad. It occurred to me that I hadn't considered how he must be feeling. Not only was this his last Mission Meeting, he was also leaving Colombia in a matter of days. And how many MKs ever came back? When we arrived at my apartment, he leaned toward me and kissed my head.

I hopped up a few stairs and turned to face him. "I just wanted you to know, I'm glad we're together."

He brightened. "Me, too. See you at the cafeteria."

We met again at breakfast then joined the youth to practice *Godspell* one last time. A few of the parents were ready to take carloads of kids to Rio Pance for a picnic lunch, and as soon as practice ended, we ran to our apartments for swimsuits and towels. Thankfully, my parents hadn't volunteered to come. As long as I didn't see them, I could almost forget about Dad's illegitimate child.

When our cars arrived at the picnic site, we hopped out and headed for the river's edge. From where we stood, watching the water tumble from the Andes Mountains above, we could see the snow-fed river wind through the trees that hung over the water, flowing over and around gray granite rocks strewn along the waterway.

Tom pointed downriver and told me, "I'd like to walk along those rocks all the way to the Caribbean Sea."

"Is that where this river ends, north of us?"

"Yeah, after it flows into the Cauca and the Magdalena. Strange, isn't it?" he said.

"I didn't know that," Anna added.

We stripped down to our suits, and I felt Tom's eyes on my red one-piece suit. It showed my flat stomach and curves without being too revealing. Anna and I plunged into the water, squealing at the bracing cold as we paddled against the gentle tug of the current.

"Are you getting in, Tom?" I asked.

"He's coming with me," Aaron answered for him. "Come on, Tom; I want to show you and Jack something."

A few minutes later, I crawled onto one of the many boulders along the river to warm up in the sun. Anna climbed up beside me, dripping onto the rock's surface. "You'll never guess who kissed me last night," she whispered.

"Aaron?" I asked, my eyes wide.

"No. Jack," she said with a smile.

I laughed. "Good. I'm glad you're over Aaron."

"Yeah, Jack's nice." She sighed.

"I wonder if he's as good a kisser as Tom is."

"He's pretty good," she said, smiling like the Cheshire cat. We were giggling about our twin boyfriends when Emily swam over to us.

"So what do you think of this year's visitors?" she asked, sitting beside us and squeezing water from her hair. "I think this was one of our less-eventful years."

"Hmm," I said, leaning back on the rock. She couldn't have been more wrong.

"Some of the kids from the States were fun," Anna said. "Like Donna and Daphne."

"That Erik is crazy." Emily cupped her hand around her mouth so the others couldn't hear her tell on the Greek god. "He bought some marijuana from a stranger behind the gas station."

"Just now, on our way over here?" Anna gasped. "That's unbelievable."

"Shh, keep your voice down," Emily scolded. "As soon as Erik got back in the car, Larry reached over and took the bag of marijuana out of his towel. Before Erik could stop him, Larry dumped the stuff in the trash. It was a really nasty trash can, too, or I bet Erik would have gone in after it. He looked real upset."

"Stupid *gringo*," Anna said. "A world of trouble is waiting for that boy. I don't care how good looking he is."

"Girls," Aunt Beth called from the picnic table. "Time for lunch. Could you track down the twins and Aaron?"

"Okay," Emily said, standing.

Anna and I followed Emily along the riverbed and around a bend. We caught sight of the three just as they plunged over a high rushing waterfall into the frothy foam below.

"What is wrong with those boys?" Emily asked. "Do they have a death wish?"

"Aaron does," I said.

Anna and I exchanged worried glances. "They'll be fine," I

told her, not really believing it myself until their heads bobbed up through the bubbles. The waterfall must've been two stories over the river.

Emily yelled over to them. "Hey, you crazy boys, time for lunch."

They whooped and splashed toward us.

"Did you see us?" Aaron asked. "That was so cool! Anna, you should try it."

"No thanks," Anna said.

I smiled at her, glad she didn't need to prove anything to Aaron anymore.

After lunch, Emily, Anna, and I climbed on our rock to soak in the noonday sun. Tom, Jack, and Aaron started splashing us, and the water felt so refreshing, we jumped in and splashed them back. When Aaron suggested a game of Chicken, I climbed on Tom's shoulders. I was more interested in feeling his strong chest under my legs than winning the game, but he didn't seem to mind. He kept wrapping his arms around my waist whenever Emily and Anna pulled me down, which was often.

After our game, we sat in the sun on a boulder along the river's edge. I was enjoying the peaceful gurgle of the water when Jack said, "So, Josie, what's green and sings?"

"I don't know. What?" I asked, already smiling.

"Elvis Parsley."

I started laughing at Jack's silly joke, and for some reason, I couldn't stop. The others shook their heads as my eyes filled with tears.

Jack shrugged. "Don't worry, Josie. I have that effect on people," he said, making me laugh even harder.

I rested on the warm rock and closed my eyes, still giggling. The laughter had been as cleansing as a good cry.

Aaron jumped in the water and turned to us. "Tom and Jack, when do you leave for Houston Baptist?"

"Didn't you hear?" Jack teased. "Tommy changed his mind. He's going to Judson."

Emily laughed. "That's an all-girl school. He only wishes he got accepted there."

"We'll be in Bogotá a few more weeks," Tom said, ignoring the joke. "Then we'll head to the States and stay with relatives until school starts."

"What are you guys majoring in?" Emily asked.

"I'm thinking of business," Jack said.

"I'm going to study religion," Tom told us.

Tom and I hadn't talked about our future at all, but it would be hard to keep up any kind of relationship when he went to college. He would meet new people and have new experiences in a world vastly different from mine. I would be doing the same things I'd always done with people I'd always known. Well, not exactly. There was Piedad Maria, after all.

"So will you two keep dating?" Aaron asked Tom and me as he paddled in the river.

"Ignore the monkey in the water," I said. "Maybe he'll wander off."

"Don't mean to bother you, Jos," Aaron said, "but you may want to move away from the snake that just joined you guys."

"Ha, ha, very funny," I said, staying in my spot in the sun.

Tom jerked my hand and pulled me into the water. For once, Aaron wasn't kidding; a three-foot snake had slithered onto our rock. Emily screamed and jumped into the water next to us as the snake retreated into a gap between the rocks.

"It's just a black snake," Anna said, but she and Jack jumped in, too, and we laughed at how silly we were.

We played in the river a little longer then walked together to the waterfall, but I couldn't shake the memory of what Blanca had said at the beginning of summer. Seeing a snake meant change was coming. And there was no telling how the existence of Pity would change my family.

Chapter Eleven

ON THE FINAL NIGHT OF Mission Meeting, the MKs and American kids wore silly, mismatched clothing and performed *Godspell* in the seminary chapel for the adults. Aaron, playing the piano onstage, was the star of the show, and my parents watched him with shining eyes. They weren't watching my acrobatics or listening to me sing, but I didn't care. Being part of the production was thrilling enough. And when we raised Jack, who was playing Jesus, over our heads and walked through the audience, the applause exploded around us.

It felt like the beginning of the end when Uncle Ted, the seminary president, stood and spoke about our time together. He had everyone laughing about overly competitive card games that lasted until one in the morning and rumors he'd heard about Capture the Flag, but he ended with a heartfelt prayer for another safe and productive year. His words reminded me that although there were benefits to the missionary life, we had to remain vigilant of the very real dangers of living in a third-world country. In the morning, these families I'd known all my life would scatter to the far reaches of Colombia. Would everyone stay safe, or would the other shoe fall for some of them? Then it hit me all over again. Although no one had died, there had been no tragic accident, and no one had been kidnapped, our luck had run out. The other shoe had fallen for us in a way no one could ever have dreamed, and I had no idea how my family would survive.

When the prayer ended, I shook off the realization and walked arm in arm with Anna to the cafeteria. With her in a purple peasant dress and go-go boots and me in jean shorts, rainbow suspenders, and a tie-dyed shirt I had made the day before, we made a crazy pair. We raced each other to the cafeteria and joined in celebrating another successful Mission Meeting with cake, ice cream, and punch.

The adults arranged their chairs in a big circle for the annual white elephant exchange, where each missionary would open an unusual gift someone else had brought. We stayed to watch, since it was guaranteed to be amusing. Sure enough, Tom's dad brandished a rubber chicken over his head, Aunt Agnes shook her cassette tape of salsa music like a maraca, and Aunt Beth refused to touch the turquoise toilet seat she unwrapped. By the time Emily's burly father, Uncle Bob, unwrapped a pair of nude panty hose, the laughter lasted almost five minutes.

Then it was my dad's turn. He opened a small gift, and when he pulled out a pacifier and a rattle, my stomach jumped to my throat. I shot a glance at my mom and saw the smile freeze on her face. My dad blushed as he gave the rattle an awkward shake, but everyone burst out laughing, and Dad recovered quickly.

"What'll I do with this thing?" he joked, studying the pacifier. "I think I got Craig's gift."

"Here's mine," Uncle Craig said, opening a deflated soccer ball. The game continued, but for the rest of the exchange, both Mom and Dad looked uneasy. Did she know about Pity? And could someone else know Dad's secret?

Afterward, Tom, Anna, and I were walking out of the cafeteria. "I wonder what my dad will do with a rubber chicken," Tom said.

"I bet Jack'll steal it," Anna answered.

Tom turned to me. "And what will your dad do with a rattle and a pacifier?"

I wasn't about to tell him.

Donna and Daphne came over to us, and Donna's eyes were wide with disbelief. "I've never seen grownups act like that before. Missionaries are weird."

Anna nodded. "Living on the edge does that to people."

We were standing on the sidewalk, the cool night alive with the sound of cicadas, when Tom reached for my hand and pulled me aside. "Let's take a walk," he whispered in my ear.

We left the others and wandered the pattern of sidewalks connecting the seminary buildings. "There's the Southern Cross," I said, stopping to point at the four stars as they glistened in the night sky.

"This has been a great Mission Meeting," Tom said, pulling me toward him.

"It *has* been great," I answered, putting my arms around him. "But I could've done without hurting my leg."

"But you were healed." He smiled. We walked to a mango tree, where he crawled up the branches and snapped a mango off a high limb. "I didn't see any ripe ones," he said, climbing down.

"I like the green ones, too," I told him, sitting on the bench under the tree.

He pulled a Swiss army knife out of his pocket and cut into the fruit. He handed me a slice, taking one for himself.

"Thanks." I bit into the crunchy mango.

Tom laughed when its sour taste made my mouth pucker. "I'm really going to miss you, Josie."

"I'll miss you, too."

"Maybe I could see you at Christmas. Jack and I are coming back to Bogotá for the break."

"Yeah. Maybe my family can visit yours." Having plans to see him again would get me through the next six months. I took another bite of the mango and looked out into the darkness. "Why are you studying religion?"

"I want to teach Biblical languages, like Uncle Ted."

"You'll know the language Jesus spoke," I said. "That'll be cool." The only thing that made sense to me in the Bible was what Jesus had to say. But I didn't tell Tom that. After a moment, I asked, "What did Jesus speak, anyway?"

"Aramaic, I think," Tom answered, cutting another piece of mango. "Maybe after high school you can come to Houston, too."

I reached around him and hugged him. "Maybe I will."

He closed the knife and pulled me onto his lap. His head was leaning against my heart, which had begun to beat faster.

"Tom, why did you break up with the most popular girl in your school?"

He was quiet for a while then said, "Well, Isabel wanted to have sex. She said everyone else was doing it, and she wanted to do it, too. I told her I wasn't going to have sex until I got married. She didn't like that, so we split up."

"She wanted to have sex, and you didn't?" I raised my eyebrows. "Usually, it's the other way around."

"My parents asked me to wait. I said I would. It's as easy as that."

"But didn't you have this enormously strong feeling to go all the way?"

"No, not really. Not when I had already decided I wasn't going to. Only the people who haven't made up their minds get in trouble." He handed me another slice of mango.

"I kind of want to have sex just so it won't be a big deal later on. But not yet. When I'm twenty or so. Besides, I figure by the time someone gets to twenty-five, they'll marry anyone to see what sex is like. Not that I've given it a lot of thought."

Tom laughed. "Sounds like you have. Anyway, I have a feeling I'll be married by twenty-five." He pulled away from me and looked into my eyes. "There's another reason I broke up with Isabel, though."

"What was that?"

"I knew I was going to see you here."

I blinked. "Really? How come I didn't know how you felt about me?"

He shrugged, and I remembered my family's recent visit to Bogotá. We had stayed with his family when Mom returned from the States after her operation. I kept catching Tom watching me, and he made sure he sat next to me when we rode the cable car to Monserrate, a mountain in the center of Bogotá. The steep ride had been frightening, and he had been there to distract me, pointing out landmarks in the huge capital city. The memory made me smile, and I reached under his shirt, thrilled by the feeling of his firm skin.

Tom shivered at my cold hands.

"Sorry," I whispered as we kissed.

He took a deep breath and pulled my hands from his shirt as he smiled down at me, his eyes soft and warm. We sat together in deep and delicious silence, but finally, as much as I didn't want the moment to end, I wanted to be the one to end it. "I guess we'd better go." I stood and reached for his hand. "You have a big day tomorrow, and I have to pack up and move all the way back across the street."

He took my hand, and we walked slowly to my apartment, where I spent a sleepless night thinking of Tom, my family, and Pity.

And then Mission Meeting was over. The next morning, everyone prepared to travel home, and the previous night's festive feeling was gone. The Americans were the first ones to leave for their early flight, and Anna and I made sure we met the group at the seminary gates to see them off and snap some pictures.

Daphne and Donna hugged Anna and me and promised to mail

interesting magazine articles to us. Martin made a point of hugging me and wishing me well, but he looked hurt as he said good-bye. I wondered if we could have been friends. *Maybe,* I thought as the van lumbered into the quiet morning. Maybe we could have kept in touch. After all, how often would I meet someone who was so easy to talk to?

I shook off the regret and walked back to the apartments, where I offered to watch Aunt Beth's daughters while she and Uncle Craig packed their Suburban. She gratefully handed Allison over to me, and I let Sarah lead me around the seminary campus. As Sarah told me about her tricycle and how she wished she had it here to ride, I saw the seminary through the eyes of a four-year-old. I remembered how much I had loved the endless maze of sidewalks under the tall shade trees.

Allison reached up and grabbed my hair, and when I looked down to untangle her chubby hand, her serious gray eyes stopped me. Could my half sister be Allison's age? Did she have blue eyes like me, or the brown eyes of a native Colombian?

When we walked past Tom's apartment, he joined us and gave Sarah a piggyback ride around the mango tree we had kissed under the night before. Sarah squealed, her little strawberry-blond ponytail bouncing on top of her head, and Allison laughed as she watched her big sister. I pushed thoughts of my half sister out of my head.

"I guess we're ready to pull out," Uncle Craig said, walking over to us. "Come on, little monkey." He hefted Sarah off Tom's back.

"Thanks for watching the girls," Aunt Beth added, taking Allison out of my arms. Aunt Beth and Uncle Craig would drive south to the valley town of Popayán, and Emily and her parents would follow them, heading farther southeast, to Tumaco.

Emily came over to me from her family's car behind Uncle Craig's. "I'm glad you and Tom are dating," she said as we hugged before the two-car caravan drove away. "You make a cute couple."

I waved her off with a smile, remembering I had wished for a boyfriend this summer, and my wish had come true. For a moment, I allowed myself to enjoy the fact that I would get to tell Aunt Rosie all about Tom, knowing she would be happy for me.

As the cars drove out of sight, I reached for Tom's hand. "Do you think you'll ever give Sarah another piggyback ride?"

"Doubtful." He shrugged. "Looks like I'm next," he added as another van pulled in, ready to take the next group to the airport.

Anna was leaving, too, so after Tom put his bag in the trunk, we climbed in the van with Anna's family. As we pulled out of the seminary, I made myself stop thinking about how quiet it would be when we returned.

"So how was this batch of American kids?" Aunt Lucy asked, turning around to face us.

"They were fine," Anna told her mother.

"No interesting stories?"

Aaron put his head down behind Anna's seat and pretended to smoke a joint, sucking in on his fingers.

I tried not to laugh at his reference to Erik. "No, ma'am," I said. "How did you like the musical last night?"

"It was great," she said. "Aaron, that was impressive piano playing."

"Thanks, I try," he said.

I rolled my eyes.

During the drive to the airport, Tom and Jack kept the trip lighthearted with Elvis Parsley-type jokes and silly songs. We were passing a brightly painted *chiva* crammed with people and their belongings when Jack leaned out of the window and offered to trade his dad's rubber chicken for a few oranges. A man nodded, so Jack threw the chicken onto the *chiva*. Jack didn't get his oranges; Aunt Lucy told Uncle Ben he'd better step on the gas or someone was going to pelt the van with fruit. We zoomed past the *chiva* as one orange bounced off our bumper.

Before long, the road veered away from the mountains, leaving us surrounded by wide-open space. Tom put his arm around me as the breeze blowing into the van grew warm and thick with the smell of sugar cane. Our group settled into a comfortable silence, and I memorized every detail of Tom's strong hand in mine.

When we reached the airport, Tom's parents were standing next to mine, waiting for us.

"Believe it or not, our flight is on time," Tom's dad told the twins. "Come on, we've got to hurry." He grabbed Tom's duffel bag and led the way to the check-in desk.

Amid a flurry of good-byes, the Westins hurried to their gate, and when Tom hugged and kissed me, I knew my parents were just finding out we were dating. I felt self-conscious at first, but I pushed them out of my mind. It was my moment, and it wouldn't last very long. I had Anna take a picture of Tom and me, then I took a picture of her with Jack. Tom smiled down at me and promised to write, hugging me one last time before walking down the long concourse, his twin beside him.

Anna and I ran up the stairs and outside in time to see Tom and Jack, both carrying bags over their shoulders and both looking handsome in jeans and black jackets. I watched Tom walk across the windswept tarmac, climb the stairs in front of Jack, and duck his head to board the large airplane without looking back. Jack turned to us and waved before following Tom inside.

The airplane taxied to the end of the landing strip and completed a slow turn. Anna and I covered our ears to soften the deafening roar of the engine, then the jet thundered down the runway and rose into the blue sky. It angled over the sun and quickly became a speck among the clouds.

"Well, that's that," Anna said.

I looked over at her and smiled through my tears.

"And it was a lot fun," she added with a nod of her head.

Aunt Lucy came and put her arm around Anna. "I didn't realize you girls were dating the Westin boys. That's really sweet."

Anna buried her face in her mom's shoulder. "Jack and I weren't really dating, but whatever it was, it's over now."

"Come now, you don't know that! Besides, you still have all the wonderful memories from this Mission Meeting."

I turned away. Anna's mom was wrong. All the memories were not wonderful, and now, faced with going home, I wasn't sure the good ones would be enough.

"It's time for us to go, too." Aunt Lucy sighed as Uncle Ben and Isaac joined us. "Back to the ranch."

"Are you sad, Mom?" Anna asked.

"Sure, I am," she said. "It's wonderful to spend time with other missionaries. They're my friends. They know what I'm going through and understand my problems. But it's time to go back. Aren't you curious to see how the horses are doing?"

"I have missed riding them," Anna said. She turned to me. "Maybe you can come visit us. Then you can see the foal."

"Remember not to name it after me," I said, smiling. "Hey, I know—call it Aaron. You'll get a kick out of bossing Aaron around."

Anna laughed. "Sounds good. You okay with that, Aaron?"

Aaron put his arm around Anna. "Yeah, call your new pony Aaron, and I'll come out there and take my namesake on a journey into the wilds of Colombia." He raised his hand, pretending to throw a lasso.

"I want to go!" Isaac said, and everyone laughed.

"Henry"—Uncle Ben turned to my dad—"how about we take our families to San Andrés for vacation this summer?"

Anna and I squealed at the idea of visiting the Colombian island in the Caribbean Sea.

"That would be fun, Dad," Aaron said.

Dad shook Uncle Ben's hand and said, "We'll see."

I hugged Anna, promising to talk Dad into it.

We all said good-bye, and after Anna's family boarded their airplane, Mom said, "Let's get going."

"Can we stay and see their plane lift off?" I asked.

She looked at her watch. "We still have to move out of the apartment and back to our house. And I have choir practice this afternoon. We better not."

Mom's choir practice depressed me more than anything. I guess it was the thought of going back to the routine of church services, choir practices, and visits to prospective converts as if nothing had changed. But everything had changed, and if Mom didn't already know, she was going to find out.

"Can I drive the van?" Aaron asked Dad.

"Sure," he answered, pulling out the keys.

"I'll go with you, Mom," I said, still not trusting myself to be around Dad.

I quickly discovered riding in the van would have been more comfortable—Aaron and Dad would have left me alone with my thoughts. Mom asked about Tom but didn't seem interested in hearing what I had to say. I asked about the other missionaries, but her answers were vague. When I mentioned I wanted to shop for some new sandals, she ignored me. Feeling like I had nothing to lose, I asked, "What happens when a missionary breaks the rules?"

"What do you mean?" She slowed to let a motorcycle scoot around our car.

"Anna and I were talking about Uncle Perry. He stole money from the church, and they fired him."

"Technically, he didn't get fired. He was asked to resign."

"But where is Jesus's forgiveness in all of that?" I asked. "Why couldn't Uncle Perry have a second chance?"

"Missionaries are held to higher standards, I guess," Mom said, shrugging. "We represent the perfect life of Jesus to the lost world."

"I bet it was pretty hard for Uncle Perry's family to leave Santa Marta," I said.

She didn't respond, and there was nothing left to talk about. The silence between us unnerved me, as if she knew I was keeping a secret from her and was torturing me until I let her in on it.

I closed my eyes and turned my face to the window, letting the breeze blow through my hair. Cali was full of smells, each connected to a memory. Some, like the burning of sugar cane, reminded me of good-byes. The smell of the city—with its diesel fuel, cigarettes, and occasional aromas of cologne and bursts of air conditioning—was the smell of excitement and possibilities. The mountains' mix of cool fresh air, rain, and coffee was sheer beauty.

But the best smell, the one I knew even with my eyes closed, was our street. The smoky smell of frying bread from the corner restaurant lingered among the fragrance of fruit trees, flowers, and mown grass. I breathed it all in, hoping we would be able to adjust to the changes coming our way and that it would be a long time before I had to say good-bye to this.

Chapter Twelve

MY FAMILY SPENT THE AFTERNOON moving back home, and although Brandy was thrilled to have us back, no doubt hoping for regular feedings again, the house felt empty without Blanca. She wouldn't return from Huila until the next day. Mom went to choir practice and was still away at suppertime, so Dad made grilled cheese sandwiches.

I leaned against the counter, watching him as he burned part of each one. "Dad, I've been thinking you should tell Aaron what happened. The longer you wait to get it out in the open, the harder it'll be. Besides, if Aaron knows first, we three can figure out how to tell Mom."

"We'll see." He pulled a bowl of fruit from the refrigerator. "Call Aaron for supper."

Aaron came into the kitchen, and we each grabbed some dinner and sat down at the table. Dad said a quick prayer, and I watched him as we ate, waiting for him to speak. He kept chewing his sandwich without a word. If he wasn't going to say something, I would. There was no way we were pretending everything was okay.

I took a deep breath and jumped in. "Dad, I think it's time."

Dad kept chewing, hunched over his plate.

"What's going on?" Aaron asked, looking from one of us to the other over the papaya slice on his fork.

Dad straightened, put his sandwich down, and looked at my brother. "Son, I made a mistake."

Aaron waited for Dad to explain, but the silence must have dragged on too long. "What? What are you talking about?"

After another long pause, Dad said, "I had an affair, and I'm really sorry and—"

"So that's it," Aaron said, looking as if he'd solved a riddle.

"What's it?" I asked.

Aaron turned to me. "Dad kept going the wrong way when he said he was visiting Ricardo." He turned back to Dad and added, "But, hey, you don't need to tell me about it. Really." Aaron stood and carried his plate to the kitchen. "This doesn't involve me. Shouldn't you be talking to Mom?"

"Mom doesn't know yet," I answered, following him. "And depending on how she reacts, it could involve us all. A lot."

"Well, maybe I don't want to hear it." Aaron set his plate in the sink.

"Aaron, listen. You have a half sister."

He froze, his hand on the water faucet, only the muscles in his jaw tightening.

"Her name is Piedad Maria."

"Really?" He looked at me. "How old is she?" He put his hand up. "Never mind. She'll never be part of my life." Aaron rinsed his plate and walked back to the breakfast room.

"That's true, son," Dad said from his place at the table. "You don't have to get involved. But you do have to know, and Josie's right. We may have to go back to the States. I could be looking for a job there soon."

"I don't want to leave Cali. I like it here." Aaron crossed his arms over his chest and leaned against the kitchen doorway. "What are you going to do?"

"I don't know." Dad pushed his plate away and put his head

in his hands. "Samara, the mother, doesn't think she can keep the baby, but I don't want Pity to end up an orphan."

"Maybe someone from church will adopt her," I offered.

"What a mess," Aaron said, shaking his head as he walked out of the room.

"Forget about Aaron." I said, sitting next to Dad. I should've known he wouldn't be any help at all. "What do you want to say to Mom?"

"I don't want to say anything to her."

"Really, Dad? Because she has to know. Do you want me to tell her?"

"No! Why does she have to know?"

I stared at him, disgusted. I wanted to shake this man, yell at him, tell him he had to make this right. But he was my father, and I couldn't deny my unnamable need to align with him, or at least make the insanity feel normal.

Our standoff lasted a full minute before he whispered, "Fine." He hung his head. "Your mom's the only one I've ever loved, Josie." His voice cracked, and chills crawled up my spine. I knew he was telling the truth.

"Do you think you should tell Mom about the money you're going to give to…" I couldn't bring myself to say her name.

"I've already given it to Samara."

"What?"

"I had time off between meetings a few days ago and took it to her."

I stood up, shaken. My dad's double life kept finding new ways to shock me, and each time, my reaction was different. This time, I retreated to my room.

When Mom pulled into the garage, I was lying on my bed, trying to read *Jonathan Livingston Seagull*. I listened to every sound: the car door slamming, the garage closing, the jingling of her keys, her footsteps into the kitchen, and the refrigerator opening. I found Dad in his office, where he was looking out the window. "We should get this over with, Dad."

He didn't answer, but he followed me.

We went to the kitchen, where Mom was putting fruit salad in a bowl.

As I lifted myself onto the counter, she said, "Don't sit on the counters, dear. The maid prepares food there."

I slid off, went to the refrigerator, and pulled out the pitcher of powdered milk. We kept the stuff cold, but it was still dreadful, not like real milk. Enough Chocavena or Milo in it made a decent glass of chocolate milk, though.

Dad leaned on the doorframe. "Astrid, you look lovely tonight."

His compliment seemed like a lame way to start the worst conversation of their marriage. She gave him a suspicious look, then she softened and thanked him.

She took a fork from the silverware drawer and carried the bowl into the dining room off the kitchen instead of the breakfast nook where we usually ate. The dining room table seated ten in leather chairs that resembled small thrones, and Mom looked like a queen sitting at the head of the table. "The three sopranos are sounding better," she told my dad as he sat beside her. "They might be ready to sing a trio soon."

"That's good," Dad said, fingering the grooves on the edge of the table.

"I noticed some cans of paint fell off the shelves in the garage," she went on. "Must've happened during the earthquake."

"I'll check on it first thing in the morning," Dad said.

Mom's fork clinked against her bowl as she ate in the uncomfortable silence. I busied myself with an old newspaper on the other end of the table.

"So, what's going on?" Mom asked. "You two don't usually join me when I eat after choir practice."

"True." Without looking up, I waited for Dad to start talking.

Finally, he reached for her hand. "Astrid, I love you. I never meant to hurt you, but I…"

She stopped chewing, her face pale. "What happened?"

"I committed adultery."

I realized, too late, that I had been an utter fool. I shouldn't have pushed Dad to tell her. It wasn't my place to say. His transgression was between the two of them, and my stomach became a knot of regret when I saw the horrible sadness that clouded Mom's eyes. This moment had nothing to do with me. I was hurt and very afraid of what the future would hold for all of us, but I couldn't know the pain Mom was feeling. I crept out of the room but not before I saw my mother's shoulders start to tremble then fall, creating the saddest memory of my life.

I couldn't bear to be alone, so I went upstairs to Aaron's room and sat on his midnight-blue rug while he flipped through a magazine and listened to Elton John's *Goodbye Yellow Brick Road*. I usually enjoyed the album, but that night, the lyrics seemed dark.

"So I feel like this is all your fault," he said, leaning back and tossing the magazine aside.

"Yeah, you would. But it's not. I just happened to overhear Dad talking on the phone. He was saying something about a baby. I made him tell me what was going on. I told him I'd assume the worst if he didn't tell me." I gave a bitter smirk. "But I can't imagine it being any worse. Dad and Mom could get fired, and we'll have to move back to the States. Are you ready for that?"

"No way. It's my senior year. All the MKs who've gone to the States for their senior year hated it. I want to graduate here, with my friends."

"I don't want to leave, either." I sighed. "I love it here."

"No, you don't, especially now that Tom is going to be in the States. You'd probably like it if we moved back."

His words plunged like knives into my heart. "You jerk!" I hissed. Anger, the kind that is too big to breathe out, forced its way through me, leaving me shaking. "For one thing," I said, failing to control my shrill voice, "we'll probably live too far from Houston for Tom to make any difference. And for another, what kind of job would Dad get? What kind of house will we live in? What about Blanca?"

I gasped for air and looked at Aaron. When he didn't meet my eyes, I went on. "Of course I'll end up living in the States. You will, too. But I'm not ready to leave here. Not yet. And do you want Mom to leave Dad?"

"Of course not! Don't you think I know Dad really screwed up?"

We were at an impasse when the front door slammed. I jumped up and hurried into my bedroom. From the window, I saw Mom running past the gate and down the street. "Dad, you have to go after her," I yelled, taking the stairs two by two.

"Why?" He was standing at the door. "Don't you think she needs time to cool off?"

"Just follow her to keep her safe!" I begged, trying to shove him out the door.

Dad hesitated then raced outside behind Mom. I sat on the front porch with Brandy by my side, waiting for their return, and as the night wore on, a million mosquitoes must have bitten me. The temperature dropped into the sixties, making me wish I had grabbed a sweatshirt, but nothing was going to move me from my post. It was my way of paying for the mistake I'd made.

I sat outside, itching and freezing, and thought about how much my life had changed. I remembered Alejandro and how, just weeks ago, what I wanted most in life was a boyfriend. Right then, I wanted my family to survive Dad's affair. And though Tom and I were dating, when I tried to picture his face, it didn't come together in my mind's eye. I could feel his arms around me, his hand on my waist, and his lips on mine, but all I could see was that hat. As much as I wanted it to work between us, doubts crept in. I pushed them away. There was enough to deal with for the moment.

I was thinking about Blanca and how good it would be to see her again when Dad and Mom finally came home, talking to each other in low voices. That was a good sign. I patted Brandy on the head one last time, stood, and went inside. When they opened the front door, I was sitting on the rug in Aaron's room again. Dad came in and sat on Aaron's bed while Mom rested against the edge of his desk.

I stared at the rug until Dad said, "Your mom and I have talked it over, and we've decided that for now, we're going to try to keep our lives as normal as possible. It would be best if we didn't involve any missionaries until we sort this out. Tomorrow, Mom will come with me to see Pity. And I'm just so sorry." He gave Mom a miserable look.

"Okay, Henry," Mom snapped. "Rule number one is no more apologizing. I don't want to hear it."

"Good answer, Mom," I told her, relieved to hear the strength in her voice.

"And you"—she pointed to me—"stay out of it." Her eyes were so angry, I felt as if I'd been slapped.

I slunk out of Aaron's room and into my own, where I gathered my rosary, the statue of Saint Michael, and the brown paper bag where I'd put the pieces of Saint Jude. I curled up in bed with them, numb and unmoving, as the lyrics of Elton John's "Candle in the Wind" washed over me.

Chapter Thirteen

I WAS SITTING AT MY DESK, finishing a letter to Aunt Rosie about Mission Meeting and Tom—I'd purposely left out Dad and Pity—when Brandy started barking. From my window, I saw Blanca set her bags down and pet him as he bounced and yapped around her dark-blue skirt. Such relief flooded me, I could almost imagine dancing around her myself.

"Blanca's home!" I called as I ran downstairs and out the door. I hugged Blanca, nearly tipping her over with my enthusiasm.

She seemed shorter, but her eyes were as bright as ever as she hugged me back.

"How was your trip?" I asked, taking her bags. "Tell me everything. Did your brothers and sisters like the clothes you made for them?"

"It was very good. Everyone loved the clothes," Blanca said as we headed into the house. She greeted Aaron, who was reading a magazine on the couch, then we walked to her room.

"How was gringo week at the seminary?" she asked, opening her suitcase on the bed.

"I have a lot to tell you," I answered, glad to be curling up in the familiar chair in her room. "I have a boyfriend."

"Really? Is it Alejandro?" she asked.

"No, it's a missionary kid. I'll get his picture." I ran upstairs and came back with a photo from our photo album. It was of Aaron,

Tom, and me during my family's trip to Bogotá. The rolls of film from Mission Meeting had been sent to the States to be developed and wouldn't arrive for another week.

"*Qué chusco,*" she said, studying the photo. "He is handsome, and you look good together."

"Yeah, but I won't get to see him much. His family lives in Bogotá, and he's going to college in the States in a few weeks."

"Too bad he is so far away." Blanca handed me the picture and pulled a dress from her suitcase, shaking it to loosen the wrinkles.

"I might get to see him at Christmas," I told her. "So I guess you missed Juan Fernando while you were gone."

"I am hoping to talk with him tonight."

"That's nice." Watching her unpack, I wondered how to tell her our family's news. I decided the best thing was to dive in. "I need to tell you something."

Blanca stopped unpacking, her eyes wide. "What happened?"

"My dad, he did a really dumb thing." I picked nervously at the armrest of my chair. "He had an affair with this girl and got her pregnant. Now I have a half sister."

"Oh, so you found out about that." Blanca turned back to her suitcase.

My jaw dropped. "You knew?"

"Yes." She didn't look up. "I overheard some telephone conversations. Your father is a good man; he just had a weak moment. And now he does not know how to handle the outcome."

"My dad's adultery was way more than a weak moment."

"It happens, *chica,*" Blanca said with a shrug.

"Not to missionaries," I said, wondering how Blanca could be taking the news so lightly. "And I'm worried about my mom," I added.

"Yes." Blanca sat on her bed, sighing. "I am worried about your mother, too. How is she taking the news?"

"She just found out yesterday, so it's hard to say."

"And you, *mija*? How long have you known?"

"Over a week. I learned the same way you did. My friend Anna and I were here one day during Mission Meeting and heard Dad talking to the woman on the phone. The baby's name is Piedad Maria."

"That is a pretty name."

"It's a strange one in English. Pity is more like sadness than mercy. And get this—my mom is going to meet the mother and baby today. Can you believe it?"

"It's not surprising," Blanca said. "Your mother wants to do the right thing, no matter what the cost."

Just then the telephone rang, and I jumped up. "That might be Tom," I said, racing to the phone. Sure enough, his voice was on the other end of the line, sounding sweet and far away, and the way he said my name melted my heart. I made him laugh, reminding him of our race to the rope swing, and he told me about his plane trip home and about the party his soccer friends were having for the graduating class. But then we had nothing more to say. I wanted to talk some more about Mission Meeting, tell him how Blanca had just come home, and get him to read the book I'd started. But I couldn't find the words, because all I really wanted was to reach through the phone lines and hold him close. After hanging up, I stared at the phone, counting the things I wished were different about my life, starting with Pity and her mother.

While my parents were visiting Samara and the baby, Aaron played the piano, each piece more energetic than the last, and I paced. Why would Mom put herself in this position? Missionaries were expected to help those in need, but she was going too far.

I flopped on my bed and tried to read *Jonathan Livingston Seagull* again but kept losing my concentration. I had gone over the same page at least three times when my parents finally pulled through the front gate. Mom rushed upstairs and slammed her bedroom door, and when I leaned against it, I heard her sobbing.

I listened to her cry, wishing there were a way to comfort her. I joined Dad and Aaron in the living room.

"Samara wants to give Pity up for adoption," Dad was saying, sitting on the sofa with his head in his hands. "But what if the baby ends up in an orphanage? What kind of life will she have? I think Samara should raise her. Don't you?"

"How did Mom and Samara get along?" Aaron ignored Dad's entreaty with a smirk. "Did Mom try to bite her head off?"

Dad gave Aaron a haggard look. "No. Your mother was fine. Until we got home, at least."

I sat in the rocking chair with my arms crossed, angry at Aaron for being so callous and at Dad for putting up with it. Dad looked at me and sighed. "I guess we need to find a family who will adopt Pity."

"Of course you do," Aaron said, turning back to the piano.

I walked out.

The next morning, I was choosing clothes to wear when Mom came into my room and sat on my bed. "I want to go shopping for some things for Pity. She doesn't have enough clothes, and she needs more diapers. Do you want to come?"

"Sure, Mom," I said, hiding my surprise at being included in her plans.

"We can take the things over to Sa… to her afterward." Mom was strong, but she was still human, and the other woman's name must have stuck in her throat. "Your father doesn't know what a baby needs, and it doesn't look like that woman knows, either. This way, you'll get to meet Pity. Or have you met her already?"

"No, I've never seen her," I whispered, feeling the sting of another slap from her words.

"We'll leave when you're ready," Mom said, walking out.

I quickly pulled on jeans and a blouse and met her at the front door.

Mom was businesslike about the shopping, but I enjoyed choosing cute baby clothes, bottles, formula, diapers, and lightweight blankets for Pity. We also bought fruit, bread, and a Colombian chocolate bar for Samara. By the time we arrived at Samara's apartment building, I was nervous enough to be nauseated, but Mom went straight to the second-floor apartment and knocked lightly. Samara answered in a housecoat, something my mother would never have done. This woman was in her early twenties, with beautiful tan skin, a full figure, and long dark hair. I couldn't help comparing Samara to my mom, who was pale and rail thin.

"*Gracias.*" Samara nodded, looking at the gifts. She put the formula and food on the kitchen counter and the diapers on the changing table.

I held up a few of the outfits we bought for her to see.

"*Ay, mire,*" she said, taking an especially cute pink dress with a big white collar from me. Her chin trembled as she admired it.

When Samara lowered the dress, she spoke softly but hurriedly, confessing she was overwhelmed by the job of taking care of the baby alone. She said her mother wasn't able to visit often since she lived over three hours away in Puracé. Most of Samara's friends were single and had jobs that kept them busy, or they were married with families of their own.

"My neighbors, they don't help." Tears rolled down Samara's cheeks. "They care more about keeping the baby quiet at night."

I looked around the place as Samara talked. Shelves fashioned from planks and bricks lined one wall, and I knew my father had made them; I had the same makeshift shelves in my room. The bedroom was only big enough for a bed, and the crib dominated the living room. As Mom and Samara talked, I gathered my courage and took the few paces to see Pity. I leaned over the crib and caught my breath when I saw her. She looked up at me with pale-blue eyes, her fragile face surrounded by wispy black hair. Tiny gold earrings glinted in her earlobes. She stared at me for a moment, then she broke into a toothless grin as she kicked her chubby legs and waved her arms. She was the most beautiful baby I'd ever seen, and I couldn't help myself. I fell in love with her.

"How old is she?" I asked, turning to Samara. Mom's eyes widened, and I gasped. Samara's answer would be loaded with information, and I wasn't ready to hear it.

"Six months," Samara said. Pity started to cry, and Samara asked my mom, "Please, would you hold her? I will get her bottle ready."

Mom smiled at Pity as she lifted the baby in her arms and sang to her, bouncing her gently as she walked around the apartment. How was it possible that these two women were so comfortable with each other? I realized, watching Mom, that it didn't matter how they were connected. This baby needed both of them. I knew, though, that Mom was calculating the six months. January.

We sat at the kitchen table as Samara fed Pity her bottle, and for a while we watched the baby slurp her milk. Finally, Mom asked, "Samara, do you really want to put Piedad Maria up for adoption?"

Samara lowered her eyes. "I had a good job. I worked in the emergency room, but I couldn't keep it when the baby came. Now I can't find any work. Nothing that pays enough. I was living with my aunt and her family, but they were too angry when…" She looked away then added, "That's why Enrique gives me money."

I saw my mom stiffen as Samara said Dad's name in Spanish. It was a window into their affair I'm sure Mom didn't want to peek into. But Mom recovered quickly and asked, "What about taking her back to your family in Puracé?"

"My father drinks too much." Samara scowled. "My mother is powerless to stop him. I left home and vowed never to go back. My child will never grow up in that place."

Suddenly, Samara was sobbing, her tears falling on the baby's head. "Piedad Maria's father will never be my husband. It's hard to find a man when I already have a baby. I need a better way."

Samara held Pity close, and the infant reached a hand to her mother's face. Milk ran down Pity's chin as she gurgled, making Samara laugh through her tears. Using a coarse white cloth, Mom wiped Pity's mouth, an unreadable expression on her face.

We were saying good-bye at the door when Samara said, "A friend set up a job interview for me at her work next week, but I can't go because I don't have anyone to watch the baby."

"We could do it," I said, looking at Mom.

Mom gave me a shushing glance.

"I'm sure something will work out," she said to Samara as we walked to the stairs. "We'll be in touch."

Mom and I rode home in silence. I was about to jump out and open the front gate for her to drive through when she put her hand on my arm. "Josie, it's important you not tell anyone about this. Not even Tom."

"I know," I said. "Anna was with me when I found out, though."

"Oh." Mom frowned.

"Can I ask you a question?"

"What is it?" she asked, wary.

"How can you stand to see Samara and that baby?"

That same incomprehensible look came over her face. "The Lord works in mysterious ways, Josie," was all she said. "Now go open the gate."

The following day was Sunday, and I awoke to the sound of Mom and Dad arguing in their bedroom, but we went to church as if nothing had changed. Dad preached a sermon on forgiveness and led the congregation in singing "Holy, Holy, Holy," the first song in the hymnal. My mother's clear voice rose above the rest, like a feather floating on a breeze. I hoped no one noticed my tears as I closed my eyes and listened, amazed by her strength.

Dad was driving us home when Mom told Aaron and me that Pity would be staying with us for a few days.

"Do you think that's a good idea, Mom?" Aaron asked.

"Of course I do," Mom insisted. "Samara needs a break, and she has a chance to go on a job interview. She really needs to find work."

Aaron shrugged. I was about to say it would be nice to see the baby again, but when I saw Dad's face, I changed my mind. Though he had no say in the matter, his lips were a thin line of disapproval.

He dropped us off at home, and I went straight to Blanca's room to ask her to go with me to La Ermita. I needed two statues: Saint Anthony, the miracle worker, and Saint Joseph, the patron saint of the family. Our family needed a miracle, and both saints were holding babies. Besides, Aunt Rosie had bought those two saints, and I needed a way to keep her memory close. I also needed to replace Blanca's statue of Saint Jude.

"My mom wants Pity to stay with us for a few days," I added.

Blanca was logical about it. "Well, your father is the baby's father, too. He should see her some of the time."

"That's true. But what do you think of Mom wanting to have Pity around? I can't help but think it's not going to go well."

"I don't know. It could be the best thing for her. Your mom seems to be a little softer now that she knows about Piedad Maria. More human. She used to be perfect at everything." Blanca smiled. "Yesterday, she burned some cookies and laughed about it."

"Please tell me she didn't burn cookies with American chocolate chips in them!" I feigned horror.

Blanca smiled. "Her life is falling apart around her, and she cannot fix it. She is just taking what comes."

"I suppose you're right," I said. "I'll get changed, and we can go, okay?"

"Okay, *mija.*"

We rode the *buseta* to the church, and I lifted my eyes to the ceiling, taking in the stained-glass panels and towering arches. I breathed in the incense, feeling a weight lift off my chest for the first time in two long weeks.

Mass had just begun, so we joined the others in the pews. The words of the priest comforted me as I watched him make the sign of the cross, and I gained more peace with every "Hail Mary" and "Our Father" the congregation recited.

When the service was over, I whispered to Blanca, "There's something I have to do." I had seen others put money in a box and use long matchsticks to light small candles on a narrow table. I did the same, saying a quick prayer for my family. We needed all the help we could get.

On our way out, I bought the statues, giving Blanca the statue of Saint Jude. She smiled and thanked me as she put it in her purse, and we stepped outside, blinking into the sunshine.

Our bus was waiting at the stop. "*¡Qué suerte!* We are lucky this time," Blanca said, finding seats for us.

We got off the bus at our street and were two houses from our home when a white car passed by. I noticed the thin woman with long brown hair driving the new Renault, though she was unaware of me. And I saw the men catching up to her on a motorcycle, their faces hidden by helmets. I heard two loud shots and looked back as the white Renault veered off the road and crashed into a huge tree. The motorcycle sped past, leaving me wondering why they hadn't stopped when the Renault crashed. The car's pitiful horn blew continuously as steam rose from its crumpled hood. Blanca grabbed my hand and pulled me to our gate.

"Stay here!" she told me then ran to the white car. I stood by the gate until someone started wailing. Then I had to know what happened.

Blanca talked to others who had gathered at the crash and didn't notice me as I walked slowly toward the accident. I wasn't sure how much I wanted to see, and without meaning to, I caught a glimpse of blood spattered on the window. Then I saw the young woman's body slumped forward, pressing against the horn. I jumped back when a man reached in and pulled her off the steering wheel. For an eerie moment, all was quiet, until a neighbor kneeled on the ground with her arms outstretched and began to sob.

Blanca walked over to where I was standing. "You should go home, *niña*."

"What happened?"

"The motorcyclist shot her, *chica*. Now go home."

"I didn't see her face."

"Good." Blanca patted my shoulder. "Go home. The police will be here soon."

"Are you coming, too?"

"I will be there soon. Go pray the rosary for her." She turned and headed toward the small crowd.

I walked home, and as I opened the gate to our house, Aaron asked, "What happened?" He was standing in the middle of the driveway, his hand on Brandy's head.

"A woman was shot. She was driving down our street, when two guys on a motorcycle rode by and shot her." I shuddered. "She had just passed us."

He walked over to see for himself while I stood under the mango tree in our front yard. I couldn't help but think about that thin woman with the long brown hair. From the split second I'd seen of her, I created her life. She mattered to people; she had children at home, maybe two young sons. She probably lived in a big house in the new part of town, a house with pink bougainvilleas and white gardenias. I shivered and wished Blanca would come back.

"The police showed up," Aaron said as he unlatched the gate. "Juan Fernando is with them, keeping the traffic moving around the scene. One of the officers said it was probably a *mafioso*'s wife."

"Should we tell Mom and Dad?" I asked, watching the crowd as it hovered in apprehension around the car.

"No, they have enough on their plate right now," he said, walking toward the door. "You should come inside."

"In a minute," I told him.

I turned to see Juan Fernando and Blanca walking my way. I rarely saw them touch, but today they had their arms around each other, and Juan Fernando's face, which always had a smile, was now gaunt.

When they arrived at our gate, I reached for Blanca's hand.

"I have to go back," Juan Fernando said to her. "Be safe, and keep her safe." He motioned to me.

"Of course," she answered.

He walked back toward the crowd, and we watched the scene awhile longer.

"We saw a dead person," I whispered to Blanca. "I saw her just before she died."

"I know," she said, putting her hand on my arm. "But my father always said life is for the living. It is the job of her family and her friends to mourn her loss. Do not forget to pray the rosary for her. Pray for her once tonight. That will be enough."

"Does it mean anything that we saw someone die?"

She sighed. "It is not a good omen. We will just have to watch what happens for a little while." She pulled me toward the house. "*Ponga atención, niña.*"

Pay attention, child.

Chapter Fourteen

"JOSIE, COME SIT DOWN," MY dad called from the dining room. Blanca slipped past me as I walked in and took a seat at the long table. Dad was at the far end, in one of the throne-like chairs, and Mom and Aaron were sitting on each side of him. Everyone was looking at me, and I assumed they were going to ask me about the shooting. Instead, my father said, "Josie, Aaron followed you today. He said you went to La Ermita and stayed for a service. Is that true?"

"Yes," I answered slowly, confused by his question. "Why? Don't you want to know about the woman who was shot outside our house?"

"No," Mom answered. "We want to know why you were at La Ermita today. It seems strange to us that you would go to a Catholic church."

My stomach clenched into a knot, but I resolved to explain. "I like going to La Ermita. It's beautiful and calming. I like the rituals in the mass, and I like the rosary. Have you noticed I don't scream in the night like I used to? It's because of the rosary."

"You pray on the rosary?" Mom asked, sounding incredulous. "What's in that bag?" She pointed at the package I held in my hands.

I pulled out the statues and stood them on the table. "This is Saint Anthony. He's the patron saint of lost articles, and also of miracles. This is Saint Joseph. He's the patron saint of families. I thought we could use some help." A giggle died in my throat when they didn't respond. "I guess I just wanted him around during these hard times." I didn't tell them Aunt Rosie had bought the same statues when she was here.

Dad picked up Saint Joseph and studied it. "What do you do with these figurines?"

"Nothing! I just have them in my room, and when I see them, it reminds me to pray about what's bothering me. Are you seriously accusing me of doing something wrong?" I could feel my face burn as I spoke. "I'd think having Pity might change a few things around here."

Dad set the statue down and faced me. "Josie, we're here to introduce God's word to the lost, not to adopt their beliefs."

"I think, Dad," I said, barely controlling the urge to yell at him, "that after what has happened with you and that woman, I can believe what I want to believe." My parents gave me a longsuffering look, and I turned to my brother. "And why were you spying on me, anyway?"

Aaron just stared at the table.

I stood and grabbed the statues. "I can't believe any of you," I said and stomped up the stairs, feeling angrier with each step.

"This isn't over, Josie," my father called after me.

I slammed my bedroom door in response and fell facedown on my bed, dropping the statues beside me. La Ermita was the only place I could go to find comfort. The mass lifted me up in ways I hadn't experienced before. Why should I give it up? My anger gave way to shuddering sobs. I felt so lonely, and my parents were being horribly unfair. I cried because everything had changed, and I cried for the poor dead woman and her family. I cried because my parents weren't going to let me go to La Ermita anymore and because Tom was so far away. Finally, I cried myself to sleep.

I jolted awake, surrounded by darkness. When my stomach

growled, I decided to go downstairs for a snack. My family was finishing dinner, and I overheard my dad saying, "She's probably the bad influence, though."

I stopped and listened.

"I don't care," Mom answered. "I can't train a new one right now. We'll just have to talk some sense into Josie."

"I shouldn't have told you guys where she went," Aaron said. He sounded remorseful, but I didn't care. My hate for him was so intense my throat closed, and I had to swallow hard to keep breathing.

"Well, it's done," Dad said. "We needed to know, I guess. I really think Blanca should leave."

They were blaming Blanca. My blood turned to ice. Before anyone could answer him, I stormed in. "You can't fire Blanca. It's not her fault."

My family stared up at me, then Dad spoke. "She shouldn't have taken you to her church, Josie."

"I guess she figured we were praying to the same God," I answered. "But I should have known better. Wait here." I raced up the stairs to my room. Blanca was more important to me than La Ermita, and I knew what I had to do.

I found the red prayer book from La Ermita and took my beautiful rosary from under my pillow. I gathered the statues, along with the pieces of Saint Jude, and carried them into the breakfast room. "I want you to see me do this," I said. "I'll stop going to La Ermita, I'll get rid of these things. Just leave Blanca out of this."

My family followed me to the kitchen, where I grabbed a box of matches. Then I led them to the backyard. I placed the missal with the statues and beads on the ground and struck a match, setting the missal on fire.

"What are you doing, Josie?" Dad cried, pulling me away as the flame leapt up, gobbling the booklet.

"I'm burning these things. Just leave Blanca out of this."

Dad was shaking his head. "You shouldn't do that, Josie."

"Why not?" I asked.

He looked wildly at Mom, whose arms were crossed in front of her. She and Aaron stared down at the fire, mesmerized. Dad put his hands to his head. "This is wrong!"

But he didn't try to stop the fire.

Watching the pile burn, I might have cried again if I hadn't been so angry and if the fire hadn't been so beautiful. As the rosary melted and Saint Michael's wings softened and blurred into a shapeless lump, the flames turned into a golden rainbow of colors then back to orange. The blaze lit Blanca's face. She was watching from her window, a hand over her mouth.

"You did the right thing," Mom said, coming over to me. She tried to put her arm around my shoulder, but I pushed her away. Her face hardened as she tightened her sweater around her shoulders and walked back to the house. Dad and Aaron followed her, but I sat down beside the fire and witnessed each statue and bead turn black and shapeless. Regret over what I'd done rose inside me and strangled my breath, but I pushed the feeling away. I had to keep Blanca.

After watching the final wisp of smoke, I stumbled inside. Everyone had gone to bed, but I lay awake deep into the night, wishing an earthquake would swallow up our house or that I would have the courage to pack up and leave my pitiful family, taking Blanca with me.

I awoke early the following morning and dressed in shorts and a T-shirt for a run in the seminary. The sun's angle played with my shadow, and I watched my ponytail swing steadily as I ran, my thoughts steering clear of the fire the night before. Over breakfast, I learned Pity would stay with us starting the next day so Samara could go on her interview. My parents would tell anyone who asked that a member of our church needed us to keep their baby for a few days.

"I'm going shopping for the baby again," Mom said. "Canned formula, disposable diapers," she listed. She might have asked me to come along, but the withering look I gave her stopped her in her tracks. There was no way in hell I was going.

Blanca barely spoke to me as she cleaned the library, Pity's temporary room. I didn't speak to her, even though I wanted to; our silence was for the best. By the end of the day, the house was ready for the baby. After everyone had gone to bed, I crept down to Blanca's room and tapped on the door. She seemed to have been expecting me, because she let me in right away, her eyes wide.

"Yo-si, *qué pasó?*" she asked, wanting to know what had happened the night before.

I plopped into my chair. "My parents don't like it that I prefer your church to mine," I said with a sardonic laugh. "They think it's your fault. They were talking about firing you, but I told them I would stop going to La Ermita and get rid of the rosary and statues if they would just leave you out of it."

Blanca sat down on her bed. "*Ay, chica*, that is horrible. I am so sorry. I should not have given you a rosary. I should not have taken you to La Ermita."

"Stop, Blanca," I said, reaching out for her hand. "If you hadn't, I'd still be worrying all the time and screaming in the night." Tears choked my throat as I added, "Thank you for the rosary. Thank you for taking me to the church." I started to cry.

"You are right," she said, patting my shoulder. "I am glad I could help you. But you should not have burned those things."

"Yeah," I said. "By the time I figured that out, it was too late."

We sat together a few minutes more, then I stood and stretched. "I'd better go to bed. Hey, can I borrow your rosary beads?" I joked. "Mine went up in smoke."

"I am so sorry, *mija*," she said, her eyes sad.

I shook my head and slipped out her door.

I stepped out of the car with Mom, grumbling. She and Dad had insisted I come with them to Samara's apartment. As soon as I slammed the door, Dad pulled away to look for a parking spot. I shoved my hands in my pockets and followed Mom upstairs to get the baby. When Mom saw Samara had packed every one of Pity's belongings in a big suitcase she said, "We won't need all of her things for three days."

"You never know what you'll need with this little one," Samara answered. Tears welled in her eyes as she kissed Piedad Maria's head and handed her to my mom.

I struggled with the luggage, hauling it out of the apartment and down the flight of stairs, while Mom followed, holding the baby close. "We'll see you in a few days," she called to Samara from the floor below. All I heard was the click of a closing door.

Mom and I climbed into the backseat of the car with Pity while Dad heaved the suitcase into the trunk, then he drove us home. As we bounced down the busy streets, I gazed at this chubby baby who stared back at me with big eyes, curious and unafraid. We studied each other's faces as I wondered how such a precious little person could cause so much suffering.

When we arrived at home, Aaron helped get Pity and her suitcase inside. "Looks like she's skipping town," he said with a laugh.

"What?" Mom said, staring at him over the suitcase. "Why would you say that?"

"All this for three days? Come on, Ma."

Mom froze, visibly shaken, and Aaron backpedaled. "It's okay. I could be wrong. I've never been wrong before, but there's always a first time."

"Just shut up," I snarled at him.

After everything was set up in her room, Aaron carried Pity around, joking about her constant drooling. He propped her on his lap as he played the piano, and she seemed fascinated by his fingers as they flew over the keys.

Someone held her all day. When Pity started fussing around five in the afternoon, Mom said, "It's time for another bottle, Josie. I've already made one for her; it just needs to be heated." She showed me how to put the bottle in warm water and check the temperature of the formula on my wrist. I sat on the couch in the living room and fed her, watching her make bubbles as she drank. Soon she was happy again, and she wrapped her hand around my finger.

Dad came home from the seminary, and I handed the baby to him. As he changed Pity's diaper, he cooed softly to her. My heart ached as I watched Pity smile at her father. She deserved to have her father in her life. Every daughter did. But at what cost?

When I carried Pity upstairs and placed her in the crate we were using as a makeshift crib, I noticed that although she had Samara's tan skin and my dad's blue eyes, there was something else in her face that reminded me of Dad. I couldn't put my finger on the particular feature, but Pity's face held some whisper of the Wales family ancestry, just as Aaron's and mine did. Again, the reality of having a half sister overwhelmed me. I had to look away.

Pity kept us awake much of the first night with her restless cries even though Mom rocked her well into the morning hours. Was the baby crying because she knew someone was missing in her life? Or did she feel the heavy weight of our family's sadness? The next day, Dad carried Pity's crate into their bedroom and officially moved his things to the guest room.

Mom borrowed a green buggy with large wheels and a canopy from a neighbor whose baby had outgrown it. Since I was too tired to run the next morning, I took Pity on a walk in the stroller through the seminary. I set pillows around her so she could see the world, and I snapped a few photos of her as we meandered along the quiet sidewalks. I thought back to Aunt Beth's daughters and how Tom had given Sarah a piggyback ride while I'd held Allison. It seemed like years had passed since then. It hadn't even been a week.

Pity started to cry when we were crossing the street to go back to the house. I was closing the front gate behind me when her cries suddenly broke off. I turned to see Brandy racing toward us, his teeth bared. Fear strangled my heart. Jumping between the dog and the baby, I caught our big mutt in a bear hug just before he attacked the stroller. I kneeled on the ground with a firm grasp on Brandy's collar and calmed him as he eyed the baby. His wet nose tickled her feet, and Pity kicked and gurgled as she watched the dog. Brandy didn't seem to know what to do with this creature, so he tore off, running and barking wildly around the yard. Aaron, Mom, and Blanca came to the front door, and we watched Brandy's antics until he flopped on the ground panting, completely worn out. Pity started to cry again, ready for another bottle.

When the day came to take Pity back to Samara, my family was groggy after three nights of little sleep. Together, we gathered her things, moving slowly.

"I'm gonna miss that little drooler," Aaron said.

"What'll we do all day?" I asked. She had simple, but constant, needs.

"I'll miss her sweet smile," Mom added, holding the baby over her head. Dad smiled at them, and I realized Pity had done the impossible—she had pulled us back together.

At Samara's apartment, I held Pity and watched as Mom knocked on the door. When there was no answer, she tried the lock then knocked harder. A neighbor opened his door and gave us a questioning look, so Mom asked if he knew where Samara might be.

"*No sé.*" He didn't know. "I saw her leave with suitcases two days ago."

Dad arrived at the top of the stairs, out of breath from lugging Pity's big suitcase. "What's wrong?" he asked when he saw we were still in the hall.

"She's not here," I told him.

He searched his pockets. "I don't have my key, but the owner of the apartment lives on the floor below." The color drained from my mom's face as he turned away, adding, "I'll go see if he'll let us in."

The sound of Dad knocking on his door floated up through the open stairwell. "Can we get into Samara's apartment?" he asked in Spanish. "We kept Piedad Maria for a few days. We're returning the child to her mother, but she's not answering the door."

The jingling keys coming up the stairs was the only response. The landlord unlocked the door, and my jaw dropped. Aaron had been right; Samara was gone. There were no knickknacks on the table. No pictures on the wall. No sheets on the bed. Nothing in the closet. Samara had given us all of Pity's possessions because she was giving us Pity, too.

"What do you think we should do?" Dad asked, sitting on the small rattan sofa in the barren apartment.

"There's only one thing we can do," Mom answered. "We have to take Pity home with us." But she didn't move.

Finally, I said, "We should take the crib and the changing table."

Mom turned to the landlord. "How much belongs to Samara, and what was in the apartment to begin with?"

"All of it belongs to her," he said.

We had been speaking in Spanish, but Dad, staring straight ahead, said in English, "She picked out the furniture, and I paid for it."

Again, my mom's face paled. She walked toward the window. "Were you there when the baby was born?" she whispered, staring out over the busy street below.

"Yes."

I thought back to January. There had been a night when Dad

had not come home until very late. Mom had paced, Aaron had played the piano, and I had watched out the window. When Dad finally came home, he said he'd lost track of time with Ricardo.

"What about May?" I asked.

Mom and Dad turned to me.

"What?" Dad asked.

"Why were you so late during the revival in May? Before school was out?"

"Pity got sick," Dad whispered. "Samara panicked, and we took her to the hospital. They gave her some shots and said she'd be fine. I didn't go to the revival that night. There *were* three converts, though."

Nobody moved until Pity started wriggling in my arms, babbling as she pulled my hair. Finally, Mom took a deep breath and became all business. In Spanish, she told the landlord we would come back for the furniture later. "Do you have another address on file for her?" she asked him.

"I don't think so, but I will check," he said. He returned a few minutes later with no information, held his hands up in surrender, then made a speedy exit.

I wished I could disappear, too.

Mom picked up two of the chairs from the small kitchen table and moved them toward the door. "I'm sure someone from church can use this stuff," she said. "Maybe we should take a load with us now."

Dad stood and grabbed the chairs. "Josie, maybe you should sit downstairs by the car with Pity and keep an eye on the stuff so no one walks off with it."

"Sure," I said, following him downstairs. Dad put the chairs on the sidewalk next to the apartment building, and I sat in one of them, holding Pity while pedestrians walked around me. As I sat by that road in Cali, Colombia, on a chair my missionary father had bought for his lover, with strangers smiling at the beautiful baby who happened to be my half sister, I knew I was having the most bizarre moment of my life.

Mom and Dad came down with the crib, changing table, and the other chairs and crammed them into the Suburban. During the long ride home, Pity fell asleep in my arms. My parents were silent, staring straight ahead. I wondered how long it would take for either of them to get over this, or if they ever would.

While Dad returned to the apartment with Aaron for the rest of the furniture, Mom and I pulled all of Pity's belongings out of the suitcase and arranged them in the changing-table compartments. When Mom checked the side pockets of the suitcase one last time, she found a picture of Samara, a dainty gold necklace with a locket, and the child's birth certificate. Dad's name wasn't on the document, but it was validation Samara wasn't coming back.

"Let's put these in a safe place," Mom told me. She pulled an envelope from her stationery set on her dresser, put the three items in it, wrote Pity's name on the outside, and tucked it into the bottom drawer of the changing table.

Dad and Aaron came home with the rest of the furniture, and Blanca and I helped them unload and store the pieces in the garage. Eager to get rid of the furniture, Dad called every member of our church until he found someone who would pick it up. Soon, a couple drove over in a rickety truck and hauled the furniture away, just as Pity started crying for her five o'clock bottle.

Chapter Fifteen

AFTER PITY MOVED IN, MY family settled into a routine of caring for the baby, attending church, and avoiding each other. Pity's presence changed our family, separating us yet making us more polite, as if we were strangers. My dad threw himself into studying the Bible, reading it in Hebrew, learning the language as he went along. Taking care of Pity fell to my mom, who continued to lead the church choir and teach Sunday school. She was usually in bed by eight o'clock.

On good days, I received letters from Tom, Aunt Rosie, or Anna. I missed the comfort of my rosary beads until I remembered my mom had a string of pearls she never wore. While she was at choir practice one afternoon, I searched her jewelry box and took the long strand. Praying the rosary wasn't the same without the medals and the crucifix, but the effort helped me sleep better at night.

One afternoon, Mom asked me to watch Pity so she could run errands in town, and I carried the baby to the kitchen to watch Blanca make *sancocho*. "I'm glad there's no necks in your soup," I told Blanca. The Colombian soup was sometimes made with every part of a chicken, and at a church dinner one night, I had ended up with a chicken neck in my bowl.

"You are missing the best part," she said.

"The best part is the *yuca*," I answered, making sure plenty of the potato-like vegetables were in the pot.

"Do you like cow's tongue?" Blanca asked, smiling. "Or chocolate-covered ants?"

"No," I said of Colombia's stranger typical foods. "And please don't serve them."

She laughed then covered the *sancocho* and grabbed her apron. "We should check for oranges in the backyard."

I put Pity in her stroller and rolled her outside with us, and I was about to snap an orange from the tree when Blanca said, "Juan Fernando found Samara."

"Really? How did he find her? Where is she?"

"I don't know how he found her," she said. "Police officers have connections." She shook a low branch, and an orange thudded to the ground. "He said she is living with relatives and has a job in a clinic."

"Sounds like she's moved on. I bet she's with the aunt she lived with before." I held an orange in front of Pity, and she stared at it, waving her arms as she sucked vigorously on her pacifier. "I guess we don't have to worry about Samara coming back to take Pity away from us. I wonder if I should tell my parents."

"No, *chica*." Blanca collected more fallen oranges and stowed them in her apron pockets. "Your parents might be angry that Juan Fernando knows about Samara and Piedad Maria."

I was about to agree with her when Aaron called for Blanca from the house.

"Out here," she answered, walking toward his voice.

Aaron stood at the back door, wearing a nice shirt and slacks. "I'm going out," he told Blanca. "If my parents ask about me, tell them I'll be home later."

He didn't seem to notice me, but when Blanca returned, I asked, "Do you know where he's going?"

"No, he has not told me. He usually leaves after dinner." Blanca looked at her watch. "His nice clothes smell like cigarette smoke and liquor when he gets home."

"And you don't know where he goes?" I asked.

"No. And do not get any ideas," she said, wagging a finger at me.

"What do you mean, Blanca?" I asked, playing the fool. We both knew I wanted to find out what Aaron was up to. I twisted a few oranges from the tree and put them around Pity in the stroller. Blanca and I laughed when the baby managed to kick some of the bright fruits out of her buggy.

In bed that night, I was reading Chaim Potok's *The Chosen* and keeping an eye out for Aaron when I heard someone creeping around downstairs. I decided to investigate and found Dad in the kitchen.

"What are you doing up so late?" I asked him.

"Hey Josie," he said, raising his bowl in greeting. "Caught me having a snack. Here, come eat some ice cream with me."

I took a spoon and bowl from the cupboard and scooped chocolate ice cream from the container. As we leaned against the counters eating, he talked about school. Summer would be over in a few weeks, and Dad wondered what courses I would be taking and if I would join the school choir.

I shrugged, not really wanting to think about the end of summer too soon.

He set his bowl and spoon in the sink and turned to me. "Josie, I just wanted to say about Pity, I'm sorry."

I put my hand up. "Dad, you're breaking rule number one again."

"Just let me apologize. Please." His eyes beseeched me.

"Does it really make you feel any better?" I gritted my teeth, trying to keep my voice down. "At night, when you're trying to sleep, does knowing that you've said 'I'm sorry' five million times change anything?"

"Yes, it does. Because it's all I can do."

I stared at him, speechless. Finally, I found the words. "How about if you just don't do that horrible thing you did? How about if you stop being so oblivious to how your actions affect everyone around you?"

I set my dishes on his in the sink and turned to go back to bed. "Good night, Dad."

He didn't answer.

When Aaron slipped into the house deep in the night, anger rose inside me. He wasn't going to get away with sneaking out—I would make sure of that.

The following Thursday night, I heard Aaron ask Blanca if his white shirt was ironed. He was getting ready to go out again, so I set my plan in motion.

I called a cab company and asked them to send a taxi to the seminary a few minutes before seven. After putting on blue jeans, a dark jacket, and tennis shoes, I left a note in my room, saying I had gone to visit a classmate down the street. Chances were good no one would even miss me. They certainly hadn't noticed Aaron's disappearances. I grabbed money from my sock drawer, shoved it in my purse, and crept out of the house while my parents were giving Pity a bath.

When my taxi arrived, I jumped in the backseat. "Can you park a few houses down the road from ours?" I asked the driver in Spanish. "I need to wait for someone."

Soon, Aaron slipped through the gates and into another taxi that had stopped at our house. My heart pounded as I hunched down and watched Aaron ride past.

"We need to follow that cab," I told the driver. "I'm not sure where it's going."

"*Bueno.* Is that your brother you follow?"

"Yes," I said. "He's been going out at night, and we want to know what he's doing."

He laughed. "Why do you not simply ask him?"

"I doubt if he'd tell the truth."

"You two do not get along?"

"We used to, sort of, but then he got me in trouble with our parents, so I'm returning the favor."

"Ahh," he said, smiling at me in his rearview mirror. "Brothers and sisters should help each other, not get each other into trouble."

"Yeah, well, you should tell him that. He's older. He's supposed to be more mature."

The driver shook his head. He followed the taxi from a safe distance, and before long, we were downtown, where it was harder to keep up. My driver had just run a red light to stay with Aaron's cab when it pulled into a parking place. Aaron hopped out and backtracked to a part of town known for its popular nightclubs, passing my taxi in the process.

I ducked out of sight and had my driver stop at the corner.

"He certainly is your brother," he said. "Are you twins?"

"No. I don't think we look anything alike."

"*Bueno*, you are safe now. He will not see you."

"Thanks," I said, paying him and sliding out of his cab. "Wish me luck."

He took my money and passed me a card. "Call this number when you want to go home. Ask for me; I'm Moises. I will come for you."

I took a better look at my driver. He was probably older than my father, with kind eyes and gray hair. "Thank you, Señor Moises," I said then realized there was no turning back as I watched him pull away.

Even though young people crowded the streets, it was easy to keep track of my tall, blond brother. I followed Aaron to a glitzy discotheque with darkened windows and a hot-pink neon sign over the black door. The club was protected by a muscular man who smiled at Aaron as he opened the door. Loud American music poured out when Aaron stepped in. I hung back in the shadows and watched as women in heels, tight dresses, and heavy makeup entered the nightclub. Men dressed in nice shirts and slacks, with gold chains around their necks, stood at the entrance. All of them smelled like cologne mixed with cigarette smoke. Every time the door opened, cold air blasted onto the street.

My parents definitely would not approve of my brother going to a nightclub, and he would get in trouble just like I had. The victory seemed hollow, though, and I stood by the entrance, thinking about what I wanted to do.

Just then, Aaron came out of the club with a beer in one hand and a slim, beautiful girl by his side. She was wearing a silvery dress and high heels; her dark-brown hair curled down her back. I squeezed into the shadow of a building, watching the two as they passed within three feet of me.

"*Oye*, Trina," the doorman called after them. "What shall I tell Lilo?"

"We are just going for a snack," the girl snapped as she grabbed Aaron's hand.

"*Si*, Pedro, we'll be right back." Aaron raised his beer to the man as he smiled down at the girl.

They stopped at an outdoor café and shared an *arepa* and the rest of Aaron's beer, laughing together. She seemed to be nervous; she looked behind her every few seconds. Suddenly, she stood and grabbed Aaron's arm. They hurried my way, and I had to move to a nearby alley to keep from getting caught. Unfortunately, Aaron and the girl turned into my alley to hide, too. They were so close that I could smell the fried bread and beer on their breaths, but they didn't see me in the darkness. I stood perfectly still; only my heart beating out of my chest would have given me away.

"That was him," the girl said in an excited voice.

"Who? Your boyfriend?" Aaron asked.

"*Si, pendejo*. Elías López."

"He doesn't look that scary." Aaron put his arms around her, but she pushed him away.

"He'll still kill us if he catches us."

They both peeked around the corner to the street. She pulled him back into the alley, and they froze as a hefty man with a long scar on his cheek walked past us, away from the club. "That was close!" she said with a giggle, looking up at Aaron.

He leaned down and kissed her. I closed my eyes and prayed I wouldn't gag.

"I've heard he's a jealous guy," Aaron said, leaning away from her.

"And it's true." Trina pulled him back in.

"I bet I can take him."

"No, you can't," she answered with finality, but Aaron didn't seem worried at all, just carelessly arrogant as he and the girl stepped into the street and walked back to the nightclub.

I took a deep breath. Aaron was dating a girl whose boyfriend was the jealous type. And the girl was urging him on. I knew Aaron liked to live dangerously, but his new gamble was ridiculous.

I stayed a few paces behind them, but before they arrived at the black door, Aaron turned around, and I ducked into the shadows again. I wanted to be the one to catch him, not have him catch me. I held my breath, praying he wasn't coming my way. Years of furtiveness in Capture the Flag were paying off.

Suddenly, a rough arm reached around my neck and jerked me deeper into the darkness. "Aaron, help!" I screamed before a foul hand covered my mouth.

As I wrestled to free myself, Aaron called, "Josie? Is that you? Where are you?" His voice was coming toward me.

I kicked the person who held me captive. "Over here! Help me!"

The man tightened his grip on me so that I could barely breathe. He yanked on my purse strap, and I tried to give my bag to him, but it was caught around my neck. The lights and sounds from the bars and passing cars seemed out of reach, and I would've fainted except for the adrenaline pumping through me, driving me to kick and scream at the person who kept pulling me farther into the darkness.

"Josie! Where are you?" Aaron called again, panic in his voice. The mugger was getting the upper hand, and his filthy arms muffled my screams as they squeezed. I tried to bite his arm, but the taste of grime and sweat made me gag.

"Pedro, help my sister," Aaron yelled.

Within moments, the guard found me in the shadows and yanked me out of the attacker's arms. Pedro pulled a pistol from his back pocket. Shouting, he opened fire, but the thug disappeared into the night. I fell into Aaron's arms and shook, too shocked to cry.

"Oh my God, Josie," Aaron said, not letting me go. "You are such a fool."

"Are you okay?" Pedro asked, walking toward us as he put his gun away and straightened his collar. He didn't wait for an answer. "This is your sister?" he asked Aaron.

"*Sí*, this is Josie," Aaron said, helping me regain my balance.

"Thank you, Pedro," I told him, my face buried in Aaron's arm. "You saved my life."

A crowd had formed, but the guard waved them away. I looked up to see the girl in the silver dress watching from the entrance of the nightclub, a scowl on her face.

"You should be more careful." Pedro spoke sternly but patted my back as he headed to his post.

Any sympathy from Aaron evaporated as he pushed me away from him. "Okay, Jos, what's this about? What are you doing here?"

"I was following you. Like you did to me."

"You followed me here?" he asked, glaring down at me. "Did Mom and Dad put you up to this?"

"No." I hung my head. "They didn't notice you were gone."

"Well, fine, you see I'm at this nightclub. Now that you didn't get kidnapped or killed, why don't you just head home?"

"But, Aaron—"

"You owe me one for getting you out of there alive," he said. "Just go on home and forget this ever happened."

He turned and walked back to Trina. She gave me a smug smile as they headed into the nightclub. I stood alone in the middle of the sidewalk, hugging my purse to me, still too dazed to move. An endless flood of people passed by. Some of them bumped into me and stared as they wondered aloud what was wrong with me. Finally, I gathered my wits and used the club's telephone to call Moises. He arrived moments later.

"I was expecting your call," Moises said when I climbed into his taxi. "Did you find out what you were wanting to know?"

"I found out way more than I wanted to know," I answered, sinking into the back of his cab. I curled into the seat and sat motionless with my eyes shut tight, barely breathing as the lights of the city flashed over me.

We were stopped in front of my house, and as I was counting pesos to give to Moises, I asked, "Do you know anyone called Elías López?"

"I think I have read about him," he answered. "He gets into trouble with the law. Do they call him Lilo?" Moises asked.

"Yes," I whispered.

"Is everything okay?" Moises studied me through the rearview mirror.

"It looks like my brother is playing with fire," I told him. "Thank you for coming to get me."

"Call me anytime, *niña*," he answered then waited to make sure I made it safely through our gate before he drove away.

I called quietly to Brandy so he would know it was me, then I ran to the backyard and knocked on Blanca's window.

"Where have you been? Why is your face so dirty?" Blanca asked as she opened the back door that led into the kitchen.

I raised my hand to my cheek. "I followed Aaron. Can we go to your room? I need to tell you what happened."

"Of course, *mija*."

Blanca sat on her bed as I took off my jacket and scrubbed my hands and face in the little bathroom in her room. Using soap and a tea towel I had never seen before made me feel like a guest in my own home. I sat in my favorite chair then stood again. Anxious energy coursed through me, and it was all I could do to stay in control as I paced back and forth, my hands making tight fists.

"I followed Aaron. He went to a nightclub downtown."

"Which one?"

"I think it was called El Jazmin. Why?"

"Juan Fernando told me about those places. Many of them have reputations for being dangerous. What happened?"

"Aaron came out with a girl. He called her Trina. I followed them and heard her say she had a boyfriend, but then they kissed."

"It sounds like he is just like your father."

I stopped and took a deep breath. Blanca couldn't have known how much her comment hurt. Not long ago, I'd thought my dad was a good man—someone who might have been absentminded and out of touch but who always meant well. I would have to get used to seeing him in a different light.

"I'm sorry, *chica*," she said, looking up at me. "*Sigue.*"

"Trina was saying her boyfriend was a very jealous person who would kill them both if he found out about Aaron. She said his name was Elías López." I paused, took a deep breath, then continued. "I was hiding in the darkness when somebody grabbed me."

Blanca's eyes widened. "*¡Dios mío!* Are you okay?"

"Yeah, yeah. The guard at the club ran him off." I started to laugh, because I remembered Aaron hadn't exactly been brave; he had called for Pedro to help me instead of saving me himself. My laughter turned to tears when I realized there was no telling what that man would have done to me if he had succeeded in dragging me away.

"It is best if you convince yourself he was only after your money," Blanca told me, standing to put her arms around me as I sobbed.

Nodding through my tears, I broke away from her hug and began pacing again. She sat on her bed, still looking worried. "Sit down and try to breathe."

"I can't. I feel like a tiger in a cage."

"Then you should keep talking to me."

"Aaron said I owed him since he saved my life, and I'd better not tell anyone where he was." I covered my face with my hands. "He doesn't know I saw him with Trina. Blanca, I think Aaron's dating a dangerous guy's girlfriend. I'm scared."

"Well, he is a fool, that is for sure. Let me think about it. I will ask Juan Fernando about that man. What was his name? Elías López?"

I nodded.

"Go to bed, *mija*." She stood again and gave me another hug. "You are safe now. Pray the rosary, and try to get some sleep."

"I don't have a rosary," I whispered. "I just have my mom's pearls."

"Take mine," she said, turning to reach for her beads.

I recoiled. "No way! And get you in trouble again?" As much as

I wanted a real rosary with the figure of Jesus on the cross, I didn't dare risk getting caught with it. "I'll just use the pearls. Thanks, Blanca."

After tiptoeing up the stairs, I took a hot shower to wash away the memory of the attack, even though I risked waking the others. But if Mom and Dad heard my longest shower ever, they didn't come to ask any questions.

In bed, I tried to imagine Tom's arms around me, but when I closed my eyes, I panicked at the memory of the city lights swirling far from me. I made myself focus on the pearls, praying fervently to Mother Mary. After I finished reciting the rosary, nothing was left to stop me from reliving the terror of the man's filthy hand on my mouth. Each time I remembered his foul smell, I ran to the bathroom to wash my face again. Finally, I fell into an exhausted sleep.

The faint slam of a car door and the quiet creak of the gate woke me around two in the morning. Aaron was home safe. Later, I awoke again to the sound of a terrifying scream. At first muffled and distant, it grew louder until I was covering my ears from the terrible noise. And only when my mother shook my shoulder and called my name, begging me to stop screaming, did I realize it was me. She looked at me with such sadness that tears stung my eyes. Then Mom left my side to console Pity, who was wailing, too.

Chapter Sixteen

MOM WOKE ME THE NEXT morning at nine. She placed Pity, dressed in a cute seersucker romper, on the bed next to me. "I have letters to write, so I need you to watch the baby," she said.

Pity looked over at me and kicked her legs.

"Okay." My throat ached from screaming in the night, and my words came out as a whisper.

"She's already had her morning bottle," Mom added, leaving the room.

I dressed in shorts and a T-shirt then carried Pity downstairs. I was pouring a glass of orange juice when the doorbell rang. I swallowed the juice, its stinging sweetness restoring my throat, and took the baby with me to look out the side window. A small boy was standing under the towering bougainvillea.

"Can I have some bread, please?" the boy asked when I opened the door.

I looked around for Brandy, who usually kept beggars off our property. "Did you see our dog?" I asked in Spanish.

"*Por favor,* can I have some bread? My mother is very sick, and she can't work. She and my sisters need food. Can you help us?"

Being approached by the impoverished of Colombia was nothing new. My parents, along with other missionaries, always kept small change and Baptist tracts in their pockets to give to beggars. But that was in the city. Having a poor child knock on our door just didn't happen. I had no excuses for this boy as I stood in the doorway of our big house filled with more than enough of anything he might want. He watched me with a serious look on his dirty face.

"*Un momento.*" I decided to give him what he asked for. I put Pity in her playpen in the living room and found a bag of sliced bread on the kitchen counter. I went back to the boy and handed it to him. "Here you go," I said, about to close the door.

"Wait," he said. "Do you think you could give us something to drink, too?"

"Okay, I'll be right back." I shut the door and went back to the kitchen for two bottles of Coke from the refrigerator. "Do you like Coca-Colas?" I asked when I returned.

"I have never had one." His eyes were round as he accepted the cold drinks. I was about to close the door again when he said, "*Por favor*, do you have any clothes to spare? My sisters, they have grown out of their clothes."

I looked at him more closely. He couldn't have been over ten years old, and his brownish-gray pants were ragged and dirty. His ripped shirt barely covered him, and his shoes were falling apart. We had a bin of unwanted clothing in the garage, so I left him again and gathered the old T-shirts, shoes, dresses, and socks in a plastic bag. "Here are some things," I said, handing the bag to him at the door. "I hope you can use them."

I was turning away from him when he whispered, "Wait. My mother, I want to give my mother a gift for her birthday. It's coming up next week. Do you have anything for her?"

At first, this boy had met my gaze with his coal-black eyes, but he stopped looking at me then quietly asked for more as if he were reading a winning lottery ticket one lucky number at a time.

"I'll see what we have." I closed the door again and took the stairs two at a time to the large closet in the bathroom. I stuffed a flowered cosmetic case with lotion, a container of cotton balls, a new lipstick, some nail polish, and my bottle of Sweet Honesty perfume Aunt Rosie had brought from the States.

Back downstairs, I offered him the case. "Here are a few things your mother might like," I said, wondering if he even had a mother or sisters. This boy was probably on his own, like most *gamines* were. But everything I gave him could be sold or traded for food.

"Thank you," he said, taking the pretty bag in his dirty hands. I knew he was going to ask for something else, but suddenly, I couldn't help him anymore. There would be no end to his needs, and there were hundreds—no, thousands—just like him, all around me.

I heard Pity whimper in her playpen, and I put up my hand. "*Pare.* You should run," I told him. "I don't know how you got past our dog, but you'd better go before he sees you. *¡Corre!*"

I closed the door and went into the living room, where I watched the boy from the window as he ambled toward the street. He was fumbling with the gate when Brandy charged at the poor boy, with fury in his bark.

The beggar was obviously familiar with this situation; he calmly opened the gate, slipped out, and closed it behind him just before Brandy came to a full stop on our side of the bars. The boy, carrying three bags and two Cokes, looked for a long second at the barking dog before moving on.

Pity had begun to cry. I lifted her and held her close, grateful she would never have to know the life of an abandoned Colombian child. She could have any life she chose. Well, almost any. Like me, she wouldn't get to be Catholic.

With Pity on my hip, I went to the kitchen and poured another glass of orange juice before strapping her into the stroller for a walk around the seminary.

That evening, Dad and Mom announced we would be going to the Caribbean island of San Andrés with Anna's family, and the next few days were an excited flurry of preparations and packing.

The morning of our departure, I was carrying my bags downstairs when Blanca called me into the kitchen. "I must talk to you," she told me, looking around to make sure no one could hear.

"Is something wrong?" I asked, leaving my bag in the hallway and following her to her room.

"Elías López." She closed the door behind me. "He is bad news. Juan Fernando told me they think he is in the mafia and that he is the reason the woman in the white car was killed."

I dropped into my chair. "The one who was shot on our street? Why did he kill her?"

She shrugged and said, "Whatever the reason, you can see he is a dangerous man. And he owns that nightclub El Jazmin. Yo-si, your brother must be warned."

"He isn't going to listen to me," I said.

"It is a very good thing you are going away for a few days. Talk to him while you are on this trip."

"I'll try, but Blanca, he does what he wants to do."

"I have noticed that." She sighed and opened the door. "I must go help your mother with the baby."

As Aaron drove us to the airport, I thought of ways to mention Elías López to him, but on the two-hour flight to Colombia's island, my excitement about seeing Anna outshined his problem. She and I could discuss my family, our twin boyfriends, and her horses. Or we could forget about all of it and have a great time. When I stepped off the plane, the salty breeze immediately put a smile on my face.

The lively town of San Andrés was surrounded by palm trees on white sandy beaches. The islanders were friendly, and their reggae music floated in the air. After we checked in at the hotel, Aaron went on an afternoon snorkeling tour with Isaac while my parents napped with the baby. Anna and I headed for the beach.

"So how is your pregnant mare?" I asked as we lounged on towels across the street from our hotel.

Anna chuckled. "Turns out she isn't pregnant, just fat! How's your summer so far?"

"Full of Pity," I joked. It was hard to take anything too seriously as we basked in the sun, the afternoon breeze keeping us cool. "What do you think of my new baby sister?"

"That is some crazy mess," she said. "She's as cute as a cream puff, though."

I smiled. "You realize you can't tell a soul. All the missionaries think a mother from church asked us to keep the baby then skipped town. I can't believe they don't see how she has Dad's eyes."

"How did your mom get talked into seeing the baby?" Anna asked.

"Believe it or not, it was her idea to meet Pity. And she was the one who wanted to keep the baby for a few days so Samara, the mother, could go on a job interview. When we tried to take Pity back to her apartment, Samara was gone."

"Wow. She really did skip town. So how is it going?"

"Fine, I guess. My mom takes care of Pity most of the time. She gets Dad to change diapers a lot, and Aaron and I play with her, but otherwise, it's her baby."

"That's so weird, your mother taking care of this child like it was her own," Anna said, rubbing suntan oil on her arms. "How is your dad doing?"

The smell of her coconut lotion filled the air as a million thoughts flooded my head. I didn't know what to say. Should I say Dad was trying to make it right? That he was still a complete jerk? The answer was somewhere in the middle...

"I'm sorry," Anna finally said. "I don't know how you're handling all this."

"I'm just glad I have you to talk to."

"I couldn't imagine my father screwing up like that," she said, returning the lotion to her bag and resting on her towel again.

"I hate to burden you with another family secret, but this one is really scary," I said after a while.

"Talk to me."

"I followed Aaron one night and saw him go to a bar."

"Do you think he was getting drunk?" Anna asked.

"Oh, he drinks," I said, recalling the beer he and Trina had shared. "That would be bad enough, but he's going out with a Colombian who already has a boyfriend, and the boyfriend's dangerous." I took a deep breath. "He may be in the mafia."

"What?" Anna sat up and pulled off her sunglasses to stare at me. "Are you sure?"

I sighed. "Yeah, I'm pretty sure. I heard the girl say her boyfriend was Elías López, and I found out there's a *mafioso* in Cali by the same name who owns the nightclub they went to."

"Good grief, Josie! Tell your parents!"

"I can't. Aaron swore me to secrecy." I told Anna how I was attacked, and since Aaron helped run the guy off, I couldn't get him in trouble. "So tell me, what do I do?"

"That night must have been horrible," Anna said, reaching for my arm.

"It was horrible." I shivered as I remembered the foul hand on my mouth.

"He could've dragged you off and raped you, then killed you, and buried your—"

"Anna!" I covered my ears. "You could really use a censor on that mouth of yours."

"You have to tell your parents." She squeezed my arm then pulled away, shaking her head. "I'm glad I didn't get involved with your brother."

"Yeah." I gave a dry laugh. "Tell me, what would you do if you were in my shoes?"

"If Isaac pulled a stunt like that, I'd knock some sense into him. You need to talk to Aaron. He's gone too far. Sorry to have to tell you this, but he could get hurt like you almost did—or even killed."

I closed my eyes and leaned back on my towel. I should have known Anna wouldn't exactly comfort me. She was right, though. I would have to confront Aaron and tell Mom and Dad, but I sure didn't want to.

I looked over to her. "Hopefully, he'll stay out of trouble while we're here. Help me keep an eye on him. Meanwhile, let's talk about happy things. How's Jack?"

"He's good. I like having a boyfriend who's far away so I can flirt with other guys but still have him in my back pocket. Is that bad?"

I laughed. "Not if you know Jack's probably doing the same thing. I get the feeling you don't think it's going to last with your twin."

"It could, but he's got a brand-new life in the States, and I don't want to hold him back. Of course if it's meant to be, it'll happen." She shrugged. "I'm not worried."

"I wish I was like you." I sighed. "I miss Tom a lot. It'd be nice to have his shoulder to cry on right now. You wouldn't believe all the letters I've written him."

"Does he know about Pity? Or Aaron?"

"No. My parents don't want anyone else to know. Anyway, I'm not even sure it'll work out between Tom and me. He's so different from me."

"Are you still thinking about that hat?" Anna asked.

I laughed, feeling sheepish. Anna knew me so well.

We were reminiscing about Mission Meeting when my parents and Pity joined us at the beach. Anna and I carried the baby down to the water's edge and splashed her legs with the salt water, careful to keep her new yellow jumper and matching hat dry. She was fascinated with the waves rolling onto the shore, never blinking as she soaked in the new experience.

Two women walking along the beach stopped to admire her. *¿Es ella su bebé?*" one of them asked.

"No, my parents..." There was no way to explain the situation, so I pointed to my mom and dad. They were sitting on towels next to each other, and Dad was rubbing suntan lotion on Mom's shoulders. My dad must have said something funny, because they were laughing. The two women smiled and moved on, and for the first time since Pity came into our lives, it seemed things between my parents might be okay after all.

That night, our families ate at an open-air restaurant on the beach where the fish had been caught minutes before they were grilled for us. Aaron and Isaac described their snorkeling trip and how Isaac thought he saw a barracuda swimming beneath them. Aaron had us laughing, telling how everyone almost walked on water to make it to the boat. Someone had even tossed Aaron the life ring to haul him in.

"I think it was a barracuda..." Isaac said, and the strained look on his face made us laugh even harder.

When our amusement finally died down, Mom handed Pity to Aaron, and he held the baby above his head. Pity giggled as he made up a song about "a sweetie named Petie," bouncing her on his knee.

"Petie," Mom said, looking at the baby. "I like it. How about we give our little Pity a new name?"

"What does Mommy mean?" Aaron asked Pity in a silly voice.

"I mean, let's not call her Pity anymore," she said, looking at my dad. "Let's call her Petie, our little sweetie."

"That's a great idea, Astrid." The relief in his voice was as refreshing as Petie's happy laugh.

Stuffed from our meal, we walked onto the beach. Uncle Ben

and Aunt Lucy strolled hand in hand, their heads turned toward the moonlit view of Johnny Key, the small island about a mile off the coast. Anna and Isaac splashed Aaron as they ran along the water's edge, and Dad carried Petie as Mom walked alongside them. I followed, breathing in the warm evening air, laughing as Aaron crawled up a palm tree and threatened to throw coconuts at Anna and Isaac. Yes, the vacation was working. Maybe, somehow, we would find our way back to normal.

My contentment continued the next morning when Dad and I snorkeled halfway to Johnny Key and floated back on the tide to the beach, staying together by holding the ends of his T-shirt between us. Through my diving mask I saw an occasional fish flash below me, but mostly, my view was seashells along the ocean's floor, swept along with us by the tide. I was in a different world, and the only sound I heard was the steady whoosh of my breath through the mask's mouthpiece.

Though danger lurked in the water around me, Dad's presence was my protection, and the calm feeling in the face of danger wasn't new. Many times during scary car rides through the Colombian Andes, in crowded city streets surrounded by strangers, and in desolate *barrios* on the outskirts of town, I'd known I would be perfectly safe if Dad was around.

Eventually, we washed ashore and stretched out on the sand. A feeling of weightlessness continued to carry me, and I stared up at the palm trees swaying in the breeze. The curves of the tree trunks and the blue sky added to the euphoria. After a few minutes, my stomach growled. I sat up and looked at my dad.

"You okay?" I asked.

"Never better." He was lying on the gritty sand, shading his eyes with his arm, and he was smiling.

"Really?"

"Really," he answered.

I pushed sand into a heap beside me. "Is it because Cali is so far away?"

He sat up. "Look around you, Josie." He motioned to the waves lapping at the shore and the fluffy white clouds in the blue sky. "We're in paradise."

I smiled and kept making my sand hill, remembering what I loved so much about my dad: he knew how to live in the moment. He rarely worried about what was ahead and easily forgot the past, and his easy-going attitude rubbed off on others around him. Dad let the present be what it would be, and for the moment, he was right. We were in paradise. So what if his carefree way of thinking got him into trouble back in Cali?

I soaked in the delicious breeze, the sand, and the view for a few more minutes.

"I'm starving," he said suddenly, jumping to his feet. "Let's go back and see what's for breakfast."

"Sounds great, Pop." I reached for the shirt and our masks, and he offered his hand to help me up. Then we raced back to the hotel, laughing as we ran.

Chapter Seventeen

AFTER BREAKFAST IN THE HOTEL'S elegant restaurant overlooking the ocean, everyone but Mom, Aunt Lucy, and Petie headed to the dock. A man from one of the local Baptist churches had offered to take us on a boat ride. After we struggled into orange life vests, Captain Edward helped us onto his wooden boat, and soon, we were skipping over the waves.

Since there was no competing with the noisy motor, we didn't speak as our boat crossed the emerald water. Captain Edward took us around San Andrés and showed us the difference between the south end of the island and the north, where our hotel was. The south end was a jungle of foliage, towering trees, and coconut palms. Red-roofed homes painted in bright blues, yellows, and pinks stood on stilts over the water, their windows propped open to catch the breeze. Native islanders waved to us from their porches, making our ten-story hotel with its fancy restaurant seem a world away.

The captain took us a few miles from the coastline and shut off the engine, letting us drift in the Caribbean, surrounded by sea, sky, and stillness. One by one, all of us except Captain Ed took off our vests and jumped overboard. Aaron swam straight down from our boat, and I followed him. Muffled silence pressed in around me with each downward stroke. As I swam deeper into the sea, the water grew colder.

When I looked up and saw how far from the surface we were, I panicked. If I didn't turn back immediately, I wouldn't have enough air to make it back. Aaron could go without breathing a lot longer than I could. My lungs tightened, and my heart raced as I kicked furiously toward the dim circle of light above me, wishing it could pull me upward. Finally, I burst out of the water, gasping for air.

"Isn't this great, Josie?" Anna paddled up to me. She hadn't noticed I was gone.

"Yeah," I wheezed, floating on the water as my heart slowly stopped pounding. I was never going to be able to keep up with Aaron. There was just no way.

Aaron lunged out of the water with a splash, swinging his hair. We all swam a little longer, but the deep water was cold, so Anna and I crawled, shivering, into the boat. Captain Ed called for the others then steered us back to San Andrés.

On land again, Anna and I rented scooters and rode around the island before pulling into a local tourist attraction. We stood on large black rocks that bordered the sea and looked out over the water, not sure what we would find. All of a sudden, a column of water shot out of a gap in the rocks next to us, soaking us as we screamed and dashed back to shore.

A man at a *tienda* nearby called out, "How d'ya li'e da blowhole, ladies?"

The musical native Islander Creole English made "thanks for everything" sound like "tanks fi eva'ting" and turned "all right" into "ol' rye." And everything was always *ol' rye*, even if we were soaking wet. Another geyser erupted where we had been standing, and from a dry distance, the sight was impressive.

The man loaned us towels and said he never tired of luring tourists into his trap. After watching the waves push water through the rocks and up into natural fountains a few more times, we thanked the man and continued our trek around the island. At the top of a large hill in the heart of the island, we puttered past a stately white Baptist church with a red roof and a steeple reaching high above the hill. Our families would be going to a service there the next day.

We took a wrong turn on our way back to town and found ourselves in the middle of a market, dodging pedestrians, cars, and other scooters. At a stoplight, I happened to see my parents in a souvenir shop on the corner. They were smiling as Dad raised a shell necklace for Mom to see. Aaron, holding Petie and looking on, seemed to be saying something. The light turned green, and Anna beeped her horn behind me, so I rode on. But the image of the four of them, so happy and connected, stayed in my mind.

The next morning, our families dressed up and took taxis to the Baptist church with the red roof, joining the beautiful island women in bright Sunday dresses and men wearing lightweight suits. Mom and Dad seemed to fit right in. Petie did, too, wearing the white-collared pink dress Samara had loved so much.

After we sang all five verses of "I Surrender All," the minister preached a sermon about God's love. His singsong voice was relaxing, and the murmurs of the congregation were soothing. The fans in the spacious sanctuary caught the sea breeze and cooled us, and I thought of how my life would be so much easier if I just accepted my parents' beliefs as my own. Sometimes, like that moment, I wanted to believe like they did. It wouldn't be hard. Surely there were others who went along with a loved one's beliefs just to keep the peace.

But the new necklace glinting around Mom's neck caught my eye, and I remembered the flash of my rosary as it burned in the fire. No, there was no going back. I would have to find a way to stay true to myself.

When the service finally ended, Isaac came over to Anna and me. "That kid will take us up to the bell tower for twenty pesos." He pointed to a small islander, who waved.

"Sounds fun," Anna said to me. "Let's do it."

The boy led us to a door and up tightly spiraled stairs then climbed a long ladder. He slid a trapdoor open and squeezed through before leaning down and motioning for us to follow.

"In our dresses?" I asked, looking at Anna.

"Isaac, you go first. Go on." Anna gave her brother a push.

Isaac climbed up and disappeared through the trapdoor. "Wow. You gotta see this!"

Anna and I followed, careful to keep the heels of our shoes from getting caught in the rungs. I rose through the trapdoor directly under a large bell suspended in the steeple, and a gust of wind tossed my hair as I took in the breathtaking view from the tower. I could see our hotel, the blowhole, the colorful houses on the water, and Johnny Key. I'd heard the water surrounding the island had seven shades of green, and as we perched on a ledge on top of the world, I could see them all. The hues along the seashore were pale, but as the Caribbean deepened, the greens took on a more emerald color, finally mixing with black. Then a lighter strip of fluorescent aqua merged the sea with the sky. More stunning, though, were the huge clouds piled one on top of another around us. There was another world in that vast sky, and I wished I had my camera to capture the beauty.

The boy who'd brought us to the lookout seemed to enjoy the view as much as we did, but after a few minutes, he broke the spell with, "Ol' rye."

"We'd better go down," Anna added. "Our parents might be looking for us."

Once outside, Anna took twenty pesos from her pocket and gave it to the boy. He ran to his friends, arms outstretched for them to see the money.

Anna, Isaac, and I joined our families at the church entrance. Together, we walked the short distance to the home of our boat captain. He had invited us to lunch, and we enjoyed the easygoing pace of island life as we sat around tables on the patio of his home and ate coconut bread and a thick stew called rundown.

After attending another service that evening in a smaller Baptist church near our hotel, Anna and I walked along the beach one last time. "I'd give almost anything to stay here," I said as we slipped out of our shoes to walk in the soft sand. "Do I have to go home?"

Anna linked arms with me, and we watched silently as the waves crashed onto the shore. Finally, Anna said, "We're going to start our new homeschool courses next week. I'm not excited about geometry, but the art class should be fun. When does your school start?"

"In a few weeks. Hard to believe."

"Are you looking forward to seeing Alejandro?"

"Alejandro hasn't crossed my mind in weeks," I said, shaking my head. "I guess Petie and Aaron have me too busy to give him a second thought. It's hard to believe all I wanted at the beginning of this crazy summer was to go out with him."

Anna put her arm around me as we walked. "Look on the bright side. It'll be fun to watch Petie grow. Soon she'll be talking, then walking."

"Yeah." I couldn't help but smile.

"Isaac was a cute baby. Don't tell him I said that, though."

I heard my name and looked toward our hotel. Aaron waved. "Josie! Mom needs you to help pack up."

"At least Aaron didn't do anything foolish on this trip," Anna said.

"That we know of."

Mom and I packed Petie's belongings, which included a few new sundresses she and Dad had bought, and set her bag by the door. The next morning would be hectic as we raced to the airport for our flights.

Petie cried much of the night, as if she knew our vacation

The Existence of Pity

was ending, and the rest of us dragged out of bed the next day, discombobulated by our lack of sleep. We were late arriving at the airport, and Anna and I only had time for a hurried good-bye at the gate.

"Write soon, and tell me how everything's going, okay?" she asked, hugging me.

"Of course. You, too."

"And you, Aaron," Anna added, turning to my brother. "Please try to stay out of trouble."

I looked at my parents to see if they caught the worried look on Anna's face, but they were looking for the tickets.

"Aaron, make sure they aren't in your bag," Mom said, holding Petie in one arm while searching her purse.

My brother gave Anna a wicked grin then pulled our airline tickets from his bag.

I gave Anna one last wave before we boarded then settled in behind Mom, Dad, and Petie. The airplane would take us back to Cali and to all the worries I had forgotten while on vacation. Aaron pushed his bag into the overhead compartment and sat down beside me. "How is it you always get the window seat?"

"Lucky, I guess." My nose was already pressed against the window.

The plane lifted off the seahorse-shaped island, and the clapboard houses, high-rise hotels, and sunny beaches shrank until the airplane banked away. Then the spot of land in the big blue sea was gone.

After a few minutes, I pulled the airline's magazine from the seat in front of me, found a pen in my purse, and wrote on a random page, "I know about Trina."

I showed it to Aaron, who grabbed the magazine and my pen. "What are you talking about?" he printed on a different page.

I took the magazine, flipped the pages again, and wrote in the pink of a model's skirt, "I saw you kiss her." Then on another page,

I wrote, "I heard her tell you her boyfriend is dangerous." I drew a skull and crossbones on the facing page.

He looked at my words for a long time. Finally, he scrawled, "Butt out!" inside my skull and crossbones. He threw the magazine onto my lap, turned away, and closed his eyes.

Across the top of the cover, I wrote, "Don't be a fool. Please." I stuffed the magazine in the seat pocket in front of him and pulled James Herriot's *All Creatures Great and Small* from my carry-on bag.

The next thing I knew, Aaron was shaking my shoulder. "Wake up. We're about to land in Cali."

Out my window, the sun was shining on the patchwork quilt that was the Colombian plain. Dark roads bordered blocks of green and golden crops, and stands of trees were scattered on the rolling hills. The island had been beautiful, but the Colombian countryside held my heart. I took a deep breath. *Home.*

Dad stopped at the post office downtown on our way home from the airport. I loved running up the well-worn marble stairs and searching through the maze of miniature doors for our gold-plated box, number 6748. It had been almost a week since we last checked the mail, and the slot was full. Walking to the car, I sorted through the stack and found a letter from Tom. I saved it to read later and flipped through the latest *National Geographic* as we rode through the familiar streets of Cali.

After helping unpack the car, I tossed my suitcase in my room and ran downstairs to talk to Blanca. She was in the kitchen, preparing dinner. "How were your *vacaciones?*" she asked.

"Really fun," I answered, grabbing a banana and hopping onto the counter. I told her about the delicious food we ate, our boat trip, and snorkeling with my dad.

Before I could tell her about the view from the steeple, she asked, "Did you speak to your brother about Elías López?"

"Sort of."

She looked up at me. "You need to talk to him."

"I know." I sighed. It would mean letting go of the relaxed feeling the island vacation had given me, but Blanca was right—I would have to face reality. "Anna thinks I should tell my parents."

Blanca stopped snapping green beans and looked at me. "I do not want you to tell them Juan Fernando knows any of this."

"I don't want to tell my parents *anything*." I slid off the counter and poured a glass of water. Then I changed the subject. "I got a letter from Tom today."

"How is he doing?"

"I haven't opened it."

"What are you waiting for, *mija*? Open it!"

"I'm just enjoying the fact that I have a letter from my boyfriend." I pulled it out of my back pocket and showed it to her. "As soon as I open it, the anticipation will be over."

"*Ay, chica*, what is wrong with you? Go read your letter." She shook her head and rinsed the beans.

"Fine," I said, but upstairs, I took my time emptying my suitcase and straightening my room before I sat on my bed to slide open the thin envelope.

Dear Josie,

How are you? I'm fine. It's been good to get your letters. I miss you. Sorry I haven't written more. It's really hot here. I like the cool weather better in Bogotá, that's for sure. Yes, staying with my cousins is fun, but they have jobs and their own friends, so Jack and I spend a bunch of time just hanging out and kicking a soccer ball around. We did go to Six Flags Over Texas last week. I won a bear for you, but this little kid was crying, so I gave it to her. Sorry! Maybe when you come up here, we can ride the roller coaster together. I'll win you an even bigger bear at the gun range.

Life in Houston isn't what I expected. People seemed impressed by how I grew up so far away and that I can speak Spanish, but then they give me strange looks when I use certain expressions or wear Colombian clothes. Everyone seems so smart here, talking about the latest TV shows and movies and politics. My cousins are into bands I've never even heard of. I feel like I don't fit in, and I'm not sure I want to. I guess this is the culture shock all the MKs talk about.

But it's not all bad. At least I can pick up a real cheeseburger and a Dr Pepper any time I want. American television is fun to watch, and I like the music on the radio. It's hard to get used to life here, but I trust God has me here for a reason.

By the way, that picture you sent is great. It's fun to show you off to my cousins. Can't wait to see you at Christmas. Take care of yourself.

Love,
Tom

I read the letter a second time, savoring Tom's words, especially that he'd written "love." I hugged the pale-blue paper, looking at my copy of the photo I had sent him. It was of us standing in the waiting area at the airport. He had his arm around me, and I remembered laughing when Anna told us to say "*queso*" instead of cheese as she took the picture.

I remembered having culture shock when I was in the states two years before. It had been awful to feel like an outsider, but I couldn't help smiling at the thought of his cousins not liking some of his clothes. That stupid hat was probably in the batch, and I wasn't going to have to be the one to tell him his colorful knit cap had to go. He would figure it out soon enough.

Chapter Eighteen

THE FOLLOWING DAY, I WALKED into the house after my early-morning run at the seminary and stopped short. Mom and Blanca were having a heated discussion in the kitchen. Driven by a fear of losing Blanca, I rushed in and asked, "*¿Qué pasa?*"

Blanca turned to me, her eyes flashing with anger. "Your mother thinks I stole her necklace."

Mom said, "I went to put my new jewelry away, and my pearls were gone."

My stomach hollowed out. I was caught. "I took the necklace, Mom." I dragged her out of the kitchen. "Here, come with me, and I'll show you."

As we climbed the stairs to my room, Mom said, "That pearl necklace is special to me. It was a gift from your Aunt Rosie when we first moved to Colombia. Why do you have it?"

I swallowed hard. "I'm sorry. I borrowed it before we left for San Andrés. I should've told you." In my room, I reached under my pillow for the necklace and offered it to her. Mom didn't ask why the necklace was under my pillow. I didn't know what I would have said if she had.

"I guess I need to apologize to the maid," she said, taking the pearls.

"Yeah," I answered, wishing she hadn't accused Blanca.

Back in the kitchen, Mom held up the pearls for Blanca to see. Mom started to say something then stopped. Her shoulders began to shake, then she burst into tears. Blanca and I stood there, watching Mom break down, not sure what to do. She never lost her composure. Finally, Blanca led her to a chair in the breakfast room and patted her arm, but my mom cried harder, shaking with silent sobs.

"Bring her a box of tissues," Blanca ordered. I raced to the bathroom, glad to be able to help. Mom grabbed a handful and held them to her eyes, continuing to cry.

"Go get your father," Blanca told me.

I checked the guest room for Dad, but it was empty. I went upstairs to check in his office, and when I passed Mom's room, I saw him, still in his pajamas, sitting on the bed with Petie in front of him, wearing a pink sleeper.

"Dad, um, Mom's downstairs crying, and Blanca and I don't know what to do. Can you help her?"

"I'll talk to her," he said. "You stay here with Petie."

He grabbed his robe and went downstairs. I sat on the bed, and Petie studied me with her big blue eyes. I played peek-a-boo with her, and as my half sister giggled, I listened to the subdued sound of my father's voice as he tried to comfort my mother.

When they came upstairs, Mom went into the shower, and Dad came into the bedroom. "Will you change Petie's diaper and get her dressed?" he asked, walking to his closet. "Your mom and I are going to take Petie and see about adopting her. Legally."

"How are you going to do that? And why would you?" I stood and lifted Petie off the bed. "No one said anything, did they? Everyone still thinks she's a child from church, right?"

"I think so." Dad turned, a shirt and tie in his hands. "But Mom doesn't want to lose the baby. We'll do whatever it takes."

After changing Petie's diaper and dressing her, I took her downstairs and let Blanca give her a bottle. I raced back upstairs and threw on jeans and a shirt so that when Mom headed downstairs, I was right behind her. Dad was in the kitchen, wiping Petie's face with a little washcloth. He must have offered to take over for Blanca, who was dusting in the living room.

"So what exactly are you going to do?" I asked my parents, taking a cereal bowl from the cabinet.

Mom and Dad looked at each other, and Dad spoke. "We've decided it's best if we confide in Uncle Ted. He and Lily have helped some of their church members adopt, so they can give us some idea of what to expect with the Colombian legal system. I just called him, and he's waiting for us at his office across the street."

Still in pajama bottoms, Aaron ambled into the kitchen and opened the refrigerator. It was eight in the morning, early for him. When no one spoke, he turned to Dad and asked, "What's going on? Why are you two dressed for church?"

"Your mother and I are on our way to talk to Uncle Ted and Aunt Lily about adopting Petie." Dad looked at the baby in his arms. "You both should know, we feel it's only right to tell them she's my child."

"What?" Aaron slammed the refrigerator door as he spun around. "It'll ruin everything!"

"Look, Aaron," Dad said, a new firmness in his voice. "We don't want to live a lie. We'll have to take our chances and pray Uncle Ted will let us stay on as missionaries. People make mistakes; it's how they fix them that counts."

"I don't think he'll be very understanding." Aaron stood eye to eye with Dad, his arms crossed over his bare chest. "You can't be a missionary and commit adultery! Uncle Ted will send us back to the States—I know it! At least wait until I've graduated from high school so I can stay with my friends. Josie, too." He waved an arm my way. "Don't make our lives miserable for your stupid mistake."

Dad took a step back, his eyes wide, but I was with my brother on this one.

"We're telling Ted the truth," Mom said, her voice icy. "It's decided, Aaron."

"No, it isn't." Aaron stepped to the kitchen's entrance, blocking her way. "Not until you walk out that door."

"Don't speak to your mother like that," Dad said, frowning at Aaron as he handed Petie to Mom.

"Just don't do this," Aaron pleaded. "Think about it. Let's sit down and talk about our options."

"Aaron, this isn't about you," Mom said. "It's something your father and I have to do. For ourselves. Come on, Henry. They're expecting us."

My hands clenched tightly in front of me as I leaned against the counter, feeling sick. I shook from cold fear as the situation reeled out of control. Blanca came to the kitchen door behind Aaron, and her eyes met mine. She backed out slowly, her hand on the silver cross at her neck.

"How about this," Aaron said. "Just for now, tell Uncle Ted you want to adopt Petie. Later, in a year or two, you can tell him the baby is yours." He was talking to Dad, the only one who seemed to be wavering.

"Aaron, we are going to tell him everything." The finality in Mom's voice dipped into fury.

"Oh, really, Mom? Everything?" Aaron asked, not moving.

"What's that supposed to mean?" She stopped and eyed him.

"Are you going to tell him about the abortion you had?"

Mom froze. Finally, she turned toward the kitchen sink and leaned against it, both arms around Petie.

For the first time in the conversation, Aaron looked down at the floor. "I heard you talking about it with Aunt Rosie. You were in the dining room one morning, and you didn't hear me come downstairs. I was about to say something, when I noticed you were crying. Look, I'm sorry. I just…"

A long silence hung in the air after Aaron sputtered to a stop.

Mom's face was hidden in Petie's neck, and the rest of us stared at her.

Dad, his face ashen, asked, "Astrid, is this true? Did you have an abortion?"

"I didn't want another child," she said. "And yes, it was yours."

Dad flinched at the contempt in her words.

She turned to Aaron and me. "I was glad I had you two, but I couldn't imagine going through the early years again. Not only that, I had a bad feeling about the baby, like something wasn't right with it. I had a test done, but it wasn't conclusive. I thought it would be okay to end the pregnancy anyway. But then..." Her voice rose as she fought back tears and kept talking. "Then after the abortion, I knew I had sinned. And I didn't know what to do."

No one even breathed until Petie cooed, her chubby hand catching in the pearls around my mother's neck. Mom finally spoke, her tone completely different. "Then, there was Pity—I mean Petie. Although it's hard to accept what happened, it's a sign that God forgave me. He gave me this new baby." Mom hugged Petie tightly, her tears falling on the baby's head. "Now I can't bear the thought of losing her."

I gripped the counter to keep from falling over. All I could think was the necklace in Petie's hand was my rosary, and I really needed it at that moment.

Aaron, on the other hand, calmly asked for details. "Isn't abortion illegal here?"

"Think, Aaron." Mom raised a hand. "I went to the States earlier this year."

Dad had begun pacing, but he stopped and stared at her. "You said your doctor recommended you have a tubal ligation, and you wanted it done in the States."

Mom glared back at Dad. "Henry, don't you dare accuse me of anything here." He continued pacing, and Mom asked us, "Do you see now why I have to adopt Petie?"

"I do," Aaron answered. "And I don't have a problem with that. But Uncle Ted won't see that God gave you a second chance to have a child. He'll only see you had an abortion and Dad committed adultery. He'll think you can't be trusted to be missionaries."

Mom lowered her head over Petie's while Dad stared at her, looking deflated and sad. Finally, he took a deep breath. "He's right, Astrid. We'd jeopardize all we have here. And Ted won't want to set that kind of precedent. If he gives us a second chance, he'll have to do the same for every other missionary. I think we should keep this to ourselves, at least for a year or so. And here's another thing. Ted may not be the one who decides if we keep our job. He'll have to tell the Mission Board in the States, and they don't even know us."

Mom put her hand up to stop him. "Okay, okay. We'll just adopt her for now. We can deal with the rest later." I moved toward her and Petie to hug them, but she pushed me away. "Let me go upstairs and freshen up. Then I'll be ready to go."

Dad stayed in the kitchen with Petie, Aaron went back upstairs, and I walked out the front door. Brandy loped over to me, and I sat down in the middle of the driveway as he wagged his tail and gave me a sloppy grin, oblivious to my shock. As the words *affair* and *abortion* swirled in my brain, unbelievably, life went on around me. Cars drove by, birds chirped in the trees, and Brandy rolled over for me to rub his stomach. His happy presence calmed me as I tried to make sense of what had happened.

Soon, Mom and Dad came outside, ready to go.

"I don't know how long we'll be gone," Dad told me.

"Okay, good luck with everything." I watched them cross the street to Uncle Ted's office in the seminary. Mom didn't look back as she pushed Petie in the stroller.

When they were out of sight, I went upstairs for my purse. I had to get to La Ermita and buy a rosary. Mom had the pearls again, and I needed to pray on something. Besides, I desperately needed to get out of the house and go somewhere to think. There was no way anyone would care if I went to La Ermita after what had just happened, but I told Blanca I was going shopping for a gift for Petie, just in case.

"Yo-si, what is going on?" she asked.

"I can't talk about it right now. I'll tell you when I get home, okay?"

Blanca raised her eyebrows in suspicion, but she wasn't coming with me on another trip to La Ermita, and I wasn't ready to talk about what had happened in the kitchen. I went outside and caught a *buseta* to my sanctuary.

I leaned my head on the window and looked out as the city rolled by. How could Mom even have considered having an abortion? I didn't know her at all. The image of Mom's face when Dad had opened his white elephant gift at Mission Meeting came to me, and I realized that seeing the baby rattle and pacifier had made her uneasy not because she had known about Petie, but because of her abortion.

It all came to me now. The abortion was why she had changed so much over the past year, why she had become so withdrawn. I had blamed myself, thinking I had done something to upset her, but the change in my mother had nothing to do with me. My thoughts turned to my father, and I fought back tears as the agony of their secrets hit me again. No, none of this had been my fault, but their mistakes would affect my life profoundly.

I hopped off the bus at my stop and walked into La Ermita, pausing to kneel and cross myself with holy water. When I entered the little shop, the nun who ran the store clasped my hands in a warm welcome. After I asked for the same rosary as before, she took the familiar black beads from the glass case and put them in my hands.

"We have some new statues. Let me show them to you." She took three small statues from the shelf: Jesus, Mary, and Saint Christopher.

"'Whoever shall behold the image of Saint Christopher shall

not faint or fall on that day,'" she recited, handing me a statue of a bearded man carrying a smiling child on his shoulder. "Saint Christopher is the patron saint of travel. And here's Mother Mary. She is the comforter." Mary was holding a child with a halo above his head. "And here is Jesus, the good shepherd." The statue of Jesus was taller than the others. He had a lamb around his neck and a loving smile on his face.

I stared at the statues, flooded with memories of my time at La Ermita: buying my first rosary, watching Aunt Rosie choose her statues, and lighting a candle for my family. "I want them all," I said. Having them would remind me of happier times.

I walked back into the sanctuary and sat down to pray on my new rosary, gladly losing myself in the comfort of the words as tears rolled down my cheeks. The simple act of prayer cleared my mind, making me see that nothing I could do would change what had happened. I could only accept the situation and make the best of it. And it wasn't all bad—I got a beautiful baby sister from it.

My plan was to visit a downtown shop for Petie's gift in case anyone questioned my trip, so I joined the stream of people outside, to look for a *tienda*. Walking in the city, surrounded by strangers who didn't know what was going on in my life, made breathing a little easier.

Thick, gray clouds rolled in, blocking the view of the three crosses on the hill, then it started to rain. I ducked into a little variety shop and bought a blue teddy bear with a bow around its neck. The owner offered an extra bag to cover my head, and I continued on, walking aimlessly, hugging my purchases. My jeans were sopping wet around my ankles, and everything seemed wrong, drab, and cold. All I wanted was to go home, but then I remembered everything at home was wrong, too.

I nearly missed Aaron's nightclub—it looked so shabby and dirty in the rain—but the J of El Jazmin caught my eye. I stopped in my tracks, looking at the black door of the dilapidated building, surprised my feet had carried me to it. This rainy-day version of the nightclub was a huge contrast to the vibrant and exciting place where I had followed Aaron. Daylight stripped it of all its glamour.

Maybe Aaron would stop coming here. Maybe he would stop being a fool.

I was about to walk by, when I heard a familiar voice call to me in Spanish. "*Oye*, aren't you Aaron's sister?"

Trina came up to me, too close. The rain off her pink umbrella was dripping on me. I backed up, and she stepped forward. She looked more beautiful than I remembered; her skin was perfectly clear, and her makeup accentuated her big brown eyes. She wore American jeans, a pretty top, and heels. Her jewelry, nails, and perfume—everything about her—was wealthy and beautiful. But when she spoke, the stench of alcohol and cigarettes accompanied her words.

It never occurred to me I might have the opportunity to talk to Trina. There was no fixing my parents' problems, but maybe Trina could help stop Aaron from getting into trouble.

"Yes, I'm Aaron's sister." I forced a smile and added, "Can we talk about my brother? I saw you with him, and, well…" I swallowed.

She laughed. "*Niña*, what do you want?"

I took a deep breath. "Would you stop going out with my brother?"

"What do you mean?" she asked, her smile fading.

"Your boyfriend is Elías López, right?" I asked. "If Elías finds out about you two, Aaron could get hurt."

Trina nodded. "Your brother could get killed."

I swallowed again, trying to steady my voice and my nerves. "Trina, if you really cared about Aaron, you'd leave him alone."

"He's the one who wanted to date me. And I do care about him. I've missed him. Maybe I will stop dating Elías for Aaron."

My head began to spin as I tried to think of how to stop the dangerous fool from going out with Aaron.

"*Hola*, Trina." Another girl walked up to us. She was dressed much like Trina and carried a matching pink umbrella.

"Marlena," Trina said to the girl, "this is Aaron's sister." They turned to me, and Trina asked, "What is your name?"

"Josie," I said, looking down at the puddles on the sidewalk. They reflected the pink cloud that was Trina and Marlena.

"Yo-si? Your brother is so cute. *¡Qué bizcocho!*" Marlena said. "Is he coming to the club tonight?"

"Yo-si wants me to stop dating Aaron," Trina said, locking arms with Marlena. "She's afraid of Elías!"

"Don't worry about Elías; he's a big sweetie." Marlena giggled.

"If Elías is such a nice guy, why did he have a woman shot as she was driving down our street?" My voice refused to stay calm, and I shook as I spoke. "Why did Elías López send two guys on a motorcycle to shoot that poor woman in the white car?"

"*Cálmate*, Yo-si. That woman was married to a bad person," Trina said.

"Well, you know what? Elías will think my brother is a bad person for trying to go out with you." I stared at Trina.

"Yes," Trina sighed. "Your brother is bad. Poor little *gringa*. You need to relax. Why don't we get you a drink?" She looked at Marlena and laughed.

I stared long and hard at Trina, but she just stared right back. Finally giving up, I shook my head and turned away.

"Tell Aaron I said hello!" Trina called after me, but I didn't answer. I jumped on the first *buseta* that came by and took a seat. As the bus drove past them, the girls waved at me from under their umbrellas, still smiling.

When they were out of sight, I slumped down in my seat and took a deep breath, still clutching my bag of purchases. After a few minutes, the bustling city changed to a long row of identical white apartments with barred windows that I had never seen before.

I was on the wrong bus.

Chapter Nineteen

THE RAIN HAD EASED TO a drizzle by the time I got off the bus. I followed the driver's directions, but instead of arriving at another bus stop, I found myself in a neighborhood with elegant old houses protected by iron fences. Well-kept 1950s Buicks and Chevrolets were parked along the narrow road, and huge trees pushed up the sidewalk in uneven slabs. I was in a different world, isolated from the frenetic city, and I studied each unique home, surrounded by the sounds of children playing inside their gates and courtyards. It didn't seem possible that these families could have the same problems my family had.

The refuge ended abruptly when the old neighborhood's road intersected with a busy four-lane street. In the *barrio*, people were gathered at the corner and around barred doorways. A man smoking a cigarette nodded toward me, and others followed his gaze. I quickly raised my hand for a cab, wishing there was a way to call Moises to pick me up.

Two men called, "*Oye, mona.*" They were walking in my direction when an old yellow taxi stopped for me. I sank into the backseat and took a deep breath. Maybe it was time to stop going downtown on my own. The clouds broke open with another round of flooding rain, and within seconds, the taxi was flying through puddles that sent water wings along both sides of the car. Although it was only noon, the sky was a slate wall, and the traffic lights reflected off the raindrops.

When we arrived at my house, I didn't have enough money in my purse to pay the cabbie. I apologized, gave him what I had, and offered my Saint Christopher statue since it was the patron saint for travelers. He smiled and pointed to the Saint Christopher medallion hanging from his rearview mirror but agreed to let the statue cover the rest of my fare.

I ran inside, shaking the rain from my clothes. A delicious smell coming from the kitchen reminded me that all I had eaten was a bowl of cereal early that morning.

"What's cooking, Blanca?" I asked, walking into the kitchen with my bag. "I'm starving."

She looked at me over the sizzling fried chicken on the stove. "Your family needs a good meal to bring you together," she said. "It will be ready soon. Go upstairs and change first."

After tugging my wet clothes off and putting on dry shorts and a T-shirt, I joined Blanca in the kitchen. I hopped onto the counter next to my bag of purchases. "I went back to La Ermita without you. You can't get in trouble again. Here's what I got."

Blanca wiped her hands on her apron and took the bag I offered, a frown on her face. "Why did you go back? I don't think your parents will be happy."

I shrugged. "They shouldn't care. My parents went to see Uncle Ted. He might help them adopt Petie."

"Your father told me," she said, turning to mash the potatoes.

"Are they home yet?"

"No, they have been gone all morning, and your mother did not take an extra bottle for the baby. She will be miserable." Blanca shook her head. "Why did Aaron not want them to go?"

It took a minute to realize Blanca understood, even though we had been speaking in English, that Aaron was trying to stop Mom and Dad. I wondered what it must be like for her to stand by, comprehending so little, with no say in the situation. She'd watched the drama from the sidelines even though it was happening in the center of her world.

"Aaron was okay with them adopting Petie," I explained. "But Mom and Dad were going to tell Uncle Ted that Petie is my dad's baby."

"I would think Señor Ted would forgive your father, since your mother has."

"Yes, but it's my dad's job to be trustworthy. If he can't do that, he shouldn't be a missionary. Don't you think?"

"I guess you are right," she said. "But a minister must tell the truth."

"Blanca, he can't tell the truth. If he does, we'd have to go back to the States. Aaron and I would have to start over at a new school, and my dad would have to find another job. You would have to find a new family, too. And what about Petie?"

Blanca washed her hands in the sink, and for the first time since she'd moved in with us, I felt her judging me and my family with her silence.

I changed the subject. "Do you know where Aaron is? I need to talk to him."

"He went to the tennis club. Why?"

"I ran into Elías López's girlfriend today. I practically begged her to leave Aaron alone, but Blanca, she was so stupid! She thinks it's funny that Aaron could get killed. She can't see how serious this is. What is wrong with her?"

"What is wrong with Aaron?"

I bristled at her accusation then sighed. She was right. If Aaron wanted to play such a dangerous game, nobody could stop him, and I needed Blanca's help. "Do you think you could ask Juan Fernando to keep an eye on Aaron? He could tell the other policemen about Aaron, too."

"I want to discuss this with Aaron first," she said, stirring the green beans. "Then we will see about calling Juan Fernando."

"Thank you, Blanca," I answered, sliding off the counter. "Here, let me set the table."

Everything shifted when Mom and Dad walked through the door. Their animated conversation about what needed to be done in order to adopt Petie filled the house with hope, even though the baby was howling with hunger. My parents worked as a team; Mom quickly prepared a bottle while Dad deftly changed the diaper, and before long, Petie was content but still snuffling as she ate.

Over our meal, we laughed at Aaron's story about being stuck at the tennis club, playing against a man who insisted on finishing his winning streak in the rain. I could see Mom and Dad leaned toward each other, no longer at odds. Their unspoken detachment had been an undercurrent in our family for so long, I had grown accustomed to it. Now that it was gone, relief made us all giddy. Our respite was short lived. Mom handed Petie to Dad, and the baby put her hand in Dad's mashed potatoes, knocking a handful onto the floor. When we laughed at the surprised look on Petie's face, she started to cry, so Mom took Petie back and rocked her. The congenial mood collapsed around us as Petie sobbed, and thunder rumbled low through the valley.

Mom calmed Petie then carried her upstairs to the nursery.

I followed. "Mom, can I ask you a question?" I wanted to understand why she'd had the abortion.

"What is it?" she asked, finding a yellow romper for Petie in the dresser.

I swallowed. Maybe I didn't want to know. I looked at her, the words strangling my throat.

"About the abortion?"

I nodded, not sure if I was relieved or disappointed that she'd read my mind.

She laid Petie on the changing table and turned to me. "Look, Josie, I don't think having an abortion is wrong. Especially if the baby has serious deformities." Mom dressed Petie, picked her up, and looked me in the eye. "There's something you need to understand. There are worse things than death."

"Then why did you say you sinned and that Petie was your second chance?"

She sighed. "Because it's not that simple. I started doubting I'd made the right decision. And I shouldn't have kept it from Henry."

"Did you go by yourself to get the… the abortion?"

"Yes." She looked down at Petie. "But when I started thinking I'd been too hasty, I told your Aunt Rosie. She agreed that I'd done what was right for me, for all of us. I'm able to help so many more people since there's no child with expensive health issues to tend to. That child would have required all of my attention and plenty of your dad's, too. And Henry would've been miserable."

"You're sure?"

A pained look clouded Mom's eyes. "I did what I thought had to be done. But when it was over, it felt like something wasn't right. Then… it was like God took pity on me." She smiled down at the baby. "Now that I'm holding this healthy, beautiful girl, I'm glad there's a baby in my life." She smiled at Petie, who reached for her face. "I can't imagine it any other way."

I stood staring at Petie, trying to absorb what Mom was saying. It still didn't make sense to me. Maybe it never would.

"There's one more thing," Mom added. "I know I'm choosing to see Petie's presence in my life this way. Petie is the result of your father's affair with another woman. That could've ended our marriage, but I'm closing my eyes to how she came to be. To me, this baby is a gift, and your father's sin is for him to live with."

She turned and walked out, cooing to the baby. "Now let's see if you'll take a nap. I know you're tired, sweetie Petie."

In my room across the hall, I stared out the window, watching drops of rain grow larger on the glass until they broke and slid down, collecting other drops with them as they fell. I would never have an abortion, I decided. It might be okay for my mom, and it was good she had come to terms with all that had happened, but I couldn't be that rational.

I sat at my desk and tried to write letters to Tom and Aunt Rosie, but there was nothing to say. Sadness and exhaustion overcame me, and I stretched on my bed. Then the wind rushing through the mango trees soothed me to sleep.

Hours later, I awoke, feeling disoriented. The gray day had turned into a black night. I reached for J. R. R. Tolkien's *The Hobbit* and read for a few minutes, but when I heard Aaron get out of the shower and go to his room, I tossed the book on my bed and went downstairs. Aaron needed to be warned about Trina.

He walked past me, dressed to go out.

"Aaron," I said, "we need to talk." I followed him to the living room.

"Haven't we all talked enough today?" He sat at the piano and played a few chords.

"Not about this."

"About what?"

Blanca walked in and stood by the piano, so I answered in Spanish. "I need to tell you what I saw the night I followed you to the nightclub."

He stopped playing and looked up at me. "Okay."

"I saw you with Trina in the alley, and I know Trina's boyfriend is Elías López."

"Why are you speaking in Spanish?" he asked in English.

"Because Blanca is worried about you, too," I continued in

Spanish. "Elías López is bad news. He's the reason that woman was shot on our street."

"Keep your voice down," Aaron said in Spanish, standing. "Mom and Dad might hear you." Aaron grabbed my hand and dragged me to the maid's quarters. Blanca followed, and Aaron shut the door behind us.

"Can't you just end it with Trina?" I asked. "I saw her today, and she was really mean. I asked her to stop dating you, and she just laughed."

"You did what?" Aaron's eyes narrowed with such anger, I was afraid he might hit me. "Why did you talk to her? You don't know anything about my life. I'm fine. *You're* the one who's living dangerously. I saw the statues you got from La Ermita today, and that string of beads. You left them sitting on the kitchen counter like a fool. You're lucky Mom and Dad didn't see that stuff. When they find out you went back to that church, they'll be furious."

"And who's going to tell them? You? Your secret is way worse than mine. Your secret could kill you."

"You're a fool, Josie." Aaron rolled his eyes. "Why do you keep going to that Catholic church? Mom and Dad are missionaries!"

I didn't know what to say. It took every ounce of my strength to hold his gaze, even though my face was burning and my brain had shut down. Had I really been stupid enough to leave my statues and rosary in the kitchen?

"Forget it," he said, walking to the door. He yanked it open and seethed. "You take care of your secrets; I'll take care of mine." He stomped to the piano and began playing a loud classical piece.

Moments later, Petie began crying, and Mom yelled down at Aaron to stop the noise. I had gone to the kitchen when I heard the front door slam. Blanca and I ran to the living room window in time to see Aaron slide a jacket over his shoulders, push Brandy down, and jam the gate shut behind him before disappearing into the darkness. I fell onto the couch and put my head in my hands.

"Who just left?" Dad asked from the top step.

"Aaron."

"Where did he go?"

"Not sure." That was sort of true. There was still a chance he would come to his senses. A very slim chance.

"I'm hungry," Dad said, ambling down the stairs. "Who wants leftovers with me?"

I slipped into the kitchen in front of him and grabbed the bear, the rosary, and the statues then hid them in Blanca's room before Dad made it to the bottom step. Mom came downstairs, too, and we filled plates with chicken and beans. We watched Petie play with a rattle as we ate.

"I wish the neighbor who loaned us the buggy would let us use their highchair," Mom said. "We'll have to buy one soon. She did tell me she has another stroller for Petie to use."

Dad smirked. "Is it as ugly as the first one?"

"Who cares?" Mom answered.

Their lighthearted banter was too much for me. I finished eating and turned on the television, looking for something to distract me. I gave up on the Colombian soap operas and variety shows a little before nine then retrieved my things from Blanca's room.

I lay in bed, praying on my new beads, but they couldn't stop me from thinking of my brother. If Aaron had gone to see Trina, all I could do was hope his luck would hold. Or maybe Trina would tire of Aaron, and they would part ways without Elías ever finding out. I sighed. "Yeah, when pigs fly," I muttered. Maybe I should have told Dad about Trina, but what if I was overreacting? If anyone could get out of a scrape, it was Aaron.

I forced myself to concentrate on praying the rosary—twice. Then I put the beads under my pillow and turned off the lamp, but I still couldn't sleep. When Aaron still had not returned at midnight, I decided it was time to do something. After dressing, I crept down the stairs.

"Blanca, *despiértese*," I whispered through the crack of her door.

She let me in her room, bleary eyed. "What is wrong?"

"We need to make sure he's okay."

Blanca dropped onto her bed. "Yo-si, you should tell your parents."

"No, not yet. I just want to check on him. Please come with me, just this once."

She held my gaze for what felt like a full minute. Finally, she acquiesced. "Okay, *chica*, but I don't like it."

I breathed a sigh of relief. "I'll call a taxi. He'll take us to the nightclub."

"I am only coming along to keep you from being pulled into an alley again," she said, leaving me with a chill running down my spine.

I set our big black phone on the floor and called Moises's cab company, silencing the sound of the rotary dial with a dish towel. When the company answered, I asked them to send Moises to our address right away. I gathered the last of my pesos from my sock drawer for the cab ride and met Blanca downstairs.

"*Tenga,*" she said, handing me a dark-blue sweater as she threw a jacket over her shoulders.

"*Gracias,*" I whispered, pulling the sweater over my shirt. I would be glad for the warmth.

We walked in darkness to the front door and slipped outside, moving away from the house before Brandy noticed us. While we waited on a bench in front of the seminary, Blanca told more stories of her childhood to pass the time.

"My older brother was like Aaron," she said. "He would roam the mountainside, hunting foxes with his friends. It was difficult to wake him the next day, and I very often had to complete his morning chores for him."

"Well, that's not fair."

She shrugged. "The goats had to be milked. But it did make

me angry, so one day, I poured a bucket of water on his head to get him out of bed."

"Blanca! You did that?" I imagined how satisfying it would be to douse my brother's sleeping head with water—and how angry my parents would be.

"It worked. That's all I can say."

"Do you two still fight?" I asked.

"No, *chica*, we are close now that we are grown." She squeezed my hand. "Maybe you will be, too."

"I don't know," I said, shaking my head. "Sometimes I want us to be close. Sometimes I want to push him off a cliff."

"Don't say things like that, *chica*."

When our cab finally pulled up, Moises asked, "*Ay, mona*, what are you doing up so late this time? Is it your brother again?"

"Yeah," I answered as we slid into the backseat. "This is Blanca."

Moises smiled at her. "So she brought you into this, too."

Blanca laughed. There was already a bond between my maid and the cab driver, an understanding I could never share, and it hit me how often I felt outside of relationships in my life. Would I always be the one looking in from a window or listening at the door? Maybe this was why it was so important to save Aaron, my only brother.

"Is he in trouble?" Moises asked, snapping me back to the moment.

"I think so," I told him. "We need to go to El Jazmin again."

He pulled into the street. Moises and Blanca made small talk for a few blocks then settled into silence until we reached the nightclub, which looked festive and exciting again. "My shift ends at one o'clock," Moises told us, "but call the cab company. Rafael is a friend of mine. He will pick you up."

"Thank you, we will call soon," Blanca said as I paid the fare, and we climbed out of the taxi.

"*Buena suerte*," he said, wishing us luck.

We walked to the big black door, and I smiled at Pedro. "Remember me?"

He looked more closely, then his eyes opened wide. "The *gringo*'s sister. Why are you here?" He quickly changed his tune. "Go on in. Of course." Americans were always welcome at the nightclubs.

"We're looking for Aaron. Have you seen him?"

"No, I haven't," Pedro said, motioning for a couple beside us to enter.

"You haven't seen him all night?" I asked.

"If he is here, he came while I was on a break." He began a conversation with some women standing behind us, so we walked in the club.

After adjusting to the loud music and flashing lights, I found Trina seated at the bar, holding an empty glass. She was wearing a shiny miniskirt and a sheer top.

I led Blanca over. "Hey, Trina, where's my brother?" I yelled over the music.

She studied me until recognition sparked in her eyes. "You are Aaron's *hermana*. I remember you!" She reached for me, almost falling off her stool. She held my arm too tightly, looking me up and down. "You need to learn how to dress for a party," she said, tipping backward as she laughed.

I pulled away, and Blanca stepped up to steady her. "Where is Aaron?" I repeated.

"Who is this *mestiza*?" Trina asked, referring to Blanca's native Colombian heritage.

I wanted to slap Trina but decided she was too drunk to give me a straight answer. Besides, then Elías would have a reason to hate me, too. I looked around, and a Colombian, his open shirt revealing a gold chain, asked if I wanted to dance. I turned him down and found Trina's friend Marlena, who was talking with a group of people.

I made my way to her through the crowd. "Marlena, do you know where Aaron is?"

Marlena recognized me immediately. "Yo-si, the *bizcocho*'s sister!" She swayed to the music. "He was here, but he left. Ask Trina." She turned to her friends.

"Wait," I said, reaching out to her. "Trina's too drunk. She won't tell me anything."

Marlena raised her hands in exasperation. "I'll be back," she told the group then walked with me back to Trina. "She can be difficult," Marlena said. She shook Trina's shoulders and asked loudly, "*Dónde está* Aaron?"

Trina looked over at me and smiled, her eyes glazed. "Aaron and Elías are friends now. Isn't that great?"

Marlena put her hands on Trina's cheeks. "*Dónde está* Aaron?"

Trina began explaining something to Marlena, but her slurred words were hard to follow. Then I heard her say Elías had taken Aaron somewhere. Blanca grabbed my hand and pulled me away, and I stumbled, trying to keep up as she pushed through the crowded nightclub and out the door. Blanca was talking to me, but I couldn't concentrate on her words because Trina's voice kept ringing in my ears. Elías had taken Aaron. Somewhere.

"Yo-si!" Blanca shouted. "Are you listening to me? We need to call Juan Fernando! Yo-si!"

Chapter Twenty

I N FRONT OF EL JAZMIN, Blanca searched her purse for change. "I will call the police department and have Juan Fernando sent here."

I followed her to a pay phone, too dazed to tell her Pedro would probably let her use the club's phone, like I had before.

Soon the police dispatcher was connecting Blanca with Juan Fernando, and she spoke to him in rapid Spanish, describing how Aaron was missing and that Elías might have him. "Come quick," she said then hung up the phone and turned to me, her face ashen.

We moved toward the front of the club to watch for the police, and people stared as we passed by. I could never go unnoticed. I usually liked the attention, but not this time, not when they seemed to pity my anxious pacing. Only Pedro's presence at the door comforted me. He would protect us.

I was about to ask Blanca how much longer we would have to wait when a police car pulled up in front of El Jazmin. Two officers jumped out and walked over to me.

"Your brother is missing?" one of them asked. He was about my height, and his badge said his last name was García.

"Sí. Elías's girlfriend told us Aaron and Elías left together."

García turned to Blanca. "Juan Fernando will be here soon."

"What about the guard?" the other officer asked me, tossing his head toward Pedro. The sturdy policeman looked mean, and he probably outranked García. His question about Pedro confused me, and I was about to tell him the guard helped me the last time I had been here, but Blanca cut in. "He may know something."

I looked at Blanca, who nodded. Pedro's thick gold chain glittered at his neck, and his black polo shirt was stretched tight across his solid arms and chest. Before, Pedro had asked Trina what he should tell Lilo when she and Aaron left the club together, and I shivered, realizing he must be one of Elías's men.

The officers sauntered over to Pedro. The mean one rested his hand on his gun and said, "*Oye,* this *gringa* tells me her brother is missing. You know anything about that?"

"*No sé nada, Capitán,*" Pedro told the officer, shaking his head fervently as people gathered to watch.

The captain leaned against the wall by the entry and said, "I think you do, and we can stay here all night, if that's what it takes to find the boy." He spat on the ground. "We are not big fans of your boss, Elías."

Looking at his partner, he added, "I wonder if our car parked in front of the nightclub will be bad for business."

García chuckled. "I hope it is. These people should be in bed at this time of night."

A man wearing an ugly suit rushed from the nightclub. "*Buenas noches, señores.* What can I do for you?" he asked. His gold pinky ring flashed as he spoke. Officer García spoke with Pedro and the other man while the captain told us to follow him. He led us to his cruiser and helped us into the backseat.

"You will be safe here," he said.

The captain contacted Juan Fernando on his radio and seemed to be planning something. The police radio garbled his voice and cut in and out, but I understood Blanca's boyfriend was close by.

Blanca and I stared at each other when we heard sirens. Distant but persistent, they quickly moved closer. They filled the air, then Juan Fernando's police car screeched to a stop behind ours. Juan

Fernando left his car running and ran straight to Pedro, pulling his gun. García and the captain backed him up, pulling their guns, too.

"Tell me where the *gringo* is," Juan Fernando yelled into Pedro's face as the other officers held the guard's bulky arms. The man in the ugly suit disappeared into the crowd. He was deserting Pedro, and for half a second, I felt sorry for the man who had saved my life.

"*¡No sé nada!*" Pedro repeated, his forehead gleaming in the neon light. He was sweating through his shirt, struggling as he stared at the gun in his face.

"Put him in my car," Juan Fernando said. "He's going to take us to Elías."

Pedro tried to fight off the cops, but they held his arms behind him while Juan Fernando patted him down. When Juan Fernando pulled a small silver pistol from Pedro's back pocket, the bouncer struggled harder, kicking the captain. The cops managed to cuff him, and just as they guided his head into the cruiser, Pedro looked my direction with fury in his eyes. I cowered in the captain's car.

The captain jumped in the front seat and sped off behind Juan Fernando. Blanca and I were quiet as we rode from the city toward Cristo Rey, and with every mile of desolate countryside, my chest tightened in fear for Aaron. I took a deep breath. There was nothing I could do but pray.

Blanca patted my knee and whispered, "Are you okay?"

"No, are you?"

After a moment, she answered, "I hope we are not too late."

We were almost to Cristo Rey when Juan Fernando drove off the road and parked. The captain pulled in behind Juan Fernando and stepped out. "Don't move," he called to us as he followed Juan Fernando, who was walking down the ravine by the side of the road.

Tears stung my eyes at the memory of Aunt Rosie's first night with us, when Aaron nearly caused a collision at this exact spot. I looked at the four white crosses my aunt had pointed out, each only three feet tall, on the edge of the deep ditch. Four people had died here. Would we be putting up a little white cross for Aaron, too?

"Oh, Blanca," I said, covering my face with my hands. "Why didn't I tell Dad so he could stop this weeks ago? Why did Aaron have to be so stupid?"

She put her arm around me and patted my shoulder, but I couldn't be consoled and didn't want to be contained. I flung open the door and stepped out of the car. Blanca grabbed my arm. "Where are you going? It isn't safe out there!"

"I have to help them find my brother."

Blanca studied my face then sighed. "*Sí, chica*, you do. I will come with you."

We found two flashlights in the car's glove compartment and shut the door behind us. The chilly air on the mountain made me shiver, and the city lights of Cali seemed years away. At the beginning of the summer when my family had taken Aunt Rosie to see the same panorama, I had loved the view. But the city seemed dangerous and distant.

"*¿Qué pasa?*" Officer García called from the car where he held Pedro captive.

Blanca walked over and spoke to him. I hiked along the road and aimed my flashlight down the deep ravine, overgrown with waist-high weeds, praying. First, I prayed to God, begging him to save Aaron for my parents' sake. I prayed the way my father did, asking for forgiveness of my sins and for mercy on all of us. Then I fell to my knees and prayed to Mother Mary the way Blanca had taught me, begging for intercession, pleading for her to watch over my brother. I swung the flashlight down the ravine again, holding my breath. But all I could make out in the darkness of the Andes Mountains were police officers searching for any sign of my brother, too.

I stood and walked into the weeds, repeating, "*Om mani padme hum*," Aunt Rosie's Buddhist prayer.

I was halfway down the ravine when Blanca flashed her light in my direction and called to me from beside the road. "*Mija*, come here."

"What is it?" I asked, running up the hill where she was studying something in her hands.

"This is Aaron's shoe," Blanca whispered.

I grabbed the shoe, hugging it to me, then leaned on Blanca and wept. The nightmare was true.

Just then, Officer García called to us, yelling over the static on the police radio. "Someone found the boy! Tell the others to come back!"

"Juan Fernando, *Capitán*, they found him!" I screamed, waving to get their attention.

We jumped into the cruisers and raced back into Cali, Juan Fernando leading with his cruiser's lights flashing but his siren off. We flew along the roads in silence, the red and blue illuminating the mountainside then the walled houses along the city streets.

"Where do you think he is?" I asked Blanca. She shook her head, her solemn profile lit by the garish flashes.

At first, it seemed we were headed for our house, but my heart sank when Juan Fernando pulled into a hospital. Our driver followed. I hated hospitals. They held memories of visits to people hurt in earthquakes, when every hall was lined with hospital patients huddled under blood-spotted sheets, gazing at us in despair.

As I walked into the emergency room, the familiar smell of ammonia mixed with fear overwhelmed me. I nearly threw up, but Blanca squeezed my hand hard and whispered in my ear, "Yo-si, you need to be strong. I will be right beside you." She led me to the information desk.

"It's her brother," Juan Fernando was saying to the woman on duty, pointing at me.

The receptionist looked over her desk and caught her breath. "A man came in with a boy who looks like her," she said, nodding toward me. "He is in intensive care, but I think he's still alive."

A high-pitched bell blasted in my ears, all the colors and lights of the emergency room darkened around me, and an icy heat filled my veins. Even though I'd never fainted before, I realized I was about to. I reached for Blanca as my knees, usually so dependable, buckled under me…

I came to on a couch in the lobby, my head on a hard pillow in Blanca's lap. She was stroking my hair, and people were talking around us. I tried to raise my head, but the pain caused me to rest again.

"When should we call her parents?" a man was asking. It took me a minute to place the voice. *Moises.* "I don't care how bad the trouble is my children get into, I want to know about it."

"That is not the case with the parents of these two," Blanca said. "What matters most is how everything looks, not how everything really is."

There was silence for a few moments, then I heard clicking heels and a nurse's voice. "He is stable. If you hadn't brought him in when you did, he would have lost too much blood. Will the parents be arriving soon? We have paperwork for them to fill out."

"Soon," Blanca told the nurse.

"How is the boy's sister?" the nurse asked.

"She'll be okay," Blanca answered, tucking my hair behind my ear. Not ready to face the situation, I pretended to sleep.

The heels clicked away again, and I heard Juan Fernando say, "Moises, tell me exactly how you found Aaron."

"When I dropped you and the girl off at El Jazmin, I saw a group of men walking away from the club with a young man," Moises said. "I didn't think anything of it until I realized the *gringo* was the girl's brother."

"How did you know?" Blanca asked.

"I had seen him before, remember? The first time I met the girl, she was following him to see where he was slipping off to," Moises explained. "Anyway, I was watching the group when they pushed the boy into a van. I followed them, and they drove up toward Cristo Rey. When fewer cars passed me, I had to slow down so the men in the van wouldn't be suspicious. I came around a curve and saw the thugs and the gringo on the side of the road. I could tell I surprised them when my lights shone on them. I honked my horn, and the boy jumped over the edge of the road into the ravine. The men shot at him, got in the van, and drove away."

"Did you see Aaron get shot?" Juan Fernando asked.

"No, I just saw them shoot toward him. I stopped the cab and ran to the ditch. I found the boy and crawled down to him. I tried to lift him, but he was too heavy."

"He is really big, close to two meters tall," Blanca said.

"Well, he's funny, too, because he looked up at me and asked, 'Are you Jesus?' I told him I was Moises, and he stared at me. Finally, he said, 'I guess my Jewish friends were right.'"

Blanca and Juan Fernando stifled laughter, and I bit the inside of my cheek to hide a smile. Leave it to Aaron to think he'd arrived at the wrong heaven.

"How did you get him up the ravine?" Juan Fernando asked.

"I convinced him he was alive and needed to get to the hospital. He was able to crawl up the ravine with my help. By the time we got there, he was very weak. He was shot in the shoulder and was bleeding badly. I shoved him in the taxi and drove here. He must have lost his shoe on the road. The last thing he told me before he lost consciousness was he would have to pay the fare later. He didn't have enough money on him."

Juan Fernando asked, "Is that when you told your dispatcher to call the police department?"

"I called the dispatcher after I arrived here. You were probably not far behind us," Moises said.

The three were quiet, and I decided it was time to join the conversation. I sat up, holding my head.

"*Hola, chica,*" Blanca said, studying my face.

"Why does my head hurt so bad?" I asked.

"You hit it on the floor when you fainted," she answered. "I tried to catch you, but you fell too fast for me. Do you need an aspirin?"

"Maybe some water," I said.

Moises walked to the front desk and returned with a glass for me. I gave him a weak smile and drank it down.

"Let us see if you can visit your brother," Blanca said, reaching for my arm.

We walked slowly to the nurses' station and asked about Aaron.

"You may see him for a short while. We need to speak to his parents, too," the nurse told me.

I nodded and turned to Blanca. "Come with me," I said, my eyes pleading.

She didn't answer, but she took my hand.

We followed a nurse through double doors and along a hallway lined with rooms. The corridor was empty, and I kept my eyes on the tan flecks of color in the green linoleum. I didn't want to see the pain inside any of the rooms, and I didn't want the people there to see mine. The nurse stopped at a room where Aaron lay, his face bruised, a large bandage wrapped around his bare chest and over one shoulder. The other arm had an IV attached to it. His eyes were closed, but his breathing was even, and I walked to the side of the bed and held his hand.

Even though his face was battered and bruised, he still looked handsome with his light-brown hair and tan skin against the white pillow. *He'll be okay this time,* I realized with relief. He would stop going out with Trina, but then it hit me. Who would be next? Or what danger would Aaron feel drawn to? There was no way someone would be there to rescue him every time he walked down that same road.

"Come," Blanca whispered after a few minutes. She pulled me into the hallway, and we thanked the nurse before returning to the waiting room. Blanca put her hand on my arm before we joined Juan Fernando and Moises. "Yo-si, they are waiting for you to call your parents."

I shuddered at the thought of making the horrible call to my parents. "Blanca, I can't."

"You have to!"

"It's just too much," I said. "They've been through too much."

"No, *you* have been through too much." She looked at me, tears glistening in her eyes. "I will call them. I will talk to them."

I rested against the wall, relieved I didn't have to cope with the tragedy alone.

"They will let us use the phone at the front desk," she said.

Above the desk, a clock read four in the morning. I listened as Blanca dialed our home number. It rang one… two… three… then four times before my dad's voice, still full of sleep, answered. My heart ached for him as Blanca told him he needed to come to the hospital, and as he began to understand why.

She hung up the phone, and we turned to Juan Fernando and Moises, who were standing by the magazine rack. I reached out to embrace Moises, and he smiled.

I wiped my eyes. "Thank you, Señor Moises, for saving my brother's life."

"I thought you didn't like your brother," he said with a wink.

"Now more than ever. When he gets out of the hospital, I'll put him back in," I joked, shaking my fist.

My Colombian friends laughed.

I asked Moises, "Can you stay until my parents get here? They will want to meet you and thank you for all you've done."

"I've been here this long," Moises answered, looking at his big Timex. "A few more minutes won't hurt."

Juan Fernando nodded, and we sat in plastic chairs in the lobby to wait. I stood and paced, even though my head throbbed, wishing I didn't have to be there when my parents found out Aaron was keeping a secret that had nearly killed him.

Chapter Twenty-One

A T 4:20, MY PARENTS BURST through the hospital doors. Mom held Petie tightly to her.

"Where is he?" Dad asked, his eyes wild and his hair disheveled.

A nurse came around the desk and put her hand on his arm.

He jerked it away, panic in his eyes. "*¿Dónde está mi hijo?* Where is my son?"

The nurse was obviously accustomed to handling frantic family members. She stood slowly and put her hand on his arm. "Señor Wales, Señora Wales, come with me."

"Should I go, too?" I asked Blanca.

"*Sí, mija.* Go." She pushed me to follow my parents through the double doors.

The corridor seemed even longer than it had before as we hurried down the hallway. In Aaron's room, someone had turned off the overhead light, making the hospital equipment hanging over his bed look ominous. When my mother saw him, she stifled a scream and handed Petie to me. I tucked the baby's blanket around her and swayed back and forth, glad to have a peaceful job to ground me. Mom and Dad stood by Aaron, crying as they looked at him. Mom touched his hand. The nurse cleared her throat, and Dad turned to her. "What are his injuries?"

"The gunshot hit his shoulder, and he broke his arm and some ribs when he fell down the hill. He needs rest. Please step back into the waiting room. I have paperwork for you to fill out."

"Can we see the doctor?" Mom asked without taking her eyes off Aaron.

"Yes. He will see you between patients."

We followed the nurse back to the waiting room. My parents signed papers while I stood with Blanca, Petie heavy in my arms.

"Mom, Dad, this is Señor Moises," I told my parents in Spanish when they joined us. "He's the man who got Aaron to the hospital."

Moises stood and reached out to shake their hands, but my parents just collapsed into chairs. Mom closed her eyes while Dad put his head in his hands.

I tried again. "I thought you'd like to meet Moises since he saved Aaron's life."

Dad glared up at me. "Tell me, Josie, what part did you play in all of this?"

I replied in Spanish, determined to include my friends. "Blanca and I followed Aaron to a bar. Señor Moises is the cab driver who saw some men take Aaron away in a van. He followed them up to Cristo Rey. He found Aaron and brought him to the hospital. Señor Moises is our hero."

Dad looked over at Moises, stood, and pulled out his wallet. "Thanks for what you did. Now would you please take Josie and Blanca home?" Dad handed him a wad of pesos and pointed for me to follow him. "Take Petie home, Josie." He turned his back on us and sat down beside Mom.

My jaw dropped. They should have been thrilled to meet Moises, grateful for all that the cab driver had done, but my dad had dismissed him like a busboy in a restaurant.

Before I could say anything more, Blanca tugged at my arm. "Come on, *chica*." She led Moises and me out the door, apologizing to Moises for my parents' behavior. "They are very upset," she said, but I heard the anger in her voice.

Outside, I breathed in the early-morning air and realized I was exhausted. "Look, Señor Moises, you don't have to drive us home." I stopped on the sidewalk. "I know you're tired, too. We can catch a different cab from here."

Moises had been quiet, still holding the money from my father in an awkward ball in his hands. He looked around and pointed to a cab near the main entrance of the hospital. "There is a taxi from my company. It looks like Miguel," he said, walking toward his coworker.

Moises and Miguel spoke for a moment, then Moises pushed the money into the hands of the other cab driver and gave him directions to our house. Moises helped Blanca into the backseat of Miguel's car, and I passed the baby to Blanca. Petie opened her eyes and looked around, her wispy brown curls encircling her gold earrings, then she shifted in Blanca's arms and went back to sleep.

"*Gracias*, Señor Moises." I squeezed his hand then slid in beside Blanca and Petie. "Thanks for everything."

"It's fine, *mija*. I'm glad I could help you." Moises closed the door with a sad smile, his hands on the doorframe. "*Cuídate*, Yo-si," he added, his eyes glittering behind his glasses as he waved us off.

Blanca and I didn't speak on the ride home. When we dragged ourselves into the house, I went straight upstairs. After laying Petie in her crib in my parents' room, I fell onto their bed. My last thought as I dropped into sleep was how good Petie had been through the ordeal.

I awoke several hours later to screaming. This time, it wasn't my own. My mother was yelling at me, shaking my shoulder. Disoriented, I jumped up and looked around my parents' room. Mom was holding the baby, whose eyes were puffy and red. Petie's breath was ragged.

"What is wrong with you?" Mom was saying, fury in her eyes.

"We tried to call, but you didn't answer the phone. When I finally came home, Petie was bawling, and you were sound asleep right next to her!"

I reached out to touch Petie's arm, but my mom jerked her away. I fell back on the bed. "What time is it?"

"It's nine in the morning. Now get up." Mom threw her words behind her as she left the room.

I walked into the bathroom and splashed water on my face, trying to remember the reason my head ached so intensely. When I went into my room, my stomach lurched. The new rosary and two new statues were sitting on my desk, staring back at me. That was not where I'd left them.

It all came back to me then. I needed to see Blanca. Something felt very wrong, and I knew Blanca could make it right. But when I raced downstairs, Mom was yelling at her, too.

"Henry wanted to let you go the first time we found out about Josie going to that Catholic church, and I said no. But this has gone too far, Blanca. We can't have you turning Josie from our faith!"

"Mom, what are you doing?" I cried, getting between them.

"What we should have done all along, Josie," Mom said, speaking to me in English as she sat down at the breakfast table to give Petie a bottle. "I'm firing Blanca."

"Are you crazy? Blanca is the saint here. Why can't you see that?" I stood between Blanca and Mom, as I looked frantically from one to the other.

"And why was Aaron out last night, anyway? To track you down again after you'd gone to your Catholic church?"

"No, Mom." I was breathless with frustration. "Aaron was out with the girlfriend of a *mafioso* named Elías López. Elías must have found out about them, because he tried to kill Aaron."

Mom furrowed her brow. "What are you talking about? That doesn't make any sense. Why would Aaron be going out with someone else's girlfriend?"

"I don't know, Mom. Maybe he wanted to be like Dad!" As soon as the words left my mouth, I regretted them, but I let them sit in the air for a few seconds before I added, "I'm sorry. That was wrong to say. But just let me explain."

"Juan Fernando told us what happened while we waited for the doctor last night," Mom snipped. "And he didn't say anything about Elías López. He just said Aaron was caught in a bad situation and Moises happened to come along and save him."

"No, no. I followed Aaron a few weeks ago—"

Mom cut me off. "Save it. Your dad is still at the hospital, and I need to get back there. And you haven't even asked how Aaron is doing." She raised her hand and kept talking. "I don't want to take Petie to the hospital, but I don't know if I can trust you to watch her."

"Mom! Of course you can." I struggled for the words to keep the situation from slipping out of control. "Please, let me explain."

"Finish giving the baby her bottle." She stood, thrust Petie in my arms, grabbed her purse, and stormed out the door. I dropped my cheek onto Petie's head, defeated.

"Tell me what happened just now," Blanca said. She grabbed a sponge and started scrubbing the breakfast table so hard, I was afraid she might rip the vinyl tablecloth.

I patted Petie on the back and reached for her bottle, stalling for time. Finally, I whispered, "Mom thinks Aaron was trying to stop me from going to La Ermita last night. She thinks it's your fault."

Blanca threw the sponge on the table. "I can no longer be part of this, Yo-si. I am leaving."

"Blanca, wait. Maybe we can fix this." My eyes filled with tears as I wondered how.

"Juan Fernando asked me to marry him," she said, sitting at the table. "We were going to wait a few years, but now things are different."

I took a deep breath and whispered, "Blanca, that's great." I set the bottle down and put my hand on hers, giving her a weak smile. "Listen, let's just take it easy. We don't have to do anything today. Let me help around the house, and maybe when Petie takes a nap, we can sleep, too." I paused. "I just have to make sure I hear the baby when she wakes up. Why didn't I hear her crying this morning?"

Blanca reached over and tickled Petie's toes. "You were very, very tired, *chica*. I did not hear her, either, but she is happy now. See?"

Petie gave me a big smile, and I smiled back, straightening the little collar of her pink-striped sleeper.

"Maybe you should take the baby on a walk," Blanca told me. "Both of you will enjoy that. When you come back, you can take a shower and rest."

"Okay," I said, putting Petie in the playpen. I changed out of the jeans and shirt I had been wearing during last night's nightmare, settled Petie in the stroller, and told Blanca we were leaving.

"Have fun," she called from the laundry room, making it sound like an order.

As we crossed the street into the seminary, I wondered if there would ever be fun in my life again. But my sadness took a backseat as I pushed the stroller and watched clouds build huge puffy formations in the sky. One looked like an elephant, its trunk and ears too big for its body. In moments, the image was gone, replaced by a lopsided teacup.

Slowly, my mind wrapped around what had happened that morning. My parents blamed me—and Blanca. In their eyes, Aaron could do no wrong. How was I going to make them believe me? I tightened my grip on the stroller. Aaron would have to tell them the truth.

And I would have to give up La Ermita once and for all, but I couldn't give up Blanca, too. I had to make my parents keep Blanca, and I had to convince her to stay.

I walked faster, bumping along the sidewalks that threaded between the seminary buildings. Petie started to giggle. She seemed to like the bumps that bounced her along. I started to run with the carriage, and she squealed with delight. I was watching Petie and didn't see the crack in the sidewalk ahead. When the wheel hit the uneven pavement, the stroller jolted out of my hands. It rolled forward then fell on its side, and I watched with horror as Petie tumbled onto the sidewalk. I had forgotten to strap her in.

I ran to Petie and picked her up. She looked up at me, her eyes as big as saucers, and for a second, I thought she was going to be okay. Then she started to scream. I tried to console her, but she screamed even louder. Furious with myself for being so careless, I righted the stroller and buckled Petie into the seat. We raced home, Petie crying the whole way.

"Blanca," I yelled, tearing into the house. "Petie fell. Help me!"

Blanca ran to the front door, where I was trying to get the baby out of the stupid stroller. She took Petie from my arms, holding her close. When Petie kept crying, Blanca said, "Get her the bear you bought her." I ran to my room and brought it to them, walking behind Blanca as she moved through the house, swaying with the baby and singing softly in Spanish, soothing us all.

Petie finally stopped crying, and Blanca carried her into the living room and sat on the couch. I'd never seen Blanca sit in the living room before, but many things were new these days. She placed Petie beside her and checked the baby over, moving her arms and legs.

"Is she hurt?" I asked.

"She will be fine," Blanca answered. "What happened?"

"I was going too fast. I hit a bump, and the carriage fell on its side. Petie fell out and screamed the whole way home."

Just then, the phone rang. Blanca and I looked at each other.

"Did someone see you run home?" Blanca asked.

The phone rang again. "Probably," I said. "Should I get it?"

"What will you say?"

I stood and picked up the phone. I would say Petie was doing well and say thanks for calling. If I had learned anything from my mother, it was how to make others think everything was just fine. But when I heard Aunt Rosie's voice, I burst into tears.

"Sweetheart!" she said, muted by the distance of continents. "What's wrong?"

"Oh, nothing. Just everything," I said, laughing and crying at the same time.

"I got your last letter. You wrote you were worried about Aaron. I thought I'd call and see what you were talking about. Is everything okay?"

"Aaron's in the hospital," I said.

"What?" She sounded flabbergasted and afraid.

"Aaron was dating this man's girlfriend. The man must've found out, because he tried to kill Aaron."

"What?" Aunt Rosie asked again, shock still in her voice. "I can't believe it!"

"Some friends of mine saved his life but not before he was hurt. He's in the hospital," I repeated.

"Josie, that's awful. Is he going to be okay?"

"Yeah, I think so, but…" I trailed off, not knowing where to begin.

"Are you there, Josie?"

"I'm here. I need to tell you more, but I might get in trouble with my parents if I do."

"Listen to me, Jos. I'm here for you. You talk as long as you need to. Who cares if it would be cheaper for me to fly down there than to spend an hour on the phone?"

I smiled. "I'll try to make it quick." I told her about Petie and how she was living with us. Aunt Rosie must have known, because she didn't sound surprised. I told her how we found out about Mom's abortion and that my parents were furious at me for going to La Ermita. Then I told her my parents thought it was my fault Aaron was in the hospital, when the truth was, if I hadn't followed him, Aaron would have died on that mountain.

Aunt Rosie was quiet, then she asked, "Where is your mother? I want to straighten her out."

"She's not here. She and Dad are at the hospital. Besides, I don't know if you should talk to her. She'll just get madder at me."

"You may be right, Josie, but they should listen to your side of the story. I wish I could come down there."

"Me, too." I wiped my eyes.

She didn't answer.

"Are you there?" I asked.

"Yes, I'm here." She sighed. "I just wish there was something I could do to help."

"Oh, Aunt Rosie, me, too. But just tell me something happy. Get my mind off everything. How are you doing?"

"Well, my wedding is next week. I would love it if you could come for that."

"Yeah, well, I think I'd have a hard time getting away right now."

"Josie, I'm really sorry you're in the middle of this mess. Just for the record, I think it's fine for you to go to that beautiful Catholic church, and it was brave of you to save Aaron's life. You could have gotten hurt yourself. But everything will be okay."

"Thanks, Aunt Rosie," I whispered. "I love you."

"I love you, too, baby. We'll work something out. I promise."

After we hung up, I shoved the horrible stroller into the garage and went to Blanca's room, where she was playing with Petie on the bed. I flopped in the overstuffed chair and told her Aunt Rosie was frustrated with my parents, too. "I wish she could come down here. She'd make everything right."

"She went with you to La Ermita once. Is that right?" Blanca said.

"Yeah. She thinks I should be allowed to go there." I sighed. "She wants me to go up to the States for her wedding next week."

Blanca stopped playing with the baby and looked at me, her eyes wide.

"Why are you looking at me like that?"

"It is nothing, *mija*." She continued playing with Petie, who seemed to have recovered and was drooling on the new bear. She had a scratch on her forehead, but that was all.

"I guess I'll take a shower," I said, standing. "Don't drop the baby, okay?"

Blanca shook her head at me, smiling.

The front gate creaked open just as I finished dressing. I looked out my window and saw Mom close the gate as Dad drove the car into the garage. My heart started pounding, but I had to be strong and make them see the truth: Blanca had to stay. I walked down the stairs and met Mom coming through the front door.

"Is Petie okay?" she asked.

"Yeah, she's sleeping in her crib." There was no way I was going to tell her about Petie's accident.

Mom eyed me suspiciously then walked past me to the kitchen. "I'm starving. Where's Blanca?"

"In her room, I guess. How is Aaron doing?"

Walking in from the garage, Dad answered my question. "Aaron will be fine, Josie, but it'll take time for him to heal." He filled a glass with water and turned to me. "Go get Blanca. We want to eat. We're tired and hungry."

I wasn't used to the angry, disappointed tone in my dad's voice. I ducked out to get Blanca, and soon, she was heating soup, cutting fresh bread, and warming beans. My parents and I ate our early supper in silence. Finally, I took a deep breath and said, "Mom, Dad, you have to believe me about Aaron. He—"

"Stop!" Mom said then continued with her voice under control. "We don't want to hear from you right now, Josie. We are both furious that you went back to that church after we told you not to. I found those statues. You can't tell me it isn't true. There's no telling when Aaron will be able to play the piano again, and I blame you."

"For the hundredth time, it wasn't my fault Aaron got hurt!" I slammed my fist on the table. "Yes, I did go back to La Ermita. I went back because everything in my life was a mess, and I had nowhere else to go." My mom had raised her hand to interrupt, but I said, "Let me finish. You both had your problems, Aaron kept sneaking out behind your back, Tom moved far away, and the only comfort I got was from La Ermita."

Dad leaned back in his chair, and Mom asked, "How could Aaron be sneaking out behind our backs? We always knew where he was."

"No, you didn't," I declared.

"Listen here, young lady," Mom said. "I've had just about enough of your attitude." She stood and pointed out the door. "You march upstairs and stay there until we're ready to talk to you."

"Fine!" I shouted before stomping up to my room and slamming the door. I sat on the bed with my head in my hands and rocked back and forth, feeling like I might throw up. I thought of the rosary, but praying on it was tainted with deceit. It couldn't soothe me now.

I heard Petie cry, then Mom knocked on my door. "We're going to a meeting at church. I need you to watch Petie." When I didn't say anything, she called again. "Josie, answer me."

I unlocked the door and took Petie from her. I brought the baby into my room and held her as I watched out the window. Dad backed the car into the street, and my mom closed the gate, shooing Brandy out of the way.

"Well, Petie, what shall we do?" I asked. It was a little after six, and the light was leaving the sky.

Petie cooed, weaving her hand through my hair and pulling it.

I disentangled her fingers. "I know. Let's visit Aaron in the hospital."

Petie looked at me with big eyes.

"Yeah. We need to straighten this mess out once and for all."

Chapter Twenty-Two

I HAD TO CONVINCE AARON TO tell Mom and Dad about Trina and Elías. If Aaron would tell the truth, Mom and Dad would understand, Blanca could stay, and everything would go back to normal. Resting my cheek on Petie's head, I watched my parents drive away. Normal was a distant memory... maybe it was gone for good.

I opened my sock drawer and searched for the cash next to my supply of American candy. There were no more Colombian pesos. Only American dollars were left. I grabbed the money, and when I stashed it in my purse, my fingers brushed against something hard and smooth. I pulled out the pet rock Tom had given me, then I sat on the bed next to Petie, overwhelmed with sadness. If only he were with me, he could tell me what to do. But what would Tom say? He had a strong bond with his brother; Tom would no doubt want me to count on my strong bond with my brother and trust Aaron to tell the truth. He would also want me to stop going to La Ermita. How could two missionary families be so different?

I put the rock back in my purse and stuffed Petie's bear in her diaper bag. After calling Moises's cab company, I carried Petie downstairs. "Blanca, I'm going to the hospital to talk to Aaron. I already called a taxi."

"Are you serious?" Blanca asked, wiping her hands on her apron as she came out of the kitchen.

"I have to. Aaron's my only hope. My parents don't believe me, but they'll listen to him."

Blanca leaned against the kitchen doorframe. "I do not think you should go."

"Am I supposed to just let everything fall apart around me?"

"At least do not take the baby," she said, taking Petie from my arms. "Exposing her to the night air is dangerous."

My parents believed this was just a Colombian superstition, that exposing babies to the night air would not hurt them, but I was glad to leave Petie with Blanca. I didn't want to take her to the hospital anyway.

Blanca dressed Petie in a sleeper and fed her a bottle while I watched for my taxi from the living room. When the familiar yellow cab pulled up to the gate, I headed for the door. "Wish me luck," I said.

"You will need more than luck," Blanca answered.

Brandy gamboled over to me as I raced across the front lawn, but I slipped through the gate before he arrived. In the cab, Moises looked at me through the rearview mirror. "It's been a long time," he joked. "How have you been?"

"I've seen better days, Señor Moises." Tears choked my throat. I had been afraid the cab company would send someone else. But Moises would always be there for me, like a guardian angel. Only he was better—I had his phone number.

"Where are we going now?" he asked. "Am I about to get you in trouble again?"

"Back to the hospital. And I hope you'll be getting me *out* of trouble. All I have is American dollars. Is that okay?"

"Of course, Yo-si," he answered, pulling away from the house.

"Thank you, Señor Moises. I want to apologize for my parents again. I'll find a way to make them see what you did. That's why I'm going to see Aaron. I need him to tell my parents the truth."

"Your brother has not told them what happened?" Moises sounded surprised.

"No," I said, looking out the cab window.

"Oh."

I tried not to hear the judgment in his voice. We were quiet until he pulled into the hospital.

"*Gracias*, Señor Moises," I said, paying him as I stepped out of the cab.

"I hope everything goes well."

"Me, too. Thanks again." *It would be impossible to thank him enough,* I thought as I walked into the hospital.

The nurse at the front desk told me visiting hours were over, but she offered to escort me to Aaron's room. I followed her, wondering if I was privileged for being American or if she'd taken pity on me.

They had moved Aaron out of the Intensive Care Unit, and the nurse led me to an elevator. On the second floor, we walked along a maze of corridors until we arrived at Aaron's room, where the nurse nodded to me and hurried out, leaving us alone. Aaron was sleeping soundly. A bandage was wrapped around his chest, and his arm, which was in a cast, had been propped up with pillows. He had a room to himself in the crowded hospital.

I sat in the chair by the window, waiting for him to wake up. For fifteen minutes, I stared at the busy street below, listening to my brother's steady breathing. A different nurse came in with a blood pressure cuff and a thermometer.

"*Buenas noches,*" she said when she saw me by the window. "I am just checking his vital signs. You must be his twin?"

I smiled. "We aren't twins, but he is my brother. How is he doing?"

"He should be able to go home soon. He will be in some discomfort with the broken ribs, but he will heal." The young nurse wrapped the cuff around his arm, and Aaron jerked awake.

"There he is," I said, standing and walking to his side.

"Is that my little sister?" he asked, lifting his head with a dazed expression.

"Yeah. I'm here to pray for your soul," I answered, only half joking.

"I know, I'm so evil." He smirked, laying his head back on the pillow. "After you pray for me, let's sing 'Kumbaya.' Maybe that will bring me back to the Lord."

After the nurse finished her routine and left, I asked, "Were you scared out of your mind, standing on that cliff?"

"Nah," he answered. "I knew you'd come along."

I realized he wasn't thinking clearly because of the pain medication, and there wasn't much time before he would fall asleep again. "Aaron, Mom and Dad think you were trying to stop me from going to La Ermita when you got shot. They don't believe Trina's boyfriend wanted you killed. They think you got hurt trying to rescue me."

"Wait. What did you say?" Aaron asked, trying to shake the grogginess.

"What kind of drugs are you on?" I asked, watching the IV drip into his arm.

"Something really nice," he drawled. "Now repeat the part about Mom and Dad thinking I'm the hero. I like that."

"Good grief, Aaron! This is important. You have to tell Mom and Dad the truth. They don't believe me, and they're talking about firing Blanca! They think I'm the one to blame, but the truth is you wouldn't be alive if it weren't for me."

"You're so melodramatic." Aaron closed his eyes. "Thank you for saving my life, but I like things the way they are. Now be a good sister and get me some ice chips."

"I should call El Jazmin and tell them you're still alive," I seethed. "I'll invite Elías López to come and finish the job himself."

For a second, Aaron's eyes widened. Then he laughed. "You would never. Now you run along." He fluttered his hand at me.

"Really, Aaron? You're not going to tell Mom and Dad what really happened?"

"Josie, Josie, Josie," he said. "There's no need to worry them about Elías. Let them think it's your little statue hang-up. You owe me that much."

"Owe you? Owe *you*?" I was angry enough to crawl out of my skin. "I don't owe you anything. You owe me for saving your life! If it hadn't been for me, you'd be dead right now!"

"Keep it down. You'll wake the patients in the morgue."

I stared at him, wondering if I could get away with ripping out his IV out and strangling him with the cord. I closed my eyes and took a deep breath.

Aaron yawned and turned away from me. "I'm tired. Don't forget the ice chips when you leave."

I stormed out of his room, wishing I could call El Jazmin and have him killed. But the only hurtful thing I could do was pass the nurses' station without getting Aaron his damn ice. Outside the hospital, I stumbled down the street until a cab pulled over and offered me a ride.

"I only have American money," I told the cab driver.

"It's okay," he said. "I work with Moises. I am Rafael."

"*Gracias*, Rafael." I opened the back door and fell onto the seat. His radio was tuned to Spanish love songs, and as he drove, we listened to the melody Tom had sung to me the night I had been healed. I tried to relive that memory but couldn't bear to bring the sweetness of that moment to the dreadful day I was having. I buried my face in my hands and didn't move until Rafael stopped and said we had arrived at the house.

I gave Rafael the last of my money and thanked him again. Noticing Mom and Dad were already home, I slipped past the gates and quietly headed toward the backyard. I was near the dining room window when I saw Mom and Blanca in an animated conversation.

"Josie shouldn't have gone to that church," Mom was saying.

I inched closer to the window to hear Blanca's reply.

"Yo-si had nowhere else to go! You have not been helpful for her when she needed you. And now you are not believing her! She deserves better than this."

My mouth dropped open. Blanca was giving my mother hell.

"How dare you speak to me that way," Mom said, her voice rising. "We had already decided to fire you, Blanca. Now I want you out of here tonight."

I peeked into the window to see Blanca. She was shaking, but she wasn't backing down.

"Oh, I am leaving," she said, determination making her voice strong. "But first, you must send Yo-si to live with her *Tía* Rosa. Your sister can take better care of the girl than you. And if you do not send Yo-si to the United States, I will tell every maid in every missionary family that your husband had a child with another woman. I will tell them Aaron is a drunken fool. And one more thing. Why is it you went to the United States for an operation and when you came home you were no longer pregnant?"

"How dare you!" Mom gasped. Her hand flew to her mouth.

"It is true what your daughter has been saying, that your son was dating someone he should not have been with," Blanca added. "And if you do not protect Yo-si by sending her to her *Tía* Rosa, I will take Yo-si home with me, and she will live in my village."

Mom was silent.

"I will do this for Yo-si." Blanca swallowed hard.

I could tell Blanca was beginning to cave under the enormity of her condemnation, so I walked around to the front door. I had to stand beside her. "What's going on?" I asked in Spanish.

"Josie," Mom said, her face ashen. "I have to talk to you."

"Petie's down for the night," Dad said, walking downstairs. He stopped when he saw Mom. He looked at me, then at Blanca in bewilderment. "What's this about, Astrid?"

Mom gestured to Blanca. "She thinks Josie would be better off living with Rosie because of everything that's gone on."

"Why is Blanca involved here? This is crazy!" Dad said, white-knuckling the railing.

"Wait, Henry. Blanca knows everything. She wants us to send Josie to Rosie, and if we don't, she'll tell the other missionaries about Petie." Mom gave me an incredulous look and asked, "Josie, why would you tell Blanca everything?"

"I didn't," I said, straightening my shoulders. "She knew about Petie before I did, and I didn't tell her about your abortion. As for Aaron, she saw him leaving the house and staying out late. She was there when he came home, smelling like cigarettes and alcohol. She lives here, Mom. She may not be related to us, but she's one of us."

Mom stared at me, and I stared right back. Finally, she asked in English, "Do you want to live with Rosie?"

"I want everything to go back to the way it was," I whispered.

"It can't go back to the way it was," Dad said.

Suddenly, a heavy cloud settled over all of us. No one moved, and yet everything changed, as if that was the moment my life started a new course.

"So what will we do?" Dad asked.

Nobody spoke.

"Wait." Dad stared at Mom. "Are we sending her off to the States? Just like that?"

"It's okay, Dad. It's for the best."

"We need to check with Rose," Mom said, still frozen.

"This is all my fault," Dad said, pacing the hall. He stopped and looked at me. "Shouldn't we just take a minute and think about this?"

"It's too late. It's too much." I stood and walked toward my room, stopping halfway up the stairs.

Dad dropped onto the couch, his head in his hands.

"Henry, should we do this?" Mom asked.

Dad didn't answer.

I went to my room and sat on the bed as my mother and her sister spoke on the phone. Aunt Rosie would be glad to take me in, and I wanted to go, but it broke my heart that Mom and Dad didn't believe me. If only I'd had a tape recorder when Aaron thanked me for saving his life…

Tears stung my eyes when I realized that being right wouldn't change anything. My family had broken, and we would never be the same again. It was a good thing I wanted to go, because I didn't have a choice. My parents would always believe I had committed the bigger crime by walking into La Ermita.

I picked up the rosary beads and the statues that had gotten me into so much trouble. I took them downstairs to Blanca's room and tapped on her door. When she let me in, I handed them to her. "Here. I want you to have these."

Blanca smiled. "I will take the statue of Jesus, but you should keep the rosary and Mother Mary. You are going where there is love for you, but you will still be lonely. They will remind you of me, like this statue of Jesus will remind me of you."

"Thank you, Blanca," I said, sitting in my oversized chair.

"I knew what I had to do." She shrugged. "You gave me the idea that you should live with your aunt. I just helped make it happen."

I smiled at the understatement. "What will we do now?"

"You will live with your aunt, and I will work for another family. For now."

After a few moments, I asked, "Blanca, how did you know my mom had an abortion?"

Blanca shook her head. "My mother had many babies, *chica*. When your mother was sick every morning, eating *saltinas* and drinking Ginger Ale, I knew. Then she went to the States, and when she came back, she was not pregnant anymore. And you and your *hermano* never knew a thing." Blanca knew so much about my family, but we knew so little of each other.

"I should see what Aunt Rosie had to say," I said, standing.

"*Sí, chica,*" Blanca answered. We hugged, and I breathed in the smell of her apricot shampoo.

Without warning, Mom barged into Blanca's room. "Josie, you'll go live with Aunt Rosie," she announced as if it were her idea. Pointing to Blanca, she added, "You will leave tonight."

"What?" I grabbed Blanca's hands as angry fear welled up inside me. "Why does she have to leave now? It's nine at night! Where will she go?"

Mom's face paled, but she set her jaw. "You'll leave tonight." She slammed the door.

I turned to Blanca, dazed. "She can't mean it," I whispered.

Blanca pulled her suitcase from under her bed and began to throw her belongings into it. "I am sure she does." Blanca's voice was choked with tears.

"What can I do?"

She shook her head, crying. I stood and hugged her again, but she pulled away, feverishly packing everything in the room: clothing, magazines, a few knickknacks, the statue of Jesus. Everything she had.

Blanca called Juan Fernando, and minutes later, he drove up and honked. He stood in the street just outside our gate, an angry gesture, it seemed. I walked beside Blanca, carrying her bag to the cruiser.

"What will you do?" I asked, still numb with disbelief.

"*No sé, mija.*"

Turning to Juan Fernando, I asked, "Can't you speak to my father? I don't want her to go. Help us make it so she can stay."

He looked at me, pity in his eyes. "There is nothing I can do. You know this."

"Blanca, don't go!" I put my arms around her again, scared to death of life without Blanca.

We hugged until Juan Fernando was finished putting Blanca's

belongings in the trunk. He pulled her away from me and helped her into the car.

"Wait, at least let me give you Aunt Rosie's address so you can write me," I said, panic choking my throat.

When I dashed back to the car, carrying a slip of paper, Blanca was settled in the front seat beside Juan Fernando. She seemed calmer as she took the paper and patted my hand. "Do not worry, *chica*. Pray the rosary and think of me. You will be in my thoughts, too."

"I love you, Blanca," I said, sobbing, holding tightly to her hand.

Juan Fernando leaned toward me. "Yo-si, you have brought excitement into our lives, enough for a lifetime."

"Yes, too much excitement," Blanca answered, but her smile was kind. "Now go. Go live a good life, Yo-si. We will meet again. You will see."

"Take care of Blanca, okay?" I asked Juan Fernando, wiping my eyes.

He smiled. "Of course I will, *niña*."

Brandy began to bark.

"Say good-bye to your dog for me," Blanca said. And just like that, she was ripped away from me, gone from my life.

They drove into the night, and I ran down the street until they were out of sight and I could barely breathe. I walked back to the house, numb from sadness. Knowing my parents didn't believe me had felt like a physical blow. But losing Blanca felt as if the earth were swallowing me whole. She was gone, and there was little hope of keeping in touch with her. Our lives were taking such different trajectories; we might as well have been moving to separate planets. No amount of devotion on my part could keep us connected.

Brandy was still barking when I opened the gate, and he rolled onto his back, begging me to rub his belly.

"Oh, Brandy," I said, falling to the ground beside him. I tried to hug him, but he wriggled out of my grasp and tilted his head, one ear flopped over, his tail wagging his whole body. I would miss him, too, and Anna. I would miss running in the seminary, living in Colombia. But it was over now. I resolved to do whatever I had to do to make it through the next few days, then I would be with Aunt Rosie again.

When I turned toward the door, I saw my father's silhouette at the window of his office upstairs, and I saw him step into the shadows.

Chapter Twenty-Three

OVER THE NEXT FOUR DAYS, Mom helped me go through my wardrobe and pack. She made sure I had enough makeup and accessories and even gave me the pearl necklace. I thanked her and stuffed it in my jewelry box. Maybe someday I would want to wear the pearls. Maybe someday I could forgive her for sending Blanca away.

Aaron came home two days after Blanca left, still sore and medicated. He lived in T-shirts and shorts until he could learn to maneuver around his cast and injuries, and he slept on the couch most of the time. I had nothing to do with him, and my parents never asked me to help him, even if it was only for a glass of water or another magazine to read.

Thinking of Blanca made my heart ache, so I stayed busy to keep her off my mind. I spent as much time as possible doing my favorite things: running in the seminary, playing with Petie, and reading. I also wrote letters to Tom and Anna, telling them about Aaron and that I was leaving Cali. I would be in the States before Tom received his letter, but it helped to put on paper what had happened.

Tom already knew my parents were adopting Petie, but I would never be able to tell him the truth about her or about my mom's abortion. Staring at the sparse details of the letter, I realized what

I said about my family didn't matter anymore. We would be living separate lives, and mine was opening up before me.

On the morning of my departure, I took a last run, saying good-bye to the seminary as I circled it. I passed the field where we'd played Capture the Flag, the bench where Tom and I had kissed on the last night, and the big tree with the rope swing. I stopped and pulled myself onto the rope, looking up at the tree and breathing in its sweet smell. After swaying back and forth a few times, my hands burned, so I jumped down and moved on.

My thoughts plunged farther back, into Mission Meetings of years past, when Anna and I played hopscotch on the sidewalk, when Mom and Dad pushed me on the swings, when I wandered the serene halls of the seminary classrooms unnoticed. Many of my most-precious moments would always live in Colombia. The Nevado del Huila, the snowcapped mountain Aunt Rosie saw on her first morning there, stayed out of sight as I rounded the last bend of my run. I headed to the house, pushing away the desperate sadness.

While I drank orange juice after my run, Aaron started playing a tune on the piano with one hand. The beauty of the original melody was overwhelming, and I closed my eyes to listen, thinking of our very complicated relationship. I loved him but hated him, too, maybe because he had our parents' affection and I had their disappointment. He fit easily into the mold they wanted him to fill, and I could not fit mine. He hadn't told Mom and Dad the truth about where he'd been that horrible night, and they didn't ask. But I didn't care anymore. One thing was sure: he would never hurt me again. My love for my brother would be a careful love, a love with one foot out the door. Aaron and my parents would have to work it out among themselves. Aaron's song floated to an end.

"You'll be there in time for Rosie's wedding," Mom said from the kitchen entrance, Petie on her hip.

I looked over at her. The fury I still felt made it difficult to speak to her, but I knew deciding to send me away could not have been easy for her. She was admitting failure, and the only way she could do that was by getting rid of Blanca first.

"I guess things aren't perfect around here," Mom continued with a shrug. "As much as I want you to stay, it must be God's will for you to go. I don't want you to leave, but…"

I took a deep breath. "Well, I want to go."

"Things got out of control, Josie. You won't be gone forever." Mom sounded as if she was trying to apologize, but I wasn't ready to hear it. I had nothing to say to her except to thank her for having a sister like Aunt Rosie who could give me the love and the freedom I needed to find my own way.

"I need to take a shower," I said, ending the conversation as I stood and walked out.

Dad had loaded my suitcases in the Suburban by the time I was dressed and ready to go. I walked outside with my final bag, and he took it from me. "We need to leave in a few minutes." He slammed the back doors. "Are you ready for this?"

"I guess," I answered, kneeling beside Brandy and rubbing his belly. "I'm not sure when I'll see you again, buddy," I told the dog.

"You'll see him at Christmas, if not before," Dad said, crouching beside me. "We're just trying to clean up a big mess. You'll be better off with your aunt for now."

I found a stick and threw it for Brandy to fetch. When he tore after it, I said, "You better take good care of the dog."

"Of course. We'll try, anyway."

"Try harder than you did during Mission Meeting?"

He laughed. "Yes, Josie."

I was about to toss the stick for Brandy to fetch again, when Dad said, "Josie, I want to know something. Why did you go?"

"Go where?"

"To La Ermita," he answered.

"I wanted a rosary."

"But why?"

I thought of screaming in the night, the reason Blanca had given me the rosary at the beginning of the summer. I wouldn't tell Dad about that now. "Praying the rosary helped me," was all I said. "And then going to La Ermita," I added slowly. "There's something special about that church for me."

"But don't you see we have a mission here?" he asked, studying me.

"I don't like how you try to change people," I answered, shaking my head. "I guess it's not my mission."

Dad stared toward the seminary. "Your mom and I feel called to help the people of this country. We want you to come back to our beliefs."

My voice trembled when I said, "You'll have to let me find my own way."

"We'll be praying."

"Good. I'm glad."

Dad was silent, and I looked around at our front yard. "I'm really going to miss Cali," I whispered.

"Yeah, I bet you will." He cleared his throat. "You won't find a more-beautiful place to live." He chuckled. "Except for Albuquerque. Now *that's* paradise."

Mom called to us from the house. "I need help with Petie. Would one of you get the diaper bag?"

"Coming," Dad answered. He headed inside while I stayed with Brandy. I noticed the driveway needed sweeping and wondered what Mom's new maid would be like. She would have to be as tough as nails.

Dad helped Aaron into the car, and Mom sat with Petie on her lap. With all of my belongings surrounding me, I looked back at our house one last time as we pulled away. I snapped a picture. Leaving my home seemed like a dream, but I wasn't waking up. During the ride to the airport, I said good-bye to the trees, the fountains, the buses, the people, and the rock-strewn river that meandered through the city, taking photos of everything along the way.

Dad made a point of driving downtown, and Mom gave him a disapproving look when he stopped the car at La Ermita so I could take pictures of the magnificent church that had been my haven. On an impulse, I jumped out of the car and ran to La Ermita's entrance. I tried the huge door, wanting to walk inside one last time. But the church was locked. It was time to go.

I settled back into my seat and noticed Mom's jaw was clenched and her cheek was wet with tears. She was so beautiful, wearing a pale-blue dress I had always liked and holding Petie on her lap. As I studied her profile, memories flooded my thoughts—her laughter at my silly antics as a child, her pride when I'd sung my first church solo, her rubbing my back when I couldn't sleep at night. All so long ago.

I sighed, realizing events beyond my control had separated us. Maybe, in the future, events would bring us back. Maybe I didn't need her as much as I'd thought. But just in case, I wanted to believe Mom would be there for me.

When we arrived at the airport, Dad carried my luggage while I held Petie. Aaron leaned on Mom's arm, and we walked to the check-in desk. I was flying alone for the first time, and although I worried I might miss a connection or lose my ticket or passport, my fears were nothing compared to my excitement for the adventure.

As we waited, I took random pictures of the oversized terminal, my parents, Aaron, Petie—anything that would keep the details of my life in Colombia alive. Cali would never be my city again.

We walked to the gate when my flight was called, and I hugged my mom for the first time in a while. We said a stiff, awkward good-bye. Then I turned to Aaron.

"Take care, sis," he said, hugging me with his good arm.

"Whatever." I smiled up at him. "Get your life together, will ya?"

"Just take care," he said again, his face serious. There even seemed to be tears in his eyes.

I reached for Petie and took her in my arms. "Bye-bye, baby girl."

She smiled, babbling at me. She looked adorable in a new sundress and bonnet, and I would miss her. She had become a big part of my life over the summer, and even though her existence was the reason behind much of what had happened, I couldn't imagine our family without her.

Mom took Petie, and when I turned to my dad, he grabbed my shoulder bag.

"I'm walking you to the plane," he said.

Together, we walked across the windy tarmac. The sound of the airplane's engines engulfed us.

Just before leaving Colombian ground and stepping onto the unsteady stairs, I turned back one last time to look for Mom, Petie, and Aaron in the crowd that had gathered to send off the airplane. When I found them, I froze. Mom and Aaron were looking at Petie and laughing at something she had done, and my heart broke all over again. Piedad Maria, Dad's child with another woman, would give my mother something I could not give her. The baby was my mother's chance to make it right. All I could do was remind her where she had gone wrong, because I couldn't believe the way she did.

Dad had walked up the stairs to the plane ahead of me, but when he realized I wasn't with him, he dodged the other passengers to come back and stand beside me. He must have seen what I saw, because he put his arm around me. "Josie, I really wish things didn't have to turn out like this."

I looked in his eyes and saw such sorrow, I fell into his arms. He was the one I should be the most angry with, and yet, he was my biggest comfort. I smiled through my tears, and we walked up the steps and into the plane.

Dad spoke to the flight attendant and found my seat before helping me put my bag in the overhead compartment as I sat down and buckled in. He patted my arm. "I love you, baby. Take good care. Call us when you get to Aunt Rosie's, okay?"

I clutched his hand, suddenly afraid.

"You'll be just fine, Josie. I promise." He looked around the cabin at the other passengers, and a woman across the aisle smiled at us.

"So, I'll see you soon, right, Dad?" I said, loosening my grip on his hand.

He smiled down at me. "Of course. Christmas. Now I'd better go."

"Good-bye, Dad," I said, choking on my tears.

"Christmas," he said again then hurried out of the plane.

Soon the plane was ready for departure, and I waved out my little window, aware that my family wouldn't know it was me. I watched the airport drop away and tried to imprint each detail of the landscape from my beloved country on my mind. But then we were beyond the misty clouds, where there was only blue sky. I leaned back and felt a strange freedom settle over me. The farther we flew from my family, the weaker their power was over me, and the stronger I felt.

I almost laughed when it occurred to me they couldn't hurt me anymore. I turned my thoughts to my future, wondering what my life would be like with Aunt Rosie. Maybe we would take yoga classes together. Maybe we would hike in the mountains, taking pictures. I would soon be part of a new family, with little step-cousins. I would camp out with them, bike around the neighborhood, swim at the community pool, and go to movies.

And there was Tom. I would have to check out a map and see just how far Houston was from Albuquerque. Maybe I could show up at his school to surprise him. The flight attendant interrupted my thoughts to offer me a Coke, and for the rest of the flight to

Miami, I stared at the clouds out my window and at the blue ocean far below, feeling freer by the minute.

The plane landed at Miami International Airport, and as I joined the overwhelming bustle of people, making it through customs and hurrying to my connecting flight, it sank in that I was really in the States. I loved Colombia, but I would love the States, too. I had thought of Colombia as home, but this was where I belonged. The English conversations, the American magazines, the Dr Pepper I bought from a vending machine—every one of these American details made me smile.

On the final flight to Albuquerque, I pulled out my rosary and began to pray to calm myself. Before long, the captain announced, in English, that we would be landing soon. From the air, my new city seemed less green and more dry than Cali, but just as alive. I gathered my belongings and walked off the airplane and into my new life.

Aunt Rosie was there to greet me. Laughing, she hugged me tightly. "I'm so glad you're here!" she said, taking my shoulder bag. "I have a surprise for you. Follow me."

"What is it? Is it Will and the kids?" I asked, trying to keep up as she hurried around groups of people, all moving toward the baggage claim area.

"They're here, too," she said, practically running. When Aunt Rosie stopped short, I recognized her fiancé, Will, and his boys, Warren and Thomas, waving and smiling at us. Then someone stepped out from behind Will, and I couldn't believe my eyes. Tom stood in front of me, his arms crossing his strong chest, a big smile on his handsome face.

I ran to him, and we hugged while Aunt Rosie and Will looked on, smiling. "How did you know I was coming?" I asked, not letting him go.

"I told Tom he had to be here when you arrived," Aunt Rosie gushed. "And here he is!"

Tom kissed me then said, "It's going to be okay, Josie." He looked at me with his beautiful blue eyes. "You know that, right?"

"Yeah, it is," I answered, resting my head on his shoulder.

We were oblivious to the world as it rushed around us, until Aunt Rosie tapped my shoulder. "No hurry, Josie, but which bags are yours?"

I turned and pointed to my bags on the carousel, and Will grabbed them as they came around. Then all six of us walked out of the airport, into the Albuquerque summer night, and when Tom pulled that stupid hat out of his back pocket and placed it on my head, my little step-cousins laughed with delight.

Acknowledgments

This book wouldn't have been written if it weren't for Chris Zokan, dear husband and best friend, who believed in me and encouraged me – and handled many family dinners that would otherwise have been cereal.

Thanks goes to the critique groups at the West Florida Literary Federation, a one-of-a-kind collection of writers in Pensacola. I cannot speak highly enough of the power of writers coming together week after week to share their work. Two of these groups were Sohbet (Lynn Huber, Andrea Walker, Joyce Smandra, Diane Skelton, and Judy Fawley) and the Portfolio Society (Diane Skelton, Victoria Franks, Judy Fawley, and Susan Feathers). KRJS (Shari Shallard, Rebecca Pappas, and Kerry Whiteley), although not part of the Federation, was a happy gathering of kindred spirits. Thank you, dear friends.

Diane Skelton's edits provided a quantum leap in my writing, and I am forever grateful for her sharp eye, dear friendship, constant support, and sense of humor.

Thank you, beta readers, which included Chris, our daughters Olivia and Natalie, and friends Gema Gomez, Brittany Jackson, Madison Allmon, Rachel Jowers, Donna Jones, Cath DePalma, and niece Aria Oliver.

Lynn McNamee made my year when she called to say Red

Adept Publishing was interested in my manuscript, and here we are. I am honored to be published by the amazing Red Adept team.

Finally, I want to thank my parents, who are nothing like the ones in this book, for their strong and beautiful faith and for taking their children along on their marvelous adventure.

About The Author

Jeannie Zokan grew up in Colombia, South America, where she read almost every book in the American school she attended. Her love of books led her to study Library Science at Baylor University then to attend The George Washington University in DC. When the chance came to head south, she took her motorcycle to Florida's Gulf Coast to write stories for the local newspaper.

She now lives ten minutes from the beach with her husband, two teenage daughters, and three pets, all of whom keep her inspired and just a little frantic. She enjoys aerial yoga, tennis, and holding NICU babies as a volunteer. But there's always writing. Writing to relive, writing to understand, writing to remember, writing to renew.

83784682R00155

Made in the USA
Columbia, SC
12 December 2017